Central African Folktales

Central African Folktales

Introduction by
Prof Enongene Mirabeau Sone

General Editor: Jake Jackson

**FLAME TREE
PUBLISHING**

This is a FLAME TREE Book

FLAME TREE PUBLISHING
6 Melbray Mews
Fulham, London SW6 3NS
United Kingdom
www.flametreepublishing.com

First published 2024
Copyright © 2024 Flame Tree Publishing Ltd

24 26 28 27 25
1 3 5 7 9 8 6 4 2

ISBN: 978-1-80417-780-8

The cover image is © copyright 2022 Flame Tree Publishing Ltd,
based on artwork courtesy of Shutterstock.com/only_vector.

All inside images courtesy of Shutterstock.com and the following:
evgo1977, Wiktoria Matynia, siloto, Gallery Aini.

The following stories are reprinted with permission from the University of Yaoundé,
first published in 'Our Mythical Childhood Survey', Warsaw: University of Warsaw, 2019,
Open Access: http://omc.obta.al.uw.edu.pl/myth-survey, within the project 'Our Mythical
Childhood... The Reception of Classical Antiquity in Children's and Young Adults' Culture
in Response to Regional and Global Challenges', 2016–2022, funded by the European
Research Council (ERC) Consolidator Grant under the European Union's Horizon 2020
Research and Innovation Programme under grant agreement No 681202:
'How the Earth (Land) Came to Be', 'Kaikiyourou', 'Meusep Nforpeyam', 'Kazaye
and the Horn of Abundance', 'Why Some Bamileke Tribes Worship Skulls'.

In addition to the above stories, the new introductions, and some modern retellings,
the text in this book is selected and edited from the following original sources:
Notes on the Folklore of the Fjort by Richard Edward Dennett, 1898 (London:
The Folk-Lore Society); *Where Animals Talk: West African Folk Lore Tales* by
Robert H. Nassau, 1912 (Boston: The Gorham Press); *My Dark Companions
and their Strange Stories* by Henry M. Stanley, 1893 (New York: Charles
Scribner's Sons); *Among Congo Cannibals* by Rev. John H. Weeks, 1913
(Philadelphia: J.B. Lippincott Company); *Congo Life and Folklore* by
Rev. John H. Weeks, 1911 (London: The Religious Tract Society).

Printed and bound in China

Contents

Series Foreword

STRETCHING BACK to the oral traditions of thousands of years ago, tales of heroes and disaster, creation and conquest have been told by many different civilizations in many different ways. Their impact sits deep within our culture even though the detail in the tales themselves are a loose mix of historical record, transformed narrative and the distortions of hundreds of storytellers.

Today the language of mythology lives with us: our mood is jovial, our countenance is saturnine, we are narcissistic and our modern life is hermetically sealed from others. The nuances of myths and legends form part of our daily routines and help us navigate the world around us, with its half truths and biased reported facts.

The nature of a myth is that its story is already known by most of those who hear it, or read it. Every generation brings a new emphasis, but the fundamentals remain the same: a desire to understand and describe the events and relationships of the world. Many of the great stories are archetypes that help us find our own place, equipping us with tools for self-understanding, both individually and as part of a broader culture.

For Western societies it is Greek mythology that speaks to us most clearly. It greatly influenced the mythological heritage of the ancient Roman civilization and is the lens through which we still see the Celts, the Norse and many of the other great peoples and religions. The Greeks themselves learned much from their neighbours, the Egyptians, an older culture that became weak with age and incestuous leadership.

It is important to understand that what we perceive now as mythology had its own origins in perceptions of the divine and the rituals of the sacred. The earliest civilizations, in the crucible of the Middle East, in the Sumer of the third millennium BC, are the source to which many of the mythic archetypes can be traced. As humankind collected together in cities for the first time, developed writing and industrial scale agriculture, started to irrigate the rivers and attempted to control rather than be at the mercy of its environment, humanity began to write down its tentative explanations of natural events, of floods and plagues, of disease.

Early stories tell of Gods (or god-like animals in the case of tribal societies such as African, Native American or Aboriginal cultures) who are crafty and use their wits to survive, and it is reasonable to suggest that these were the first rulers of the gathering peoples of the earth, later elevated to god-like status with the distance of time. Such tales became more political as cities vied with each other for supremacy, creating new Gods, new hierarchies for their pantheons. The older Gods took on primordial roles and became the preserve of creation and destruction, leaving the new gods to deal with more current, everyday affairs. Empires rose and fell, with Babylon assuming the mantle from Sumeria in the 1800s BC, then in turn to be swept away by the Assyrians of the 1200s BC; then the Assyrians and the Egyptians were subjugated by the Greeks, the Greeks by the Romans and so on, leading to the spread and assimilation of common themes, ideas and stories throughout the world.

The survival of history is dependent on the telling of good tales, but each one must have the 'feeling' of truth, otherwise it will be ignored. Around the firesides, or embedded in a book or a computer, the myths and legends of the past are still the living materials of retold myth, not restricted to an exploration of origins. Now we have devices and global communications that give us unparalleled access to a diversity of traditions. We can find out about Native American, Indian, Chinese and tribal African mythology in a way that was denied to our ancestors, we can find connections, match the archaeology, religion and the mythologies of the world to build a comprehensive image of the human experience that is endlessly fascinating.

The stories in this book provide an introduction to the themes and concerns of the myths and legends of their respective cultures, with a short introduction to provide a linguistic, geographic and political context. This is where the myths have arrived today, but undoubtedly over the next millennia, they will transform again whilst retaining their essential truths and signs.

Jake Jackson
General Editor

Introduction to Central African Folktales

S INCE THE ADVENT OF MANKIND, humanity has puzzled over the constitution of the universe and wondered what controls it. People have pondered over the elemental features and their various functions, especially those regarding birth and death, reincarnation and other rhetorical questions and ontological issues. These and many other questions arouse the consciousness and imagination that led storytellers to interpret and find suitable answers to their problems through folktales.

Folktales are important in the life of every African. From childhood onwards, African children see the folktale as the first type of oral literature they were exposed to; this ultimately prepares them for formal education and for the task of being responsible people in society. A folktale belongs to its community and is handed down from generation to generation. This gives rise to the theory of polygenesis. Interestingly, this situation does not seem to reduce the aesthetics and efficacy of the folktale. Each story told is very relevant to the society at large and has a unique function for children and adults alike. Beyond their role as entertainment, folktales kindle the imagination of a child and help to communicate appropriate cultural and societal traits to him or her, making an important contribution to the educational process. Writers have also shown considerable interest in folktales, as evidenced in a plethora of works on this important genre.

The central African sub-region, which is our concern in this collection, is home to hundreds of different groups distinguished by language, lifestyle and culture. Located in a continent known for its orality, it is also home to vibrant and still-active traditions of oral performance and narrative, although the march of modernization is imperilling these traditional forms. Despite the enormous opportunities presented by this wealth of variety, the collection and study of central African folktales has lagged behind other parts of the continent, in part because of the very challenges of the traditional material. The diversity of local languages in which the stories are told, the effort required to transpose these stories from an oral medium to writing, usually with a translation into a European language, and the diverse languages in which scholarship is published make the task of studying these folktales daunting. Thousands of folktales have been collected from all parts of the central African sub-region over the past centuries. However, the collections are not fully supported by tools such as tale-type or motif indexes, or the study of individual narrators' repertoires and life histories. Much work remains to be done, and the bringing together of this collection is a welcome initiative.

Locating Central Africa

'Central Africa' is a sub-region of the African continent that comprises various countries according to different definitions. Middle Africa is an analogous term used by the United Nations in its geoscheme for Africa. It consists of the following countries: Angola, Burundi, Cameroon, Central African Republic, Chad, Democratic Republic of the Congo, Republic of the Congo, Equatorial Guinea, Gabon, Rwanda, and São Tomé and Príncipe. These 11 countries are all members of the Economic Community of Central African States (ECCAS). Six of them (Cameroon, Central African Republic, Chad, Equatorial Guinea, Gabon and Republic of the Congo) are also members of the Economic and Monetary Community of Central Africa (CEMAC) and share a common currency, the Central African franc (CFA).

In this book the following countries will be considered as being part of the central African sub-region: Democratic Republic of the Congo, Republic of the Congo, Equatorial Guinea, Gabon, Cameroon, the Central African Republic and western Uganda (to a certain extent). This is because these different countries in the sub-region have similar cultures and traditions – especially the two Congos, from where most of the tales in this collection come. The folktales herein derive from the following ethnic groups: Basoko, Boloki, Bushongo, Songora (Democratic Republic of the Congo), Kongo (Republic of the Congo and Democratic Republic of the Congo), Mpongwe

(Gabon), Benga (Equatorial Guinea and Gabon), etc. Quite a significant number of the tales featured here come from the Lower Congo Basin, but most derive from the Kongo ethnic group which straddles the two countries, the Democratic Republic of the Congo and Republic of the Congo, and the entire sub-region. Because it is a fluidly defined area we will not capitalize 'central' in order to differentiate it from more political definitions.

It is worth noting that, despite the diversity of ethnic groups in the sub-region, their beliefs and worldviews closely resemble those in other parts of Africa. As a result, most of the folktales in this book have echoes to those from beyond the borders of the central African sub-region. In other words, what is true of the folktales of the sub-region is also true, to a large extent, of the folktales of other communities in Africa.

The Origin of Folktales

Close research on the study and concept of the folktale reveals the following questions: Who tells folktales in the world now? What stories are told and for what audience? How are the stories narrated, through which media and for what purpose? If in the past the folktale belonged to the hearths of peasant and rural societies, in whose artistic library or arena are modern stories inspired, created and transmitted? It is an axiom in folklore studies that the old stories did not belong to individual creators, hence the very name 'folktale' – that is, an anonymous tale owned and transmitted by the folk, the ordinary people of various societies. These days, with the evolution of new technology and the primacy given to copyrights, most storytellers are identified. Yet are the stories narrated in modern electronic media and channels amenable to be classified as 'folktales'? In other words, do the context, audience and media of storytelling affect the generic status of the folktale?

Generally speaking, folktales originated among peasants and villagers without much formal education. These stories were shared among generations as a way of presenting everyday life lessons and useful information in a format that was easy to understand. Perhaps we should return to the basics by recalling the generic antiquity of the folktale. It is all bound up to what Chinua Achebe has described in *What Has Literature Got to Do With It?* (2008) as '… the compulsive urge of humanity to signify, renew and immortalise itself through stories'. In his own words

> *The creative rondo resolves on people and stories. Was it stories first, then people, or the other way round?*

Achebe's insights here are of clear theoretical significance for the study of literature. A careful analysis of the Achebean thesis shows that stories are created by human beings for the entertainment and edification of others.

The answer to Achebe's question above, asking whether stories came before humanity or human beings invented stories, can be answered with reference to the anthropology of the human race, or *homohabilis*, *homo erectus* and *homo sapiens*. Surely humanity evolved first before it fashioned the medium of stories to narrate and interpret its environment; in the process, it educated and entertained itself. The themes, characters and images in stories are metaphorical reflections and refractions of human desires and behaviours. One can therefore reason that human beings arrived first, before stories came to celebrate them. The phenomenon of myths and legends lends credence to this deductive conclusion.

This point may appear to be contradicted by narratives in which divine or celestial forces dominate or overwhelm humans. Examples are creation stories, in which the appearance of humans is depicted as proceeding from the pre-existence of gods or the divine. Yet these are only metaphorical projections of the human mind: the gods or divine orders that take priority over humans are themselves fictive images of the fertile human imagination.

We can take the next logical step by stating that the art of stories or folktales originated in Black Africa (Sub-Saharan Africa), a point established beyond doubt by specialist archaeological studies. Evidence reveals that the origin of the human race occurred in the Olduvai Gorge near the Great Lakes Region in northern Tanzania, around approximately 3.6 million years ago. All of humanity and its variegated colours – black, white, and yellow – subsequently spread and peopled the rest of the earth from this original site. The Senegalese Egyptologist Cheikh Anta Diop has provided proof of this in his works, especially in *Civilisation or Barbarism: An Authentic*

Anthropology (1991). Human language and verbal communication also evolved from this 'African Garden of Eden'. The Hebrew story about the other Garden of Eden, the one that hosted Adam and Eve as described in the Judaeo-Christian Bible, came several million years after the African one. African people are therefore not the offspring of the Adamic family.

Early and Later Folktale Collections in the Central African Sub-region

The systematic collection of central African folktales began in the nineteenth century as Christian missionaries, and later colonial administrators and travellers, began to penetrate the societies in the sub-region. They sought to learn the languages and record the observations of the cultures they encountered. Traders, whose contacts go much further back, rarely wrote down what they experienced. So it is to the period of missionaries and colonial adminstrators mentioned above, which continued until roughly 1940, that we owe several influential collections from which folktales have been widely anthologized. Many of these collections offer versions of the stories in their original language. However, few provide reliable information on the informant or on the circumstances of their collection.

Some collections of folktales made during this time could be considered as classics. This is the case for most of the collections from missionaries that are in French, such as *Contes et Légendes de Pygmées* (*Pygmy Tales and Legends*, 1931) by H. Trilles, Joseph Van Wing and Clement Scholler's *Légendes de Bakongo Orientaux* (*Legends of the Eastern Bakongo*, 1940) and A. de Rop's *Versions et fragments de l'épopée Mongo* (*Versions and Fragments of the Mongo Epic*, 1987). Some of the scholarship is in Flemish, however, reflecting the Belgian origin of the collectors.

In the period since the 1960s, the era of independence for many African countries, including central African nations, the enterprise was renewed, albeit under a somewhat different premise. The collections were no longer intended to assist administrators in understanding their colonial subjects or to assist missionaries in learning the local languages; they were rather intended to preserve and present the national heritages of oral literature and the collective wisdom and worldview of the given people. For the Francophone countries in the sub-region (Gabon, Cameroon and the Central African Republic), the French government subsidized (in the name of the Francophonie) the publication of folktale collections, usually presented in bilingual formats. From the Congo, the Centre d'études ethnographiques du Bandundu (CEEBA: Bandundu Centre for Ethnographic Studies) published over a dozen collections of tales of peoples in the sub-region.

Another important intergovernmental organization created in the central African sub-region to collect folktales for African cultural heritage is the Centre International de Recherche et de Documentation sur les Traditions et les Langues Africaines (the International Centre for Research and Documentation on African Traditions and African Languages). Known by its French acronym as CERDOTOLA and established in 1977 with the support of UNESCO, this institution promotes co-operation in scientific research for the preservation, dissemination and enhancement of African heritage. CERDOTOLA was established on the initiative of 10 central African countries. It now works for sub-regional co-operation in the fields of culture and human and social sciences, campaigning for the protection, safeguarding and promotion of African cultural heritage. CERDOTOLA's member states are Angola, Burundi, Cameroon, the Central African Republic, Chad, Congo, the Democratic Republic of the Congo, Equatorial Guinea, Rwanda and São Tomé and Principe. Its headquarters are in Yaoundé, Cameroon.

Two significant difficulties with all collections of folktales from the central African sub-region are those of availability and access. Many works have been published in limited print runs and restricted distribution. There are also, without doubt, countless tales transcribed and translated but not yet published; these still reside in the collections of the generations of researchers who have worked in the sub-region.

The Concept of the Folktale

The folktale is a delectable verbal art form that has charmed humanity through the ages. Its etymology indicates that it is a conflation of two ideas, namely folk (meaning the people or community) and a tale, a narrative or story. Although the art of the folktale has existed in Africa from time immemorial, African scholars of the genre were inducted into it by European traditions of cultural and folklore studies. As with other domains of intellectual production, the folktale is largely viewed in these studies as being artistically inferior to stories narrated and transmitted in written formats. European interest in the folktale form derived from anthropological and cultural studies conducted in the milieu of colonialism from the mid-nineteenth century, according to Okpewho in *African Oral Literature: Backgrounds, Character and Continuity* (1992). At first the term 'folklore' was used as a 'catch all' term to embody nearly everything in oral cultures.

The term 'folklore' was coined in 1846 by the English archivist William Thoms to refer to endangered elements and expressions of oral and popular culture under the pressure of capitalist industrialization. In England and part of Western Europe, this was the age of Romanticism in the arts and literature. Students of culture sought to preserve these vanishing traditions by making them subjects worthy of academic enquiry. Godini Darah, in an article entitled 'A Survey of Studies on African Folklore', published by the *Nigerian Journal of Oral Literature* (2013), has described how European agents in Africa made frantic efforts to record and translate field materials classified as 'folklore'.

Many of the stories in this collection came as a result of these European efforts. However, the political motive was to unravel systems of thought and worldviews encoded in the narratives – not to safeguard them, but to use the knowledge to confirm a prevailing racist view of Africans as the 'primitive' and 'uncivilized' children of the human race. This theory of Social Darwinism framed much of the anthropological and sociopolitical policies applied in Africa by European colonial regimes. Consequently, early studies in the folktale art form suffered from this racist prejudice. The damage inflicted on the African intellectual imagination by this biased approach to folktale scholarship has been examined in detail in works by Adeboye Balalola (1966), John Mbiti (1966), Ruth Finnegan (1970), Isidore Okpewho (1979, 1983, 1992,

1998), Kashim Tala (1989, 1999), Godini Darah (2013), Enongene Sone (2018) and many other scholars.

It is important to note that despite the differences in the oral narrative genres, as I discussed in my introduction to *Southern African Folktales* in this same series (2023), the term 'folktale' is used in this collection – and in the many cultures and traditions of the central African sub-region – to embrace all kinds of oral narratives such as myths, legends and the traditional folktale.

Also despite the differences noted above, folktales in the cultures and traditions of the central African sub-region constitute the moral and ethical component of the people's culture and philosophy. They constitute the traditional beliefs and customs passed on orally, either during moonlit nights or around the fire at night. In some cases folktales are accompanied by songs, adding beauty and drama to the story to hold the audience's concentration and attention.

The characters in folktales range from human beings through animals to spirits. Each character is portrayed in all the features of its existence. It is made to act, speak and communicate according to the archetypal characteristics of the personality being portrayed, whether this is a spirit, an animal or a human being. As a result these characters co-mingle, with the setting and situation causing them to understand one another. In a typical folktale trees talk and animals converse with human beings and each other; they also engage with spirits in a unique way. Such communication is based on the uniqueness of the situation. As has been hinted above, folktales are crucial for the imparting of appropriate knowledge to the younger generation.

The Enchantment of Storytelling

For centuries, humans have used storytelling as a means of communicating, connecting and relationship-building. We create our lives and the world around us through the stories we tell each other and what they mean to us.

We can enlarge Achebe's view of the power of stories by examining that of another Nigerian master storyteller, Ben Okri. His novel *Famished*

Road won the Booker Prize for Literature in 1991, making him both the youngest and the first Black author to win the award. I would like to refer to his description of the storyteller as contained in his book, *A Way of Being Free* (1997).

> *The earliest storytellers were magi, seers, bards, griots, shamans. They were, it would seem, as old as time, and as terrifying to gaze upon as the mysteries with which they wrestled. They wrestled with the mysteries and transformed them into myths which coded the world and helped the community to live through one more darkness, with eyes wide open, and with hearts set alight.*
>
> *[...] The storyteller's art changed through ages. From battling dread in words and incantations before their people did in reality, they became repositories of the people's wisdom and follies. They became the living memory of a people. Often, conscripted by kings, they became the memory of a people's origins, and carried with them the long line of ancestries and lineages. Most important of all, they were the living libraries, the keepers of legends and lore. They knew the causes and mutations of things, the herbs, trees, plants, cures for diseases, causes of wars, causes of victory, the ways in which victory often precipitates defeat, or defeat victory, the lineages of gods, the rites humans have to perform to the gods. They knew of follies and restitutions, were advocates of new and old ways of being, were custodians of culture, recorders of change. They kept the oldest and truest dreams and visions of their people alive. They also kept alive the great failings, the healing tragedies of the never-ending journey towards their utopias, the ever-moving dream of happiness.*

As if anticipating the death of storytelling, Okri adds:

> *When great storytellers die, a thousand years of unconfronted journeys, unguided journeys towards the deceptive lights of future civilisations also perish in their silence.*

This statement echoes the lament by the Malian folklorist Amadou Hampâté Bâ that 'every old person who dies in Africa is like a library destroyed by fire'.

Relating the enchanting power of stories to the reading of books, Okri observes that the first joy, therefore, is the joy of service. Stories enrich the world and stories can change lives. He adds:

> stories, as can be seen from my choice of associate images, are living things; and their real life begins when they start to live in you.

Further poignant points may be drawn from Okri's work. He says that even when it is tragic, storytelling is always beautiful. It tells us that all fates can be ours. It wraps up our lives with the magic that we only see long afterwards. Storytelling reconnects us to the great sea of human destiny, human suffering and human transcendence. He also observes that there are two essential joys in storytelling: the joy of the telling (that is, of the artistic discovery) and the joy of the listening (that is, of the imagination). Both joys are magical and important. Of the two joys, the first teaches us humility while the second deepens our humanity.

In sum, this collection emanated from the tradition of storytelling in the central African sub-region and the effect that this tradition, including narratives, has on its people and communities. This tradition continues to be vibrant in Africa as a whole and in central Africa in particular, although this vibrancy is relative as one moves from one ethnic group or community to the other. While modernity, expressed through modern forms of entertainment and information technology, is taking a toll on this tradition in some communities in the central African sub-region, the degree of its entrenchment and its perceived relevance have in many ways largely accounted for its survival.

So long as the many cultures of the central African sub-region remain largely oral, storytelling will continue to occupy centre stage in the lives of the people. As for its relevance, so long as people continue to be baffled by the wonders of creation and have to confront the vicissitudes of life, so long as they seek ways in their culture to increase leisure time and lessen boredom, and appreciate the rate at which the world is becoming a global village in which everyone is his brother's keeper, storytelling will continue to have a place in the life of individuals and their communities. For stories are not merely chronicles of what happened or fancies of the imagination; they are more about the meanings that we find in life itself.

Enongene Mirabeau Sone (Introduction) is Professor of English and African Literature as well as Folklore Studies at Walter Sisulu University in South Africa. Prof. Sone holds a BA, MA and MPhil in African literature from the University of Dschang in Cameroon and completed his PhD in African oral literature studies from the University of KwaZulu-Natal, South Africa. He has taught in many universities in Africa and has published extensively on various aspects of African oral literature and folklore in reputable academic journals across the globe. His collaboration with leading world and African folklorists led to the publication of two seminal books in oral literature and folklore studies: *The Challenge of Folklore to the Humanities* (2021) edited by Dan Ben-Amos, and *The Palgrave Handbook of African Oral Traditions and Folklore* (2021) edited by Akintunde Akinyemi and Toyin Falola. He is a C2 rated researcher by the South African National Research Foundation (NRF).

Life & Death,
Creation & Origins

THIS SECTION CONSISTS of myths that deal with creation and the origin of life, death and the afterlife. The stories occupy a higher place in the pyramidal structure of oral narratives; they deal more with human beings and the forces above them. Some of the stories in this section recount how the world came into being, who the various gods are and what powers they control; they describe how the actions of these gods affect the world and people, and the means by which people in turn can propitiate these powers. In stories such as 'Why some men are white and others black' and 'Why the dog became a friend of man', we gather how through the activities of the gods a reality came into being.

Such stories attempt to explain the metaphysical phenomena of life. The ideas in the stories in this section, presented originally as literature, are exciting and stimulating; they throw new light on man's relationship to God and on his attempt to come to terms with the supernatural and the inevitable. Furthermore, stories such as 'The fight between the fetishes: Lifuma and Chimpukela', as well as 'The fetish of Chilunga', provide important evidence about 'fetishes'. These are both supernatural spirits and the power of those spirits embodied in a physical object of some kind among Kongo people. Some of the stories deal with the activities of a cultural hero in illo tempore (essentially the mythical time before recorded history, or 'once upon a time') by revealing to human beings anything that is beneficial to them: the arts, sources of food, the use of fire and the establishment of values by which a people is to live.

In other words, they embody the values of a people and guide the individual towards the standards and goals of his culture.

Lastly, some of the stories explain the origin of natural phenomena: day and night, the dry season and the rainy season, thunder and lightning, etc. A case in point is the story of 'Why the Congo Robin has a Red Breast'. Such stories use analogical reasoning, relating the familiar to the unfamiliar by means of likeness. We can conclude that despite their elements of fantasy, fictitiousness and probably falsity, this category of stories of 'life and death, creation and origins' plays a meaningful role in people's growth, survival and existence in the sub-region. The psychosocial behaviour and comportment of human beings are partly accounted for by their emotional and philosophical attachment to this cosmic environment which oversees their existence.

How the Earth (Land) Came to Be
(From the Batanga people, Cameroon, told by Nson Ngambi, storyteller)

IN THE BEGINNING, the earth was just a vast body of water. Three gods lived in the sky: Mabea the Noble, Mabea the Labourer and Mabea the Silent. As time went by, Mabea the Noble and Mabea the Labourer created an axe which was used to build canoes in which they could sail the waters, but they did not have wood with which to build the canoes.

Since the three gods were curious to know if there existed a piece of land beyond the water, Mabea the Silent was asked by the other two to go to the earth and find out since he had the ability to see beyond the ordinary. He transformed into a fish, went into the water, explored and discovered there was no land surface in it. He only discovered a white spot on the surface of the water, but he didn't know whether to consider it as a hard surface or not. He finally went back and told his brothers what he saw, and they decided to go back seven days after to confirm what it was. When they went back, they saw that the water had disappeared leaving a marshy surface on which birds could perch. Mabea the Labourer then threw stones from the sky and filled the empty surface, and it finally became earth.

After the creation of the first land, Mabea the Silent continued to study the white spots which gradually became a hard substance and as a result became land; but it was just a vast surface with no vegetation. In order to give vegetation to the empty surface, Mabea the Noble gave Mabea the Labourer the seed of a creeping plant which he planted and not long after, the plant covered all the land's surface, growing into different kinds of trees and grasses. "What we lack on this earth now is inhabitants", said Mabea the Silent. "Go and cut a branch of the creeping grass", said Mabea the Noble. Mabea the Labourer went and cut the creeping plant and as each drop of liquid from the plant touched the earth, different kinds of creatures came into being, both human and animal. That is how the first inhabitants on earth were mysteriously created.

Kaikiyourou
(From the Hadjarai peoples, Chad, told by Siddi Hamadou, storyteller)

IN A VERY LONG DISTANT PAST in Hadjarai in the Northern part of Chad, a basket-maker met Mr Death, who was going to the market to sell his teeth. When Death realized that the basket-maker was lacking one tooth, he offered her a tooth, which she tried to fit in. Once she put the tooth in the hollow space in her mouth, it stuck and couldn't come out. Death cried: "Give back my tooth". The basket-maker tried in vain to remove the tooth. She promised to give Death a stable full of goats as compensation, but Death rejected this offer. She then proposed to offer him a herd of oxen, which Death turned down again. In the third offer, the basket-maker said, "I will give you the most precious thing I have, that is, Kaikiyourou, my son. He is a brave hunter, who is very successful in hunting game with his seven dogs." Death accepted this third offer. The arrangement was that Death would encounter Kaikiyourou, his gift, as the latter returned home from a hunting expedition on a specified evening. On that evening, Death stood on the way where hunters walk back home from hunting, waiting to see Kaikiyourou with the following song:

"I have offered the woman (basket-maker) my tooth and the tooth got stuck in her mouth. In compensation she gave a stable full of goats and a herd of oxen, which I refused. She offered me Kaikiyourou, the hunter, and she said he was a very brave hunter who would kill many games for me with his seven dogs."

The first hunters who heard him told him Kaikiyourou was not among them, and that he would come later. Death kept waiting until he saw Kaikiyourou coming with his seven dogs and a game on his shoulder. Death repeated the song above and when Kaikiyourou heard his name, he said: "I am Kaikiyourou." Death said: "Put down your belongings and let us fight." (The tricky thing here is that Death cannot own Kaikiyourou in his human form, Kaikiyourou must die to belong to Death.) The fight began and Kaikiyourou overpowered Death. When Death felt his defeat he said to Kaikiyourou: "It is not right and just. We have to fight gently. Do not treat me violently." The fight continued, and this time Kaikiyourou was overpowered by Death, who seized and strangled him by the throat. Kaikiyourou called four of his seven dogs, namely Kidabilbiljui, Kodokoussou, Dyindonafjui, and Bodomarjay, who immediately rushed to his rescue and together they fought, defeated and killed Death.

As Kaikiyourou was about to go home, he was stopped by the spirit of Death. To prevent Death appearing to him in spirit again, Kaikiyourou burnt his corpse. After this he tried to go away and again he was stopped by a voice coming from the ashes saying: "You are going nowhere." To this voice, Kaikiyourou poured water on the ashes until it was washed away completely, and he went back home this time successfully. While at home, Kaikiyourou met his mother, who was singing: "I am a queen. I found a tooth and I gave my son as compensation." On hearing this song, Kaikiyourou gave a slap on her lips and the tooth fell out and disappeared.

Origins of the Ivory Trade
(From the Benga people, Equatorial Guinea and Gabon)

UKANAKÂDI LIVED in his great house, having with him his many wives. One of them bore him a son whom he named Lombolokindi.

As time passed on, the child grew in size, and strength and skill. Because of this, his mother was treated by Ukanakâdi with special favor. This aroused the jealousy of one of the other wives. She took the child one day, and secretly gave him a certain evil medicine, which caused him to be constantly hungry, hungry, hungry. Even when he ate enormously, no amount of food could fill his stomach or satisfy his appetite.

Ukanakâdi finally was angry at the child, and said to the mother, "All the food of my plantations is finished, eaten up by your child. We have no more plantains, no more cassava, no more eddoes, nor anything else in our plantations or in our kitchen gardens. You have brought a curse upon us! Go away to your father's house!" (He said this, not knowing that a Fetish-Medicine had caused all the trouble.)

So the mother went away with her child to her father's house. But there too, the boy ate up all the food of the gardens, until there was none left. Then her father said to her, "All my food is done here; go with your child to your grandfather, and find food there."

So, she went to her grandfather's. But there the same trouble followed.

After she had been there some time, and the child was now a stout lad, and she saw that they were no longer welcome, she said to herself, "Alas! It is so! All my people are weary of me! I will not longer stay at grandfather's. I will go wandering into the forest, and, with the child, will see what I can get."

Taking with her only two ears of corn, she went far off with the lad into the forest. After much wandering, and eating only wild fruits, she selected a spot without having any idea of the locality, and built a shed for a camp in which to stay. At this place, she planted the corn. It quickly sprang up, and bore abundantly. And she planted other gardens. After a time came very many birds; and they began to eat up the corn. She exclaimed, "My son and I alone have come here, and have planted our corn. How is this that all the birds have come so soon to destroy it?" And the son, who by this time had grown to be almost a young man, said to her, "Mother, why do you allow the birds to eat? Why don't you do something?" She replied, "Why do the birds thus destroy the corn? What can I do?" So he came out of the shed into the yard in front of their house and shouted at the birds, "You birds, who have come here to spoil my corn! With this stick I will kill you all!" But the birds jeered at him, saying, "No! Not all! Only one shall die!"

The young man went into the house, took up a magic spearhead he owned, fitted it onto a stick as a shaft; and going out again, he hurled it at the birds. The spear flew at them, pursuing each one, and piercing every one of them in succession. Then it flew on and on, away out into the forest.

The young man took up another medicine charm that he had with him, and, calling to his spear by name, shouted after it, "Tombeseki-o-o! Come back, back, back, here! Again, again, again, return!" The spear heard him, and obeyed, and came back. He laid hold of it, and put it again in the shed. So, he and his mother lived there. She planted a very large garden of plantains, cassava, and many other vegetables, a very large quantity. And her gardens grew, and bore fruit in plenty.

Then there came all kinds of small animals, hogs, antelopes and gazelles, very many; and they spoiled the gardens, eating the fruit, and breaking down the stalks. The mother exclaimed, "My son! The animals have finished all my food of the gardens; everything is lost! Why is this?" He replied, "Yes, it is so! And when they come again tomorrow, I know what I will do to them!"

When they came the next day, he went into the house, took the spear, flung it; and it flew from beast to beast, piercing all of them in succession. Then it went off, flying into the forest, as before. He called after it to return. The spear heard, and obeyed, and came back to the house.

Then he and his mother sat down in the house, complaining of their hunger, and how the animals had spoiled their gardens. So the mother went out, and gathered up what little remained, brought it into the house, and cooked it, leaves and all.

When the mother had planted a third garden, and it had grown, a herd of elephants came to destroy it. She cried out, "Ah! Njâku! What shall I do? You have come to destroy all my gardens! Shall I die with hunger?" The son brought out his spear, and shouting at the elephants, threatened to kill them all. But the herd laughed and said, "When you throw that spear, only one of us shall fall." He threw the spear at the one that spoke. It struck him and all the elephants in succession; and they all died. The spear kept on in its flight into the forest. The young man cried after it, "Spear! Spear! Come back, come back!" And it came to him again.

Each time that the spear had thus gone through the forest, it had mowed down the trees in its path; and thus was made the clearing which the mother had at once utilized for the planting of her successive gardens.

After the elephants, mother and son sat down again in their hunger; they had nothing to eat but leaves. These she cooked; and they ate them all at once.

Then she planted another garden, thinking that now there were no more beasts who would come to ravage. But she did not know that there was still left in the forest one very, very large elephant that had not been in the company of the herd that the son had killed.

There was also, in that forest, one very, very large ox. When the gardens had grown, that ox came, and began to destroy. The young man hurled his spear at the ox. It was wounded, but did not fall; and it went away into the forest with the spear sticking in its side. The young man pursued the ox, following, following, following far away. But he did not overtake it.

On his way, he reached unexpectedly a small, lonely hut, where an old woman was living by herself. When she saw him, she said to him, "Do not follow any longer. That ox was a person like yourself. He is dead; and his people have hung up that spear in their house."

The young man told the old woman that he was very hungry. So she cut down for him an entire bunch of plantains. He was so exceedingly hungry that he could not wait; and before the plantains were entirely cooked, he began to eat of them, and ate them all. The old woman exclaimed, "What sort of a person is this who eats in this way?" In her wisdom, thinking over the matter, she felt sure it was some disease that caused his voracity.

The man, being tired with his journey, fell asleep; and she, by her magic power, caused him to hear or feel nothing. While he was in this state, she cut him open. As she did so, his disease rushed out with a whizzing sound; and she cut away, and removed a tumor, that looked like a stone of glass. That was the thing that had caused his excessive hunger all his life. By her power, she closed the wound.

When he awoke, she cooked food for him, of which he ate, and was satisfied with an ordinary amount like any other person. She then told him what she had done, and said, "As you are now cured, you may pursue that ox. You will reach his town, and you will obtain your spear. But, as you go there, you must make a pretense. You must pretend that you are mourning for the dead. You must cry out in wailing, 'Who killed my uncle-o-o! Who killed my uncle-o-o!'" Thus he went on his way; and finally came to a town where was a crowd of people gathered in and about a house of mourning. Beginning to wail, he went among the mourners. They received him, with the idea that he was some distant relative who had come to attend the funeral.

He walked up the street of this town of the Ox-Man, and entering into the house of mourning, said, "Had not the way been so long, my mother also would have come; but, I have come to look at that thing that killed my Uncle." They welcomed him, commended his devotion, and said, "You will not go today. Stay with us. Sleep here tonight; and tomorrow you shall see and take away with you, to show to your mother, that thing."

So, the next day, they gave him the spear, and said, "Go, but do not delay. Return for the closing ceremony (the "Washing") of the mourning." He went away, and came again to the old woman. She said to him, when he showed her the spear, "I told you truly that you would obtain it. But, go with it and this bundle I have made of the tumor of your disease, and show them to your mother."

So he came back to his mother. She rejoiced; and, not knowing that he was cured, she cooked a very large and unusually varied quantity of food, for his unusual hunger, two whole bunches of plantains, and eddoes, and potatoes and yams, etc. Of this he ate only a little, sufficient for an ordinary hunger. As he had not yet told her of his being cured, she cried out in surprise, "What is this? My son will die, for not eating!" And she asked him, "What is the matter?" He replied, "No, I have eaten, and am satisfied. And, mother, this bundle is what I was cured of." Then he told her of what that old woman had done.

On another day, that great elephant that had remained in the forest, came and began to eat in the garden. The son said, "Mother! What shall I do? I thought I had killed all the elephants. I did not know there was this great big one left!" (Nor did he just then know there were left a very great many more.)

Taking his spear, he hurled it, and wounded the elephant. It did not fall, but went away with the spear in its side. The man followed, followed, followed, pursuing the elephant, not, as the other animals had gone, into the forest, but away toward the sea; and it died on the sea beach. There the man found it and his spear.

The sea was new to him; he had not seen it since his childhood. He climbed up on the elephant's body, in order to see all around. As he turned his eyes seaward, he saw a ship coming on the horizon. Also, the people on this ship were looking landward, and they said, "There is something standing on the shore like a person. Let the vessel go there, and see what is ashore."

So, the ship anchored, and a surfboat was launched into the water to go ashore. When the crew landed, they saw the carcass of the elephant, and a person standing with a spear who warned them, "Do not approach near to me!" But they replied, "We do not want you, nor will we hurt you. But we want these tusks of ivory of this elephant. We want elephants." Wondering at this wish, he cut out the tusks, and gave them to the strangers, adding, "Off in the forest are very, very many more tusks, more than I can number. You seem to like them; but they are of no use to me." They earnestly said, "But, bring them, bring them! We will buy them of you with abundance of goods." He agreed, and promised, "I am going now; but, let your ship wait, and I will bring all of those things as many as it is possible for me to carry."

So, he went back to his mother; and he and she carried many, many tusks. They filled the ship full; and the crew of the ship sent ashore an immense quantity of goods. When the vessel went away, it left ashore two carpenters, with direction to build a fine house, and have it completed before the vessel should come again.

The man remained there awhile with the carpenters, after the ship had gone.

One day, looking, on a journey down the coast, at a point of land, he was surprised to recognize his father's town, where he and his mother had lived in his childhood. He said to himself, "That's my father's town! I want them to come to me, and live at my town!" He sent word to them; they removed, and all of them came to live with him. And he married one of their young women. (In the meanwhile, he had brought his mother from the forest.)

While he was living at his new home, one day looking seaward, he saw the promised ship coming to get more ivory, and to give more goods. And he went off to the vessel.

Among the women who were still living of his father's people who had known him as a child, was the one who had given him the evil "medicine" long ago; her object in giving it having been to kill him. After he had gone off to the vessel, this woman came to his wife's home, and, seeing the spear hanging tied from the roof, said, "What is that thing tied there?" His wife replied, "It is a kind of "medicine" of my husband's. It must not be touched." But the woman said, "I know that thing; and what it does." Then she seized it, and put into it its handle the man had removed. She hurled the spear out to sea, and it went on and on, passing over the ship. The man sitting in the saloon, said to the crew, as he recognized the spear in its flight, "I saw something pass over the ship!" He went up on deck, and called after it, "My spear! Come back! Come! Come! Come back!" And he told all the people of the vessel to go below lest they should be injured. The spear turned and came back to him; and he took possession of it. Then said he to the crew, "Come! Escort me ashore!" They landed him ashore, and waited to see what he intended doing.

He called all his father's family, and asked, "Why is it that you have tried to kill me today with this spear! For this, I will this day kill all of you." He summoned all the people to come together. When they had come, he had his mother bring out that tumour bundle, and said, "This is the thing of long ago with which that woman (pointing to the one who in childhood had given him the evil disease) tried to injure me. And, for the same reason, she threw the spear today; thus trying a second time to kill me. None of you have rebuked her. So, I shall kill you all as her associates."

Though they were of his father's family, he attacked and killed them all. The whole town died that day, excepting himself, his wife, his mother and his sister. These four, not liking to remain at that evil place, went off and took passage on the ship.

So, he journeyed, and came to the country of the white people at Manga-Maněně; and never returned to Africa. But, he kept up a trade in ivory with his native country. But for him, that trade would not have been begun. For, besides his having brought the first elephant to the seacoast, he told the people of Manga-Maněně beyond the Great Sea, about the tribes of people, and about the elephants that were so abundant, in Africa. And that is all.

The Creation of Man
(From the Congo and central Africa)

IN THE OLD, OLD TIME, all this land, and indeed all the whole earth was covered with sweet water. But the water dried up or disappeared somewhere, and the grasses, herbs and plants began to spring up above the ground, and some grew, in the

course of many moons, into trees, great and small, and the water was confined into streams and rivers, pools and lakes, and as the rain fell it kept the streams and rivers running, and the pools and lakes always fresh.

There was no living thing moving upon the earth, until one day there sat by one of the pools a large Toad. How long he had lived, or how he came to exist, is not known; it is suspected, however, that the water brought him forth out of some virtue that was in it. In the sky there was only the Moon glowing and shining – on the earth there was but this one Toad. It is said that they met and conversed together, and that one day the Moon said to him:

"I have an idea. I propose to make a man and a woman to live on the fruits of the earth, for I believe that there is rich abundance of food on it fit for such creatures."

"Nay," said the Toad, "let me make them, for I can make them fitter for the use of the earth than thou canst, for I belong to the earth, while thou belongest to the sky."

"Verily," replied the Moon, "thou hast the power to create creatures which shall have but a brief existence; but if I make them, they will have something of my own nature; and it is a pity that the creatures of one's own making should suffer and die. Therefore, O Toad, I propose to reserve the power of creation for myself, that the creatures may be endowed with perfection and enduring life."

"Ah, Moon, be not envious of the power which I share with thee, but let me have my way. I will give them forms such as I have often dreamed of. The thought is big within me, and I insist upon realizing my ideas."

"And thou be so resolved, observe my words, both thou and they shall die. Thou I shall slay myself and end utterly; and thy creatures can but follow thee, being of such frail material as thou canst give them."

"Ah, thou art angry now, but I heed thee not. I am resolved that the creatures to inhabit this earth shall be of my own creating. Attend thou to thine own empire in the sky."

Then the Moon rose and soared upward, where with his big, shining face he shone upon all the world.

The Toad grew great with his conception, until it ripened and issued out in the shape of twin beings, full-grown male and female. These were the first like our kind that ever trod the earth.

The Moon beheld the event with rage, and left his place in the sky to punish the Toad, who had infringed the privilege that he had thought to reserve for himself. He came direct to Toad's pool, and stood blazingly bright over it.

"Miserable," he cried, "what hast thou done?"

"Patience, Moon, I but exercised my right and power. It was within me to do it, and lo, the deed is done."

"Thou hast exalted thyself to be my equal in thine own esteem. Thy conceit has clouded thy wit, and obscured the memory of the warning I gave thee. Even hadst thou obtained a charter from me to attempt the task, thou couldst have done no better than thou hast done. As much as thou art inferior to me, so these will be inferior to those I could have endowed this earth with. Thy creatures are pitiful things, mere animals without sense, without the gift of perception or self-protection. They see, they breathe, they exist; their lives can be measured by one round journey of mine. Were it not out of pity for them, I would even let them die. Therefore for pity's sake I propose to improve somewhat on what thou hast done: their lives shall be lengthened, and such intelligence as malformed beings as these can contain will I endow them with, that they may have guidance through a life which with all my power must be troubled and sore. But as for thee, whilst thou exist my rage is perilous to them, therefore to save thy kin I end thee."

Saying which the Moon advanced upon Toad, and the fierce sparks from his burning face were shot forth, and fell upon the Toad until he was consumed.

The Moon then bathed in the pool, that the heat of his anger might be moderated, and the water became so heated that it was like that which is in a pot over a fire, and he stayed in it until the hissing and bubbling had subsided.

Then the Moon rose out of the pool, and sought the creatures of Toad: and when he had found them, he called them unto him, but they were afraid and hid themselves.

At this sight the Moon smiled, as you sometimes see him on fine nights, when he is a clear white, and free from stain or blur, and he was pleased that Toad's creatures were afraid of him. "Poor things," said he, "Toad has left me much to do yet before I can make them fit to be the first of earthly creatures." Saying which he took hold of them, and bore them to the pool wherein he had bathed, and which had been the home of Toad. He held them in the water for some time, tenderly bathing them, and stroking them here and there as a potter does to his earthenware, until he had moulded them into something similar to the shape we men and women possess now. The male became distinguished by breadth of shoulder, depth of chest, larger bones, and more substantial form; the female was slighter in chest, slimmer of waist, and the breadth and fulness of the woman was midmost of the body at the hips. Then the Moon gave them names; the man he called Bateta, the woman Hanna, and he addressed them and said:

"Bateta, see this earth and the trees, and herbs and plants and grasses; the whole is for thee and thy wife Hanna, and for thy children whom Hanna thy wife shall bear unto thee. I have re-made thee greatly, that thou and thine may enjoy such things as thou mayest find needful and fit. In order that thou mayest discover what things are not noxious but beneficial for thee, I have placed the faculty of discernment within thy head, which thou must exercise before thou canst become wise. The more thou prove this, the more wilt thou be able to perceive the abundance of good things the earth possesses for the creatures which are to inhabit it. I have made thee and thy wife as perfect as is necessary for the preservation and enjoyment of the term of life, which by nature of the materials the Toad made thee of must needs be short. It is in thy power to prolong or shorten it. Some things I must teach thee. I give thee first an axe. I make a fire for thee, which thou must feed from time to time with wood, and the first and most necessary utensil for daily use. Observe me while I make it for thee."

The Moon took some dark clay by the pool and mixed it with water, then kneaded it, and twisted it around until its shape was round and hollowed within, and he covered it with the embers of the fire, and baked it; and when it was ready he handed it to them.

"This vessel," continued the Moon, "is for the cooking of food. Thou wilt put water into it, and place whatsoever edible thou desirest to eat in the water. Thou wilt then place the vessel on the fire, which in time will boil the water and cook the edible. All vegetables, such as roots and bulbs, are improved in flavour and give superior nourishment by being thus cooked. It will become a serious matter for thee to know which of all the things pleasant in appearance are also pleasant for the palate. But shouldst thou be long in doubt and fearful of harm, ask and I will answer thee."

Having given the man and woman their first lesson, the Moon ascended to the sky, and from his lofty place shone upon them, and upon all the earth with a pleased expression, which comforted greatly the lonely pair.

Having watched the ascending Moon until he had reached his place in the sky, Bateta and Hanna rose and travelled on by the beautiful light which he gave them, until they came to a very large tree that had fallen. The thickness of the prostrate trunk was about twice their height. At the greater end of it there was a hole, into which they could walk without bending. Feeling a desire for sleep, Bateta laid his fire down outside near the hollowed entrance, cut up dry fuel, and his wife piled it on the fire, while the flames grew brighter and lit the interior. Bateta took Hanna by the hand and entered within the tree, and the two lay down together. But presently both complained of the hardness of their bed, and Bateta, after pondering awhile, rose, and going out, plucked some fresh large leaves of a plant that grew near the fallen tree, and returned laden with it. He spread it about thickly, and Hanna rolled herself on it, and laughed gleefully as she said to Bateta that it was soft and smooth and nice; and opening her arms, she cried, "Come, Bateta, and rest by my side."

Though this was the first day of their lives, the Moon had so perfected the unfinished and poor work of the Toad that they were both mature man and woman. Within a month Hanna bore twins, of whom one was male and the other female, and they were tiny doubles of Bateta and Hanna, which so pleased Bateta that he ministered kindly to his wife who, through her double charge, was prevented from doing anything else.

Thus it was that Bateta, anxious for the comfort of his wife, and for the nourishment of his children, sought to find choice things, but could find little to please the dainty taste which his wife had contracted. Whereupon, looking up to Moon with his hands uplifted, he cried out:

"O Moon, list to thy creature Bateta! My wife lies languishing, and she has a taste strange to me which I cannot satisfy, and the children that have been born unto us feed upon her body, and her strength decreases fast. Come down, O Moon, and show me what fruit or herbs will cure her longing."

The Moon heard Bateta's voice, and coming out from behind the cloud with a white, smiling face, said, "It is well, Bateta; lo! I come to help thee."

When the Moon had approached Bateta, he showed the golden fruit of the banana – which was the same plant whose leaves had formed the first bed of himself and wife.

"O Bateta, smell this fruit. How likest thou its fragrance?"

"It is beautiful and sweet. O Moon, if it be as wholesome for the body as it is sweet to smell, my wife will rejoice in it."

Then the Moon peeled the banana and offered it to Bateta, upon which he boldly ate it, and the flavour was so pleasant that he besought permission to take one to his wife. When Hanna had tasted it she also appeared to enjoy it; but she said, "Tell Moon that I need something else, for I have no strength, and I am thinking that this fruit will not give to me what I lose by these children."

Bateta went out and prayed to Moon to listen to Hanna's words – which when he had heard, he said, "It was known to me that this should be, wherefore look round, Bateta, and tell me what thou seest moving yonder."

"Why, that is a buffalo."

"Rightly named," replied Moon. "And what follows it?"

"A goat."

"Good again. And what next?"

"An antelope."

"Excellent, O Bateta; and what may the next be?"

"A sheep."

"Sheep it is, truly. Now look up above the trees, and tell me what thou seest soaring over them."

"I see fowls and pigeons."

"Very well called, indeed," said Moon. "These I give unto thee for meat. The buffalo is strong and fierce, leave him for thy leisure; but the goat, sheep and fowls, shall live near thee, and shall partake of thy bounty.

There are numbers in the woods which will come to thee when they are filled with their grazing and their pecking. Take any of them – either goat, sheep or fowl – bind it, and chop its head off with thy hatchet. The blood will sink into the soil; the meat underneath the outer skin is good for food, after being boiled or roasted over the fire. Haste now, Bateta; it is meat thy wife craves, and she needs naught else to restore her strength. So prepare instantly and eat."

The Moon floated upward, smiling and benignant, and Bateta hastened to bind a goat, and made it ready as the Moon had advised. Hanna, after eating of the meat which was prepared by boiling, soon recovered her strength, and the children throve, and grew marvellously.

One morning Bateta walked out of his hollowed house, and lo! A change had come over the earth. Right over the tops of the trees a great globe of shining, dazzling light looked out from the sky, and blazed white and bright over all. Things that he had seen dimly before were now more clearly revealed. By the means of the strange light hung up in the sky he saw the difference between that which the Moon gave and that new brightness which now shone out. For, without, the trees and their leaves seemed clad in a luminous coat of light, while underneath it was but a dim reflection of that which was without, and to the sight it seemed like the colder light of the Moon.

And in the cooler light that prevailed below the foliage of the trees there were gathered hosts of new and strange creatures; some large, others of medium, and others of small size.

Astonished at these changes, he cried, "Come out, O Hanna, and see the strange sights without the dwelling, for verily I am amazed, and know not what has happened."

Obedient, Hanna came out with the children and stood by his side, and was equally astonished at the brightness of the light and at the numbers of creatures which in all manner of sizes and forms stood in the shade ranged around them, with their faces towards the place where they stood.

"What may this change portend, O Bateta?" asked his wife.

"Nay, Hanna, I know not. All this has happened since the Moon departed from me."

"Thou must perforce call him again, Bateta, and demand the meaning of it, else I shall fear harm unto thee, and unto these children."

"Thou art right, my wife, for to discover the meaning of all this without other aid than my own wits would keep us here until we perished."

Then he lifted his voice, and cried out aloud upward, and at the sound of his voice all the creatures gathered in the shades looked upward, and cried with their voices; but the meaning of their cry, though there was an infinite variety of sound, from the round, bellowing voice of the lion to the shrill squeak of the mouse, was:

"Come down unto us, O Moon, and explain the meaning of this great change unto us; for thou only who madest us can guide our sense unto the right understanding of it."

When they had ended their entreaty unto the Moon, there came a voice from above, which sounded like distant thunder, saying, "Rest ye where ye stand, until the brightness of this new light shall have faded, and ye distinguish my milder light and that of the many children which have been born unto me, when I shall come unto you and explain."

Thereupon they rested each creature in its own place, until the great brightness, and the warmth which the strange light gave faded and lessened, and it was observed that it disappeared from view on the opposite side to that where it had first been seen, and also immediately after at the place of its disappearance the Moon was seen, and all over the sky were visible the countless little lights which the children of the Moon gave.

Presently, after Bateta had pointed these out to Hanna and the children, the Moon shone out bland, and its face was covered with gladness, and he left the sky smiling, and floated down to the earth, and stood not far off from Bateta, in view of him and his family, and of all the creatures under the shade.

"Hearken, O Bateta, and ye creatures of prey and pasture. A little while ago, ye have seen the beginning of the measurement of time, which shall be divided hereafter into day and night. The time that lapses between the Sun's rising and its setting shall be called day, that which shall lapse between its setting and re-rising shall be called night. The light of the day proceeds from the Sun, but the light of the night proceeds from me and from my children the stars; and as ye are all my creatures, I have chosen that my softer light shall shine during the restful time wherein ye sleep, to recover the strength lost in the waking time, and that ye shall be daily waked for the working time by the stronger light of the Sun. This rule never-ending shall remain.

"And whereas Bateta and his wife are the first of creatures, to them, their families, and kind that shall be born unto them, shall be given pre-eminence over all creatures made, not that they are stronger, or swifter, but because to them only have I given understanding and a gift of speech to transmit it. Perfection and everlasting life had also been given, but the taint of the Toad remains in the system, and the result will be death – death to all living things, Bateta and Hanna excepted. In the fullness of time, when their limbs refuse to bear the burden of their bodies and their marrow has become dry, my first born shall return to me, and I shall absorb them. Children shall be born innumerable unto them, until families shall expand into tribes, and from here, as from a spring, mankind will outflow and overspread all lands, which are now but wild and wold, ay, even to the farthest edge of the earth.

"And hearken, O Bateta, the beasts which thou seest, have sprung from the ashes of the Toad. On the day that he measured his power against mine, and he was consumed by my fire, there was one drop of juice left in his head. It was a life-germ which soon grew into another toad. Though not equal in power to the parent toad, thou seest what he has done. Yonder beasts of prey and pasture and fowls are his work. As fast as they were conceived by him, and uncouth and ungainly they were, I dipped them into Toad's Pool, and perfected them outwardly, according to their uses, and, as thou seest, each specimen has its mate. Whereas, both thou and they alike have the acrid poison of the toad, thou from the parent, they in a greater measure from the child toad, the mortal taint when ripe will end both man and beast. No understanding nor gift of speech has been given to them, and they are as inferior to thyself as the child toad was to the parent toad. Wherefore, such qualities as thou mayst discover in them, thou mayst employ in thy services. Meantime, let them go out each to its own feeding ground, lair or covert, and grow and multiply, until the generations descending from thee shall have need for them. Enough for thee with the bounties of the forest, jungle and plain, are the goats, sheep and fowls. At thy leisure, Bateta, thou mayst strike and eat such beasts as thou seest akin in custom to these that will feed from thy hand. The waters abound in fish that are thine at thy need, the air swarms with birds which are also thine, as thy understanding will direct thee.

"Thou wilt be wise to plant all such edibles as thou mayest discover pleasing to the palate and agreeable to thy body, but be not rash in assuming that all things pleasant to the eye are grateful to thy inwards.

"So long as thou and Hanna are on the earth, I promise thee my aid and counsel; and what I tell thee and thy wife thou wilt do well to teach thy children, that the memory of useful things be not forgotten – for after I take thee to myself, I come no more to visit man. Enter thy house now, for it is a time, as I have told thee, for rest and sleep. At the shining of the greater light, thou wilt waken for active life and work, and family care and joys. The beasts shall also wander each to his home in the earth, on the tops of the trees, in the bush, or in the cavern. Fare thee well, Bateta, and have kindly care for thy wife Hanna and the children."

The Moon ended his speech, and floated upward, radiant and gracious, until he rested in his place in the sky, and all the children of the Moon twinkled for joy and gladness so brightly, as the parent of the world entered his house, that all the heavens for a short time seemed burning. Then the Moon drew over him his cloudy cloak, and the little children of the Moon seemed to get drowsy, for they twinkled dimly, and then a darkness fell over all the earth, and in the darkness man and beast retired, each to his own place, according as the Moon had directed.

A second time Bateta waked from sleep, and walked out to wonder at the intense brightness of the burning light that made the day. Then he looked around him, and his eyes rested upon a noble flock of goats and sheep, all of whom bleated their morning welcome, while the younglings pranced about in delight, and after curvetting around, expressed in little bleats the joy they felt at seeing their chief, Bateta. His attention was also called to the domestic fowls; there were red and white and spotted cocks, and as many coloured hens, each with its own brood of chicks. The hens trotted up to their master – cluck, cluck, clucking – the tiny chicks, following each its own mother – cheep, cheep, cheeping – while the cocks threw out their breasts and strutted grandly behind, and crowed with their trumpet throats, "All hail, master."

Then the morning wind rose and swayed the trees, plants and grasses, and their tops bending before it bowed their salutes to the new king of the earth, and thus it was that man knew that his reign over all was acknowledged.

A few months afterwards, another double birth occurred, and a few months later there was still another, and Bateta remembered the number of months that intervened between each event, and knew that it would be a regular custom for all time. At the end of the eighteenth year, he permitted his first born to choose a wife, and when his other children grew up he likewise allowed them to select their wives. At the end of ninety years, Hanna had born to Bateta 242 children, and there were grandchildren, and great-grandchildren and countless great-great-grandchildren, and they lived to an age many times the length of the greatest age amongst us nowadays. When they were so old that it became a trouble to them to live, the Moon came down to the earth as he had promised, and bore them to himself, and soon after the first-born twins died and were buried in the earth, and after that the deaths were many and more frequent. People ceased to live as long as their parents had done, for sickness, dissensions, wars, famines, accidents ended them and cut their days short, until they at last forgot how to live long, and cared not to think how their days might be prolonged. And it has happened after this manner down to us who now live. The whole earth has become filled with mankind, but the dead that are gone and forgotten are far greater in number than those now alive upon the earth.

Ye see now, my friends, what mischief the Toad did unto all mankind. Had his conceit been less, and had he waited a little, the good Moon would have conceived us of a nobler kind than we now are, and the taint of the Toad had not cursed man. Wherefore abandon headstrong ways, and give not way to rashness, but pay good heed to the wise and old, lest ye taint in like manner the people, and cause the innocent, the young and the weak to suffer. I have spoken my say. If ye have heard aught displeasing, remember I but tell the tale as it was told unto me.

"Taking it as a mere story," said Baraka, "it is very well told, but I should like to know why the Moon did not teach Bateta the value of manioc, since he took the trouble to tell him about the banana."

"For the reason," answered Matageza, "that when he showed him the banana, there was no one but the Moon could have done so. But after the

Moon had given goats and sheep and fowls for his companions, his own lively intelligence was sufficient to teach Bateta many things. The goats became great pets of Bateta, and used to follow him about. He observed that there was a certain plant to which the goats flocked with great greed, to feed upon the tops until their bellies became round and large with it. One day the idea came to him that if the goats could feed so freely upon it without harm, it might be also harmless to him. Whereupon he pulled the plant up and earned it home. While he was chopping up the tops for the pot his pet goats tried to eat the tuber which was the root, and he tried that also. He cut up both leaves and root and cooked them, and after tasting them he found them exceedingly good and palatable, and thenceforward manioc became a daily food to him and his family, and from them to his children's children, and so on down to us."

"Verily, that is of great interest. Why did you not put that in the story?"

"Because the story would then have no end. I would have to tell you of the sweet potato, and the tomato, of the pumpkin, of the millet that was discovered by the fowls, and of the palm oil nut that was discovered by the dog."

"Ah, yes, tell us how a dog could have shown the uses of the palm oil nut."

"It is very simple. Bateta coaxed a dog to live with him because he found that the dog preferred to sit on his haunches and wait for the bones that his family threw aside after the meal was over, rather than hunt for himself like other flesh-eating beasts. One day Bateta walked out into the woods, and his dog followed him. After a long walk Bateta rested at the foot of the straight tall tree called the palm, and there were a great many nuts lying on the ground, which perhaps the monkeys or the wind had thrown down. The dog after smelling them lay down and began to eat them, and though Bateta was afraid he would hurt himself, he allowed him to have his own way, and he did not see that they harmed him at all, but that he seemed as fond as ever of them. By thinking of this he conceived that they would be no harm to him; and after cooking them, he found that their fat improved the flavour of his vegetables, hence the custom came down to us. Indeed, the knowledge of most things that we know today as edibles came down to us through the observation of animals by our earliest fathers. What those of old knew not was found out later through stress of hunger, while men were lost in the bushy wilds."

When at last we rose to retire to our tents and huts, the greater number of our party felt the sorrowful conviction that the Toad had imparted to all mankind an incurable taint, and that we poor wayfarers, in particular, were cursed with an excess of it, in consequence of which both Toad and tadpole were heartily abused by all.

The Prince Who Insisted on Possessing the Moon
(From the Congo and central Africa)

THE COUNTRY NOW inhabited by the Basoko tribe was formerly known as Bandimba. A king called Bahanga was its sole ruler. He possessed a houseful of wives, but all his children were unfortunately of the female sex, which he considered to be a great grievance, and of which he frequently complained. His subjects, on the other hand, were blessed with more sons than daughters, and this fact increased the king's grief, and made him envy the meanest of his subjects.

One day, however, he married Bamana, the youngest daughter of his principal chief, and finally he became the father of a male child, and was very happy, and his people rejoiced in his happiness.

The prince grew up to be a marvel of strength and beauty, and his father doted on him so much, that he shared his power with the boy in a curious manner. The king reserved authority over all the married people, while the prince's subjects consisted of those not yet mated. It thus happened that the prince ruled over more people than his father, for the children were, of course, more numerous than the parents. But with all the honour conferred upon him the prince was not happy. The more he obtained, the more he wished to possess. His eyes had but to see a thing to make him desire its exclusive possession. Each day he preferred one or more requests to his father, and because of his great love for him, the king had not the heart to refuse anything to him. Indeed, he was persuaded to bestow so many gifts upon his son that he reserved scarcely anything for himself.

One day the prince was playing with the youth of his court, and after the sport retired to the shade of a tree to rest, and his companions sat down in a circle at a respectful distance from him. He then felt a gush of pride stealing over him as he thought of his great power, at the number and variety of his treasures, and he cried out boastfully that there never was a boy so great, so rich and so favoured by his father, as he had become. "My father," said he, "can deny me nothing. I have only to ask, and it is given unto me."

Then one little slender boy with a thin voice said, "It is true, prince. Your father has been very good to you. He is a mighty king, and he is as generous as he is great. Still, I know of one thing that he cannot give you – and it is certain that you will never possess it."

"What thing is that which I may not call my own, when I see it – and what is it that is not in the king's power to give me?" asked the prince, in a tone of annoyance.

"It is the moon," answered the little boy; "and you must confess yourself that it is beyond the king's power to give that to you."

"Do you doubt it?" asked the prince. "I say to you that I shall possess it, and I will go now and claim it from my father. I will not give him any peace until he gives it to me."

Now it so happens that such treasures as are already ours, we do not value so much as those which we have not yet got. So it was with this spoiled prince. The memory of the many gifts of his father faded from his mind, and their value was not to be compared with this new toy – the moon – which he had never thought of before and which he now so ardently coveted.

He found the king discussing important matters with the old men.

"Father," said he, "just now, while I was with my companions I was taunted because I did not have the moon among my toys, and it was said that it was beyond your power to give it to me. Now, prove this boy a liar, and procure the moon for me, that I may be able to show it to them, and glory in your gift."

"What is it you say, my son, you want the moon?" asked the astonished king.

"Yes. Do get it for me at once, won't you?"

"But, my child, the moon is a long way up. How shall we be ever able to reach it?"

"I don't know; but you have always been good to me, and you surely would not refuse me this favour, father?"

"I fear, my own, that we will not be able to give you the moon."

"But, father, I must have it; my life will not be worth living without it. How may I dare to again face my companions after my proud boast before them of your might and goodness? There was but one thing that yonder pert boy said I might not have, and that was the moon. Now my soul is bent upon possessing this moon, and you must obtain it for me or I shall die."

"Nay, my son, speak not of death. It is an ugly word, especially when connected with my prince and heir. Do you not know yet that I live only for your sake? Let your mind be at rest. I will collect all the wise men of the land together, and ask them to advise me. If they say that the moon can be reached and brought down to us, you shall have it."

Accordingly the great state drum was sounded for the general palaver, and a score of criers went through the towns beating their little drums as they went, and the messengers hastened all the wise men and elders to the presence of the king.

When all were assembled, the king announced his desire to know how the moon could be reached, and whether it could be shifted from its place in the sky and brought down to the earth, in order that he might give it to his only son the prince. If there was any wise man present who could inform him how this could be done, and would undertake to bring it to him, he would give the choicest of his daughters in marriage to him and endow him with great riches.

When the wise men heard this strange proposal, they were speechless with astonishment, as no one in the Basoko Land had ever heard of anybody mounting into the air higher than a tree, and to suppose that a person could ascend as high as the moon was, they thought, simple madness. Respect for the king, however, held them mute, though what their glances meant was very clear.

But while each man was yet looking at his neighbour in wonder, one of the wise men, who appeared to be about the youngest present, rose to his feet and said:

"Long life to the prince and to his father, the king! We have heard the words of our king, Bahanga, and they are good. I – even I – his slave, am able to reach the moon, and to do the king's pleasure, if the king's authority will assist me."

The confident air of the man, and the ring of assurance in his voice made the other wise men, who had been so ready to believe the king and prince mad, feel shame, and they turned their faces to him curiously, more than half willing to believe that after all the thing was possible. The king also lost his puzzled look, and appeared relieved.

"Say on. How may you be able to perform what you promise?"

"If it please the king," answered the man, boldly, "I will ascend from the top of the high mountain near the Cataract of Panga. But I shall first build a high scaffold on it, the base of which shall be as broad as the mountain top, and on that scaffold I will build another, and on the second I shall build a third, and so on and so on until my shoulder touches the moon."

"But is it possible to reach the moon in this manner?" asked the king doubtingly.

"Most certainly, if I were to erect a sufficient number of scaffolds, one above another, but it will require a vast quantity of timber, and a great army of workmen. If the king commands it, the work will be done."

"Be it so, then," said the king. "I place at your service every able-bodied man in the kingdom."

"Ah, but all the men in your kingdom are not sufficient, O king. All the grown-up men will be wanted to fell the trees, square the timber and bear it to the works; and every grown-up woman will be required to prepare the food for the workmen; and every boy must carry water to satisfy their thirst, and bark rope for the binding of the timbers; and every girl, big and little, must be sent to till the fields to raise cassava for food. Only in this manner can the prince obtain the moon as his toy."

"I say, then, let it be done as you think it ought to be done. All the men, women and children in the kingdom I devote to this service, that my only son may enjoy what he desires."

Then it was proclaimed throughout the wide lands of the Bandimba that all the people should be gathered together to proceed at once with the work of obtaining the moon for the king's son. And the forest was cut down, and while some of the workmen squared the trees, others cut deep holes in the ground, to make a broad and sure base for the lower scaffold; and the boys made thousands of rope coils to lash the timbers together, out of bark, fibre of palm and tough grass; and the girls, big and little, hoed up the ground and planted the cassava shrubs and cuttings from the banana and the plantain, and sowed the corn; and the women kneaded the bread and cooked the greens, and roasted green bananas for food for the workmen. And all the Bandimba people were made to slave hard every day in order that a spoiled boy might have the moon for his toy.

In a few days the first scaffolding stood up as high as the tallest trees, in a few weeks the structure had grown until it was many arrow flights in height, in two months it was so lofty that the top could not be seen with the naked eye. The fame of the wonderful wooden tower that the Bandimba were building was carried far and wide; and the friendly nations round about sent messengers to see and report to them what mad thing the Bandimba were about, for rumour had spread so many contrary stories among people that strangers did not know what to believe. Some said it was true that all the Bandimba had become mad; but some of those who came to see with their own eyes, laughed, while others began to feel anxious. All, however, admired the bigness, and wondered at the height of the tower.

In the sixth month the top of the highest scaffold was so high that on the clearest day people could not see halfway up; and it was said to be so tall that the chief engineer could tell the day he would be able to touch the moon.

The work went on, and at last the engineer passed the word down that in a few days more it would be finished. Everybody believed him, and the nations round about sent more people to be present to witness the completion of the great tower, and to observe what would happen. In all the land, and the countries adjoining it, there was found only one wise man who foresaw, if the moon was shifted out of its place what damage would happen, and that probably all those foolish people in the vicinity of the tower would be destroyed. Fearing some terrible calamity, he proposed to depart from among the Bandimba before it should be too late. He then placed his family in a canoe, and, after storing it with sufficient provisions, he embarked, and in the night he floated down the River Aruwimi and into the big river, and continued his journey night and day as fast as the current would take him – far, far below any lands known to the Bandimba. A week later, after the flight of the wise man and his family, the chief engineer sent down word to the king that he was ready to take the moon down.

"It is well," replied the king from below. "I will ascend, that I may see how you set about it."

Within twenty days the king reached the summit of the tower, and, standing at last by the side of the engineer, he laid his hand upon the moon, and it felt exceedingly hot. Then he commanded the engineer to proceed to take it down. The man put a number of cool bark coils over his shoulder and tried to dislodge it; but, as it was firmly fixed, he used such a deal of force that he cracked it, and there was an explosion, the fire and sparks from which scorched him. The timber on which the king and his chiefs were standing began to burn, and many more bursting sounds were heard, and fire and melted rock ran down through the scaffolding in a steady stream, until all the woodwork was ablaze, and the flames soared upward among the uprights and trestles of the wood in one vast pile of fire; and every man, woman and child was utterly consumed in a moment. And the heat was so great that it affected the moon, and a large portion of it tumbled to the earth, and its glowing hot materials ran over the ground like a great river of fire, so that most of the country of the Bandimba was burnt to ashes. On those who were not smothered by the smoke, nor burnt by the fire, and who fled from before the burning river, the effect was very wonderful. Such of them as were grown up, male and female, were converted into gorillas, and all the children into different kinds of long-tailed monkeys. After the engineer of the works, the first who died were the king and the prince whose folly had brought ruin on the land.

If you look at the moon when it is full, you may then see on a clear night a curious dark portion on its face, which often appears as though there were peaky mountains in it, and often the dark spots are like some kind of horned animals; and then again, you will often fancy that on the moon you see the outlines of a man's face, but those dark spots are only the holes made in the moon by the man who forced his shoulders through it. Now ever since that dreadful day when the moon burst and the Bandimba country was consumed, parents are not in the habit of granting children all they ask for, but only such things as their age and experience warn them are good for their little ones. And when little children will not be satisfied by such things, but fret and pester their parents to give them what they know will be harmful to them, then it is a custom with all wise people to take the rod to them, to drive out of their heads the wicked thoughts.

The Goat, the Lion and the Serpent
(From the Congo and central Africa)

A GOAT AND A LION were travelling together one day on the outskirts of a forest, at the end of which there was a community of mankind comfortably hutted within a village, which was fenced round with tall and pointed stakes. The Goat said to the Lion:

"Well, now, my friend, where do you come from this day?"

"I have come from a feast that I have given many friends of mine – to the leopard, hyena, wolf, jackal, wild cat, buffalo, zebra and many more. The long-necked giraffe and dew-lapped eland were also there, as well as the springing antelope."

"That is grand company you keep, indeed," said the Goat, with a sigh. "As for poor me, I am alone. No one cares for me very much, but I find abundance of grass and sweet leafage, and when I am full, I seek a soft spot under a tree, and chew my cud, dreamily and contentedly. And of other sorrows, save an occasional pang of hunger, in my wanderings I know of none."

"Do you mean to say that you do not envy me my regal dignity and strength?"

"I do not indeed, because as yet I have been ignorant of them."

"What? Know you not that I am the strongest of all who dwell in the forest or wilderness? that when I roar all who hear me bow down their heads, and shrink in fear?"

"Indeed, I do not know all this, nor am I very sure that you are not deceiving yourself, because I know many whose offensive powers are much more dangerous, my friend, than yours. True, your teeth are large, and your claws are sharp, and your roar is loud enough, and your appearance is imposing. Still, I know a tiny thing in these woods that is much more to be dreaded than you are; and I think if you matched yourself against it in a contest, that same tiny thing would become victor."

"Bah!" said the Lion, impatiently, "you anger me. Why, even today all who were at the feast acknowledged that they were but feeble creatures compared with me: and you will own that if I but clawed you once there would be no life left in you."

"What you say in regard to me is true enough, and, as I said before, I do not pretend to the possession of strength. But this tiny thing that I know of is not likely to have been at your feast."

"What may this tiny thing be that is so dreadful?" asked the Lion, sneeringly.

"The Serpent," answered the Goat, chewing his cud with an indifferent air.

"The Serpent!" said the Lion, astounded. "What, that crawling reptile, which feeds on mice and sleeping birds – that soft, vine-like, creeping thing that coils itself in tufts of grass, and branches of bush?"

"Yes, that is its name and character clearly."

"Why, my weight alone would tread it until it became flat like a smashed egg."

"I would not try to do so if I were you. Its fangs are sharper than your great corner teeth or claws."

"Will you match it against my strength?"

"Yes."

"And if you lose, what will be the forfeit?"

"If you survive the fight, I will be your slave, and you may command me for any purpose you please. But what will you give me if you lose?"

"What you please."

"Well, then, I will take one hundred bunches of bananas; and you had better bring them here alongside of me, before you begin."

"Where is this Serpent that will fight with me?"

"Close by. When you have brought the bananas he will be here, waiting for you."

The Lion stalked proudly away to procure the bananas, and the Goat proceeded into the bush, where he saw Serpent drowsily coiled in many coils on a slender branch.

"Serpent," said the Goat, "wake up. Lion is raging for a fight with you. He has made a bet of a hundred bunches of bananas that he will be the victor, and I have pledged my life that you will be the strong one; and, hark you, obey my hints, and my life is safe, and I shall be provided with food for at least three moons."

"Well," said Serpent, languidly, "what is it that you wish me to do?"

"Take position on a bush about three cubits high, that stands near the scene where the fight is to take place, and when Lion is ready, raise your crest high and boldly, and ask him to advance near you that you may see him well, because you are short-sighted, you know. And he, full of his conceit and despising your slight form, will advance towards you, unwitting of your mode of attack. Then fasten your fangs in his eyebrows, and coil yourself round his neck. If there is any virtue left in your venom, poor Lion will lie stark before long."

"And if I do this, what will you do for me?"

"I am thy servant and friend for all time."

"It is well," answered the Serpent. "Lead the way."

Accordingly Goat led Serpent to the scene of the combat, and the latter coiled itself in position, as Goat had advised, on the leafy top of a young bush.

Presently Lion came, with a long line of servile animals, bearing 100 bunches of bananas; and, after dismissing them, he turned to the Goat, and said:

"Well, Goatee, where is your friend who is stronger than I am? I feel curious to see him."

"Are you Lion?" asked a sibilant voice from the top of a bush.

"Yes, I am; and who are you that do not know me?"

"I am Serpent, friend Lion, and short of sight and slow of movement. Advance nearer to me, for I see you not."

Lion uttered a loud roaring laugh, and went confidently near the Serpent – who had raised his crest and arched his neck – so near that his breath seemed to blow the slender form to a tremulous movement.

"You shake already," said Lion, mockingly.

"Yes, I shake but to strike the better, my friend," said Serpent, as he darted forward and fixed his fangs in the right eyebrow of Lion, and at the same moment its body glided round the neck of Lion, and became buried out of sight in the copious mane.

Like the pain of fire the deadly venom was felt quickly in the head and body. When it reached the heart, Lion fell down and lay still and dead.

"Well done," cried Goat, as he danced around the pile of bananas. "Provisions for three moons have I, and this doughty roarer is of no more value than a dead goat."

Goat and Serpent then vowed friendship for one another, after which Serpent said:

"Now follow me, and obey. I have a little work for you."

"Work! What work, O Serpent?"

"It is light and agreeable. If you follow that path, you will find a village of mankind. You will there proclaim to the people what I have done, and show this carcase to them. In return for this they will make much of you, and you will find abundance of food in their gardens – tender leaves of manioc and peanut, mellow bananas and plenty of rich greens daily. True, when you are fat and a feast is to be made, they will kill you and eat you; but, for all your kind, comfort, plenty and warm, dry housing is more agreeable than the cold, damp jungle, and destruction by the feral beasts."

"Nay, neither the work nor the fate is grievous, and I thank you, O Serpent; but for you there can be no other home than the bush and the tuft of grass, and you will always be a dreaded enemy of all who come near your resting place."

Then they parted. The Goat went along the path, and came to the gardens of a village, where a woman was chopping fuel. Looking up she saw a creature with grand horns coming near to her, bleating. Her first impulse was to run away, but seeing, as it bleated, that it was a fodder-eating animal, with no means of offence, she plucked some manioc greens and coaxed it to her, upon which the Goat came and spoke to her.

"Follow me, for I have a strange thing to show you a little distance off."

The woman, wondering that a four-footed animal could address her in intelligible speech, followed; and the Goat trotted gently before her to where Lion lay dead. The woman, upon seeing the body, stopped and asked, "What is the meaning of this?"

The Goat answered, "This was once the king of beasts; the fear of him was upon all that lived in the woods and in the wilderness. But he too often boasted of his might, and became too proud. I therefore dared him to fight a tiny creature of the bush, and lo! The boaster was slain."

"And how do you name the victor?"

"The Serpent."

"Ah! You say true. Serpent is king over all, except man," answered the woman.

"You are of a wise kind," answered the Goat. "Serpent confessed to me that man was his superior, and sent me to you that I might become man's creature. Henceforth man shall feed me with greens, tender tops of plants, and house and protect me; but when the feast day comes, man shall kill me, and eat of my flesh. These are the words of Serpent."

The woman hearkened to all Goat's words, and retained them in her memory. Then she unrobed the Lion of his furry spoil, and conveyed it to the village, where she astonished her folk with all that had happened to her. From that day to this the goat kind has remained with the families of man, and people are grateful to the Serpent for his gift to them; for had not the Serpent commanded it to seek their presence, the Goat had remained forever wild like the antelope, its brother.

The City of the Elephants
(From the Congo and central Africa)

A BUNGANDU MAN named Dudu, and his wife Salimba, were one day seeking in the forest a long way from the town for a proper redwood tree, out of which they could make a wooden mortar wherein they could pound their manioc. They saw several trees of this kind as they proceeded, but after examining one, and then another, they would appear to be dissatisfied, and say, "Perhaps if we went a little further we might find a still better tree for our purpose."

And so Dudu and Salimba proceeded further and further into the tall and thick woods, and ever before them there appeared to be still finer trees which would after all be unsuited for their purpose, being too soft, or too hard, or hollow, or too old, or of another kind than the useful redwood. They strayed in this manner very far. In the forest where there is no path or track, it is not easy to tell which direction one came from, and as they had walked round many trees, they were too confused to know which way they ought to turn homeward. When Dudu said he was sure that his course was the right one for home, Salimba was as sure that the opposite was the true way. They agreed to walk in the direction Dudu wished, and after a long time spent on it, they gave it up and tried another, but neither took them any nearer home.

The night overtook them and they slept at the foot of a tree. The next day they wandered still farther from their town, and they became anxious and hungry. As one cannot see many yards off on any side in the forest, an animal hears the coming step long before the hunter gets a chance to use his weapon. Therefore, though they heard the rustle of the flying antelope, or wild pig as it rushed away, it only served to make their anxiety greater. And the second day passed, and when night came upon them they were still hungrier.

Towards the middle of the third day, they came into an open place by a pool frequented by Kiboko (hippo), and there was a margin of grass round about it, and as they came in view of it, both, at the same time, sighted a grazing buffalo.

Dudu bade his wife stand behind a tree while he chose two of his best and sharpest arrows, and after a careful look at his bowstring, he crept up to the buffalo, and drove an arrow home as far as the guiding leaf, which nearly buried it in the body. While the beast looked around and started from the twinge within, Dudu shot his second arrow into his windpipe, and it fell to the ground quite choked. Now here was water to drink and food to eat, and after cutting a load of meat they chose a thick bush-clump a little distance from the pool, made a fire, and, after satisfying their hunger, slept in content. The fourth day they stopped and roasted a meat provision that would last many days, because they knew that luck is not constant in the woods.

On the fifth they travelled, and for three days more they wandered. They then met a young lion who, at the sight of them, boldly advanced, but Dudu sighted his bow, and sent an arrow into his chest which sickened him of the fight, and he turned and fled.

A few days afterwards, Dudu saw an elephant standing close to them behind a high bush, and whispered to his wife:

"Ah, now, we have a chance to get meat enough for a month."

"But," said Salimba, "why should you wish to kill him, when we have enough meat still with us? Do not hurt him. Ah, what a fine back he has, and how strong he is. Perhaps he would carry us home."

"How could an elephant understand our wishes?" asked Dudu.

"Talk to him anyhow, perhaps he will be clever enough to understand what we want."

Dudu laughed at his wife's simplicity, but to please her he said, "Elephant, we have lost our way; will you carry us and take us home, and we shall be your friends forever."

The Elephant ceased waving his trunk, and nodding to himself, and turning to them said:

"If you come near to me and take hold of my ears, you may get on my back, and I will carry you safely."

When the Elephant spoke, Dudu fell back from surprise, and looked at him as though he had not heard aright, but Salimba advanced with all confidence, and laid hold of one of his ears, and pulled herself up on to his back. When she was seated, she cried out, "Come, Dudu, what are you looking at? Did you not hear him say he would carry you?"

Seeing his wife smiling and comfortable on the Elephant's back, Dudu became a little braver and moved forward slowly, when the Elephant spoke again, "Come, Dudu, be not afraid. Follow your wife, and do as she did, and then I will travel home with you quickly."

Dudu then put aside his fears, and his surprise, and seizing the Elephant's ear, he ascended and seated himself by his wife on the Elephant's back.

Without another word the Elephant moved on rapidly, and the motion seemed to Dudu and Salimba most delightful. Whenever any overhanging branch was in the way, the Elephant wrenched it off, or bent it and passed on. No creek, stream, gulley, or river stopped him, he seemed to know exactly the way he should go, as if the road he was travelling was well known to him.

When it was getting dark he stopped and asked his friends if they would not like to rest for the night, and finding that they so wished it, he stopped at a nice place by the side of the river, and they slid to the ground, Dudu first, and Salimba last. He then broke dead branches for them, out of which they made a fire, and the Elephant stayed by them, as though he was their slave.

Hearing their talk, he understood that they would like to have something better than dried meat to eat, and he said to them, "I am glad to know your wishes, for I think I can help you. Bide here a little, and I will go and search."

About the middle of the night he returned to them with something white in his trunk, and a young antelope in front of him. The white thing was a great manioc root, which he dropped into Salimba's lap.

"There, Salimba," he said, "there is food for you, eat your fill and sleep in peace, for I will watch over you."

Dudu and Salimba had seen many strange things that day, but they were both still more astonished at the kindly and intelligent care which their friend the Elephant took of them. While they roasted their fresh meat over the flame, and the manioc root was baking under the heap of hot embers, the Elephant dug with his tusks for the juicy roots of his favourite trees round about their camp, and munched away contentedly.

The next morning, all three, after a bathe in the river, set out on their journey more familiar with one another, and in a happier mood.

About noon, while they were resting during the heat of the day, two lions came near to roar at them, but when Dudu was drawing his bow at one of them, the Elephant said:

"You leave them to me; I will make them run pretty quick," saying which he tore off a great bough of a tree, and nourishing this with his trunk, he trotted on the double quick towards them, and used it so heartily that they both skurried away with their bellies to the ground, and their hides shrinking and quivering out of fear of the great rod.

In the afternoon the Elephant and his human friends set off again, and sometime after they came to a wide and deep river. He begged his friends to descend while he tried to find out the shallowest part. It took him some time to do this; but, having discovered a ford where the water was not quite over his back, he returned to them, and urged them to mount him as he wished to reach home before dark.

As the Elephant was about to enter the river, he said to Dudu, "I see some hunters of your own kind creeping up towards us. Perhaps they are your kinsmen. Talk to them, and let us see whether they be friends or foes."

Dudu hailed them, but they gave no answer, and, as they approached nearer, they were seen to prepare to cast their spears, so the Elephant said, "I see that they are not your friends; therefore, as I cross the river, do you look out for them, and keep them at a distance. If they come to the other side of the river, I shall know how to deal with them."

They got to the opposite bank safely; but, as they were landing, Dudu and Salimba noticed that their pursuers had discovered a canoe, and that they were pulling hard after them. But the Elephant soon after landing came to a broad path smoothed by much travel, over which he took them at a quick pace, so fast, indeed, that the pursuers had to run to be able to keep up with them. Dudu, every now and then let fly an arrow at the hunters, which kept them at a safe distance.

Towards night they came to the City of the Elephants, which was very large and fit to shelter such a multitude as they now saw. Their elephant did not linger, however, but took his friends at the same quick pace until they came to a mighty elephant that was much larger than any other, and his ivories were gleaming white and curled up, and exceedingly long. Before him Dudu and Salimba were told by their friend to descend and salaam, and he told his lord how he had found them lost in the woods, and how for the sake of the kindly words of the woman he had befriended them, and assisted them to the city of his tribe. When the King Elephant heard all this he was much pleased, and said to Dudu and Salimba that they were welcome to his city, and how they should not want for anything, as long as they would be pleased to stay with them, but as for the hunters who had dared to chase them, he would give orders at once. Accordingly he gave a signal, and ten active young elephants dashed out of the city, and in a short time not one of the hunters was left alive, though one of them had leaped into the river, thinking that he could escape in that manner. But then you know that an elephant is as much at home in a river as a Kiboko (a hippopotamus), so that the last man was soon caught and was drowned.

Dudu and Salimba, however, on account of Salimba's kind heart in preventing her husband wounding the elephant, were made free of the place, and their friend took them with him to many families, and the big pa's and ma's told their little babies all about them and their habits, and said that, though most of the human kind were very stupid and wicked, Dudu and Salimba were very good, and putting their trunks into their ears they whispered that Salimba was the better of the two. Then the little elephants gathered about them and trotted by their side and around them and diverted them with their antics, their races, their wrestlings and other trials of strength, but when they became familiar and somewhat rude in their rough play, their elephant friend would admonish them, and if that did not suffice, he would switch them soundly.

The City of the Elephants was a spacious and well-trodden glade in the midst of a thick forest, and as it was entered one saw how wisely the elephant families had arranged their manner of life. For without, the trees stood as thick as water reeds, and the bush or underwood was like an old hedge of milkweed knitted together by thorny vines and snaky climbers into which the human hunter might not even poke his nose without hurt. Well, the burly elephants had, by much uprooting, created deep hollows, or recesses, wherein a family of two and more might snugly rest, and not even a dart of sunshine might reach them.

Round about the great glade the dark leafy arches ran, and Dudu and his wife saw that the elephant families were numerous – for by one sweeping look they could tell that there were more elephants than there are human beings in a goodly village. In some of the recesses there was a row of six and more elephants; in another the parents stood head to head, and their children, big and little, clung close to their parents' sides; in another a family stood with heads turned towards the entrance, and so on all around – while under a big tree in the middle there was quite a gathering of big fellows, as though they were holding a serious palaver; under another tree one seemed to be on the outlook; another paced slowly from side to side; another plucked at this branch or at that; another appeared to be heaving a tree, or sharpening a blunted ivory; others seemed appointed to uproot the sprouts, lest the glade might become choked with underwood.

Near the entrance on both sides were a brave company of them, faces turned outward, swinging their trunks, napping their ears, rubbing against each other, or who with pate against pate seemed to be drowsily considering something. There was a continual coming in and a going out, singly, or in small companies. The roads that ran through the glade were like a network, clean and smooth, while that which went towards the king's place was so wide that twenty men might walk abreast. At the far end the king stood under his own tree, with his family under the arches behind him.

This was the City of the Elephants as Dudu and Salimba saw it. I ought to say that the outlets of it were many. One went straight through the woods in a line up river, at the other end it ran in a line following the river downward; one went to a lakelet, where juicy plants and reeds throve like corn in a man's fields, and where the elephants rejoiced in its cool water, and washed themselves and infants; another went to an ancient clearing where the plantain and manioc grew wild, and wherein more than two human tribes might find food for countless seasons.

Then said their friend to Dudu and Salimba: "Now that I have shown you our manner of life, it is for you to ease your longing for a while and rest with us. When you yearn for home, go tell our king, and he will send you with credit to your kindred."

Then Dudu and his wife resolved to stay, and eat, and they stayed a whole season, not only unhurt, but tenderly cared for, with never a hungry hour or uneasy night. But at last Salimba's heart remembered her children, and kinfolk and her own warm house and village pleasures, and on hinting of these memories to her husband, he said that after all there was no place like Bungandu. He remembered his long pipe, and the talk-house, the stool-making, shaft-polishing, bow-fitting and the little tinkering jobs, the wine trough and the merry drinking bouts, and he wept softly as he thought of them.

They thus agreed that it was time for them to travel homeward, and together they sought the elephant king, and frankly told him of their state.

"My friends," he replied, "be no longer sad, but haste to depart. With the morning's dawn guides shall take you to Bungandu with such gifts as shall make you welcome to your folk. And when you come to them, say to them that the elephant king desires lasting peace and friendship with them. On our side we shall not injure their plantations, neither a plantain, nor a manioc root belonging to them; and on your side dig no pits for our unwary youngsters, nor hang the barbed iron aloft, nor plant the poisoned stake in the path, so we shall escape hurt and be unprovoked." And Dudu put his hand on the king's trunk as the pledge of good faith.

In the morning, four elephants, as bearers of the gifts from the king – bales of bark cloth, and showy mats and soft hides and other things – and two fighting elephants besides their old friend, stood by the entrance to the city, and when the king elephant came up he lifted Salimba first on the back of her old companion, and then placed Dudu by her side, and at a parting wave the company moved on.

In ten days they reached the edge of the plantation of Bungandu, and the leader halted. The bales were set down on the ground, and then their friend asked of Dudu and his wife:

"Know you where you are?"

"We do," they answered.

"Is this Bungandu?" he asked.

"This is Bungandu," they replied.

"Then here we part, that we may not alarm your friends. Go now your way, and we go our way. Go tell your folk how the elephants treat their friends, and let there be peace forever between us."

The elephants turned away, and Dudu and Salimba, after hiding their wealth in the underwood, went arm in arm into the village of Bungandu. When their friends saw them, they greeted them as we would greet our friends whom we have long believed to be dead, but who come back smiling and rejoicing to us. When the people heard their story they greatly wondered and doubted, but when Dudu and Salimba took them to the place of parting and showed them the hoof prints of seven elephants on the road, and the bales that they had hidden in the underwood, they believed their story. And they made it a rule from that day that no man of the tribe ever should lift a spear, or draw a bow, or dig a pit, or plant the poisoned stake in the path, or hang the barbed iron aloft, to do hurt to an elephant. And as a proof that I have but told the truth go ask the Bungandu, and they will say why none of their race will ever seek to hurt the elephant, and it will be the same as I have told you. That is my story.

The Fowl and the Hippopotamus; or, the Cause of the Enmity among Birds and Animals
(From the Boloki people, Congo)

A FOWL, on returning from a trading journey, hid one of his legs under his wing and said: "I sold my leg for two thousand brass rods in the towns I have been visiting."

A greedy hippopotamus, hearing this, said: "If the Fowl could receive two thousand brass rods for his small leg, how much shall I receive for mine?" So calling some of his friends they entered a canoe and paddled downriver to the towns. On arriving, the leg of the Hippopotamus was cut off, carried ashore, and sold for a large number of brass rods.

When the Hippopotami returned to the canoe, after selling the leg, they discovered that their friend had bled to death, so they picked up their paddles in great anger and returned to their town.

On arriving at their town they sought out the Fowl and charged him with the death of their friend, for they said, "Because of your lying deception he went and sold his leg."

In their anger they called on the Hawks and Kites to swoop down and carry off the chickens belonging to the Fowls; and they told the wild bush-cat that whenever he found the door of the Fowl house open he was to creep in and kill the Fowls.

In this way so many Fowls were killed, that in defense the Fowls called on the Crocodiles to bite the Hippopotami and wound them to death; and they asked Man whenever he saw a Hippopotamus to hurl his spear at it and kill it. Thus, through the Fowl's one deception, enmity, quarrels and death were first introduced among the birds and animals.

The Punishment of the Inquisitive Man
(From the Boloki people, Congo)

MOTU MADE A LARGE garden, and planted it with many bananas and plantain. The garden was in a good position, so the fruit ripened quickly and well. Arriving one day at his garden he found the ripe bunches of bananas and plantain had been cut off and carried away.

After that he did not go once to his garden without finding that some of the fruit had been stolen, so at last he made up his mind to watch the place carefully, and hiding himself he lay in ambush for the thief.

Motu had not been in hiding very long before he saw a number of Cloud-folk descending, who cut down his bananas, and what they could not eat they tied into bundles to carry away. Motu rushed out, and, chasing them, caught one woman whom he took to his house, and after a short time he married her, and gave her a name which meant Favourite.

Although Favourite had come from the Cloud-land she was very intelligent, and went about her housework and farming just like an ordinary woman of the earth. Up to that time neither Motu nor the people of his village had ever seen a fire. They had always eaten their food raw, and on cold, windy, rainy days had sat shivering in their houses because they did not know anything about fire and warmth.

Favourite, however, told some of the Cloud-folk to bring some fire with them next time they came to visit her, which they did. And then she taught the people how to cook food, and how to sit round a fire on cold days.

Motu was very happy with his wife, and the villagers were very glad to have her among them, and, moreover, Favourite persuaded many of the Cloud-folk to settle in her husband's village.

One day Favourite received a covered basket, and putting it on a shelf in the house she said to her husband, "We are now living with much friendship together; but while I am away at the farm you must not open that basket, if you do we shall all leave you."

"All right," replied the husband, "I will never undo it."

Motu was now very glad in his heart, for he had plenty of people, a clever wife, and the villagers treated him as a great man. But he had one trouble: Why did his wife warn him every day not to open the basket? What was in that basket? What was she hiding from him? And foolish-like he decided to open it. Waiting therefore until his wife had gone as usual to the farm he opened the basket, and – there was nothing in it, so laughingly he shut it up and put it in its place.

By and by Favourite returned, and, looking at her husband, she asked him: Why did you open that basket?" And he was speechless at her question.

On the first opportunity, while Motu was away hunting, Favourite gathered her people, and ascended with them to Cloud-land, and never again returned to the earth.

That is how the earth-folk received their fire and a knowledge of cooking; and that is also how Motu through being too inquisitive lost his wife, his people, and his importance as a big man in the village.

Mbungi and His Punishment
(From the Boloki people, Congo)

MBUNGI ONE DAY SAID to his wife: "Dig up some cassava, prepare it, and cut down some plantain, for we will go hunting and fishing."

The wife did as she was told, and in a short time everything was ready for the journey. They put their goods into a canoe and paddled away to their hunting and fishing camp.

After resting, the man went and dug a hole and set his traps; and the next morning he found an antelope and a bush pig in the hole. These he took to the camp, cut up, and gave to his wife to cook. By and by when all was cooked she brought the meat to her husband, and as she was taking her portion he said: "Wait, I will ask the forest-folk (or spirits) if you may eat it."

He went and pretended to ask the forest-folk, and brought back a message that if she ate the meat the traps would lose their luck and catch no more animals. In this way the selfish husband had all the meat for himself and his wife went hungry. Mbungi found many animals in his traps, and the woman, because of the prohibition, did not have her share of them.

One day the woman made some fish traps and set them, and on her return to the camp the husband wanted to know where she had been, but she refused to tell him. Next day she went to look at her traps and found many fish in them, which she brought to the camp and cooked. Mbungi, however, returned unsuccessful from his traps; but when he saw his wife's fish he laughed and said: "Bring the fish here for me to eat."

"Wait," answered the woman, "I will ask the forest-folk if you may eat the fish." And she brought back a reply that he was not to eat the fish, for if he did so the fish traps would lose their luck.

It was now Mbungi's turn to be hungry. Days and days passed and he caught no more animals; but his wife always had plenty of fish. He became

66

very thin and angry. One day he drew his large knife, and cutting off the head of his wife he buried the head and the trunk together in the ground, and departed for his town.

Mbungi had not gone very far on his way when he heard a voice shouting: "Mbungi, wait for me, we will go together!" He wondered who was calling him, so he hid himself, and in a little time he saw the head of his wife coming along the road calling after him.

He went, and catching the head he cut it into small pieces and buried it again; but before he had gone far he heard it shouting: "Mbungi, wait for me, we will go together!" He cut and buried it again and again, but it was no use, it continued to follow and call after him.

Mbungi reached his town, and his wife's family asked him: "Where is your wife?" "Oh, she is coming on behind," he replied. They accused him of killing her, but this he strongly denied. While he was denying the charge of murder the head came right into the town; and when the family saw it they immediately tied up Mbungi and killed him.

This was how murder was first introduced into the world.

Nkengo Fails to
Obtain Lasting Life
(From the Boloki people, Congo)

NKENGO WAS THE SON of Libuta, and he noticed that the people were dying daily in great numbers. So one day he called out loudly: "You Cloud-folk, throw me down a rope!"

The Cloud-folk heard and threw him a rope. Nkengo held on to it and was pulled up to the Cloud-land.

When he arrived there Nkengo had to wait one day, and in the morning the Cloud-folk said to him: "You have come here to receive lasting life (*lobiku*) and escape from death. You cannot make your request for seven days, and in the meantime you must not go to sleep."

Nkengo was able to keep awake for six days, but on the seventh day he nodded and went to sleep. The Cloud-folk woke him up, saying: "You came here to receive lasting life and escape from death. You were able to keep awake six days. Why did you abandon your purpose on the seventh day?" They were so angry with him that they drove him out of Cloud-land and lowered him to the earth.

The people on the earth asked him what had happened up above, and Nkengo replied: "When I reached Cloud-land they told me that in order to gain lasting life I must keep awake for seven days. I did not sleep for six days and six nights; but on the seventh day I nodded in sleep; whereupon they drove me out, saying: "Get away with your dying; you shall not receive lasting life, for every day there shall be death among you!"

His friends laughed at him because he went to receive lasting life and lost it through sleeping. That is the reason why death continues in the world.

The Two Bundles
(From the Congo and central Africa)

WHILE A MAN was working one day in the forest a little man with two bundles – one large and one small – went to him and asked: "Which of these two bundles will you have? This one" (taking up the large bundle) "contains looking glasses, knives, beads, cloth, etc.; and this one" (taking up the little bundle) "contains lasting life."

"I cannot choose by myself," answered the man; "I must go and ask the other people in the town."

While he was gone to ask the other people some women arrived, and the choice was put to them. The women tried the edges of the knives, bedecked themselves in the cloth, admired themselves in the looking glasses, and without more ado they selected the big bundle and took it away. The little man, picking up the small bundle, vanished.

On the return of the man from the town both the little man and his bundles had disappeared. The women exhibited and shared the things, but death continued on the earth. Hence the people say: "Oh, if those women had only chosen the small bundle, we folk would not be dying like this!"

Why the Fowl and Dog Are
Abused by the Birds
(From the Boloki people, Congo)

There was a time when all the birds and animals lived in the sky. One day it was very rainy and cold – so cold that they were all shivering. The birds said to the Dog: "Go down and fetch us some fire to warm ourselves."

The Dog descended, but seeing plenty of bones and pieces of fish lying about on the ground he forgot to take the fire to the shivering birds.

The birds and animals waited, and the Dog not returning they sent the Fowl to hasten him with the fire.

The Fowl, however, on arriving below, beheld plenty of palm nuts, pea nuts, maize and other good things, so he did not tell the Dog to take up the fire, and did not take any himself.

This is the reason why you can hear of an evening a bird that sings with notes like this, *"Nsusu akende bombo! Nsusu akende bombo!"* which means, The Fowl has become a slave! The Fowl has become a slave!

And the Heron sometimes sits on a tree near a village and cries, *"Mbwa owa! Mbwa owa!"* – Dog, you die! Dog, you die!

This is why you hear these birds jeer at and abuse the Fowl and Dog, because they left their friends to shiver in the cold while they enjoyed themselves in warmth and plenty.

Why the Water Snake Has No Poison
(From the Boloki people, Congo)

WHEN THE PYTHON had given birth to all the snakes she said to them: "You have no poison now, but another day I will call you, and give to each of you a proper share of poison."

After a time the day arrived, and the Python called all her children to receive the promised gift. The green snake, the viper, the whip snake, the diamond-headed snake all arrived, and each received his share of the poison so as to defend himself from his enemies. Wherever these snakes went on a journey everybody jumped out of their way, for if they did not they were bitten and suffered much pain.

The water snake, however, instead of obeying his mother's call, went off to the river to fish. By and by he became tired of fishing, and thought he would go and hear what his mother the Python wanted.

As he went he met the other snakes returning, and heard that they had received their gifts from their mother. On his arrival he asked her for his share of the poison.

But the Python said: "No, I called you, and instead of coming you went fishing, so now you have lost your share of the poison through disobedience."

That is why the water snake is only laughed at when he bites, and no one thinks of moving out of his way, for he has no poison through disregarding his mother's call.

The Heron and the Parrot are Unbelieving
(From the Boloki people, Congo)

WHEN THE HERON and the Parrot entered into the bonds of blood-brotherhood the Heron put the Parrot under a ban, saying: "Friend Parrot, you must always remain in the

treetops, and never alight on the ground. If you do so you will not be able to fly again, for you will be caught, killed, and eaten; and even if you are not killed the folk who catch you will tame you, and you will lose your power to fly again in the air."

The Parrot said: "Friend Heron, you must never build a house to sleep in it; if you do you will die."

After some time the Heron began to doubt the words of the Parrot, and he said to himself: "Perhaps my friend told me a lie about sleeping in a house. I will test his words, and if I die my family will know that the words of the Parrot are true, and they will never sleep in a house."

That evening the Heron entered a house (nest), and next morning his family found him lying dead. Ever since that time the Herons have always slept on the branches of the trees.

The Parrot also doubted the power of the Heron's prohibition, and said to himself: "I will alight on the ground, and if I am unable to fly again my family will know the Heron's words are true ones."

So down the Parrot flew, and alighting on the ground he found there plenty to eat, but when he tried to rise again he was not able to use his wings. Some people caught him and tamed him, and he remained a slave in their town.

That is the reason why the Parrots always fly high above the treetops and never alight on the earth, because of the prohibition of their friend the Heron.

How the Dog Came to Live with Man
(From the Bushogo people, Congo)

THERE WAS A TIME, long ago, when the Dog and the Jackal lived together in the wilderness as brothers. Every day they hunted together and every evening they laid out on the grass whatever they had caught, making sure to divide the meal equally between them. But there were evenings when they both returned from a day's hunting empty-handed, and on these occasions, they

would curl up side by side under the stars dreaming of the bush calf or the plump zebra they had come so close to killing.

They had never before gone without food for longer than two days, but then, without warning, they suffered a long spell of bad luck and for over a week they could find nothing at all to eat. On the eighth day, although they had both searched everywhere, they returned to their shelter without meat, feeling exhausted and extremely hungry. To add to their misery, a bitterly cold wind blew across the bush, scooping up the leaves they had gathered for warmth, leaving them shivering without any hope of comfort throughout the long night ahead. Curled up together, they attempted to sleep, but the wind continued to howl and they tossed and turned despairingly.

"Jackal," said the Dog after a while. "Isn't it a terrible thing to go to bed hungry after all the effort we have put in today, and isn't it an even worse thing to be both hungry and cold at the same time?"

"Yes, it is brother," replied the Jackal, "but there's very little we can do about it at the moment. Let's just curl up here and try to sleep now. Tomorrow, as soon as the sun rises, we will go out hunting again and with any luck we will be able to find some food to satisfy us."

But even though he snuggled up closer to the Jackal, the Dog could not sleep, for his teeth had begun to chatter and his stomach rumbled more loudly than ever. He lay on the cold earth, his eyes open wide, trying to recall what it was like to be warm and well-fed.

"Jackal," he piped up again, "man has a village quite close to this spot, doesn't he?"

"Yes, that is true," answered the Jackal wearily. "But what difference can that make to us right now?"

"Well," replied the Dog, "most men know how to light a fire and fire would keep us warm if we crept near enough to one."

"If you are suggesting that we take a closer look," said the Jackal, "you can forget about it. I'm not going anywhere near that village. Now go to sleep and leave me in peace."

But the Dog could not let go of the idea and as he thought about it more and more he began to imagine the delicious meal he would make of the scraps and bones left lying around by the villagers.

"Please come with me," he begged the Jackal, "my fur is not as thick as yours and I am dying here from cold and hunger."

"Go there yourself," growled the Jackal, "this was all your idea, I want nothing to do with it."

At last, the Dog could stand it no longer. Forgetting his fear, he jumped up and announced boldly:

"Right, I'm off, nothing can be worse than this. I'm going to that village to sit by the fire and perhaps I'll even come across a tasty bone. If there's any food left over, I'll bring you some. But if I don't return, please come and look for me."

So the Dog started off towards the village, slowing down when he had reached the outskirts and crawling on his belly so that nobody would notice him approach. He could see the red glow of a fire just up ahead and already he felt the warmth of its flames. Very cautiously he slid along the earth and had almost reached his goal when some fowls roosting in a tree overhead began to cackle a loud warning to their master.

At once, a man came rushing out from a nearby hut and lifting his spear high in the air, brought it down within an inch of where the dog lay.

"Please, please don't kill me," whimpered the Dog. "I haven't come here to steal your chickens or to harm you in any way. I am starving and almost frozen to death. I only wanted to lie down by the fire where I could warm myself for a short while."

The man looked at the wretched, shivering creature and could not help feeling a bit sorry for him. It was such a cold night after all, and the Dog's request was not so unreasonable under the circumstances.

"Very well," he said, withdrawing his spear. "You can warm yourself here for a few minutes if you promise to go away again as soon as you feel better."

The Dog crept forward and lay himself down by the fire, thanking the man over and over for his kindness. Soon he felt the blood begin to circulate in his limbs once more. Slowly uncurling himself, he stretched out before the flames and there, just in front of him, he noticed a fat and juicy bone, thrown there by the man at the end of his meal. He sidled up alongside it and began to devour it, feeling happier than he had done for a very long time.

He had just about finished eating when the man suddenly reappeared:

"Aren't you warm enough yet?" he asked, rather anxious to be rid of his visitor from the bush.

"No, not yet," said the Dog, who had spotted another bone he wished to gnaw on.

"Just a few more minutes then," said the man, as he disappeared inside his hut once more.

The Dog grabbed hold of the second bone and began crushing it in his strong jaws, feeling even more contented with himself. But soon the man came out of his hut and asked again:

"When are you going to get up and go? Surely you must be warm enough by now?"

But the Dog, feeling very reluctant to leave the comfort of his surroundings, pleaded with his host:

"Let me stay just a little while longer and I promise to leave you alone after that."

This time the man disappeared and failed to return for several hours, for he had fallen asleep inside his hut, quite forgetting about his guest. But as soon as he awoke, he rushed out of doors to make certain that the Dog had left him as promised. Now he became angry to see the creature snoozing by the fire in exactly the same position as before. Prodding him with his spear, he called for the Dog to get up at once. The Dog rose slowly to his feet and summoning every ounce of his courage, he looked directly into the man's eyes and spoke the following words:

"I know that you want me to go away, but I wish you would let me stay here with you. I could teach you a great many things. I could pass on to you my knowledge of the wild, help you hunt the birds of the forests, keep watch over your house at night and frighten off any intruders. I would never harm your chickens or goats like my brother, the Jackal. I would look after your women and children while you were away. All I ask in return is that you provide me with a warm bed close to your fire and the scraps from your table to satisfy my hunger."

The man now stared back into the Dog's eyes and saw that his expression was honest and trustworthy.

"I will agree to this," he replied. "You may have a home here among the villagers if you perform as you have promised."

And from that day, the Dog has lived with man, guarding his property, protecting his livestock and helping him to hunt in the fields. At night when the Dog settles down to sleep, he hears a cry from the wilderness, "Bo-ah, Bo-ah", and he knows that it is his brother, the Jackal, calling him back home. But he never answers the call, for the Dog is more than content in his new home, enjoying the comforts Jackal was once so happy to ignore.

Why the Fowls never Shut Their Doors
(From the Lower Congo Basin)

THERE LIVED ONCE a chief who owned a large number of Fowls. On arising early one morning he found that the door of their house had been left open all night. He thereupon woke up the Head Cock and asked why he had not shut the door.

The Cock replied: "We did not go to sleep very early last night, as we quarrelled over who should shut the door. I told one to do it, and he told another, and at last we became so angry with each other that no one would shut the door, so we went to sleep leaving it open."

The owner snapped his fingers in speechless surprise at the Fowl's excuse, and walked away.

Another day the chief went to see his wives' farms and found them all clean and well weeded, but the road leading to the farms, which was nobody's work, was choked with tall grass and weeds. That evening the chief called out loudly so that all the town could hear: "You women, I went to your farms today, and found the road covered with tall grass and weeds. Truly you are near relatives of the fowls, who sleep with open door because each tells the other to shut it. Tomorrow all of you go and clear the road."

When the Fowls heard these remarks they were very vexed, and the Cock said: "You have heard what our owner has shouted out to the whole town. He has held us up as a bad example to all in the place, yet when I went to a neighbouring town the day before yesterday I saw a buffalo rotting by the roadside."

"Why was it rotting there?" asked the Black Hen of her husband.

75

The Cock replied: "When I reached the town the other day I heard that Don't-care, who is the son of Peter Pay-if-you-like, went outside his house and saw a buffalo; he aroused his companions and told them to go and shoot it; but they said: 'Go and shoot it yourself.' 'What?! Am I to see the buffalo and shoot it also?' he asked. Thereupon Wise-man fired at the buffalo, and told another to go and see if it were killed. He came back and said it was wounded; so another went and killed it; but he would not cut it up; and another went and cut it into pieces. Then each thought that the other should carry the flesh into the town; consequently it was left in the bush, and that was why the buffalo meat rotted at the roadside."

The Black Hen said: "Indeed, is that so?" But the Speckled Hen observed: "That it would be better for human beings if they looked better after their own business, instead of poking their noses into affairs belonging to Fowls, and holding them up as a bad example to their women."

The Head Cock said: "That from that day neither he, nor his children, nor his grandchildren should ever shut the doors of their houses, no matter how cold it might be, or what risks they might run of being eaten by wild animals." Thus it is that Fowls never shut their doors at night. They are angry that human beings, who conduct their own affairs so badly, should find fault with the way in which Fowls look after theirs.

Why the Dog and the Palm-rat
Hate Each Other
(From the Lower Congo Basin)

ONE DAY THE DOG, the Palm-rat, the Hawk, and the Eagle arranged to take a journey together, but before starting they agreed not to thwart each other in any matter.

They had not gone very far when the Eagle saw a bunch of unripe palm nuts, and said: "When these palm nuts are ripe, and I have eaten them, then we will proceed on our way."

They waited many days until the palm nuts ripened and were eaten by the Eagle, then they started again, and by and by the Hawk espied the bush (a great space covered with tall grass, canes and stunted trees), and said: "When this bush is burnt, and I have eaten the locusts, and drunk in the smoke from the fire, then we will go."

So they waited while the bush dried, and was burnt, and the Hawk ate his locusts, and drank in the smoke from the burning grass, then they were ready to start again; but when the Palm-rat saw the bush was burnt, he said: "We remain here until the grass and canes have grown again, so that I may eat the young canes, for remember we agreed not to thwart or oppose each other on this journey."

They waited there some months until the canes grew again, and the Palm-rat had eaten them.

Once more they started on their travels, and on reaching a large forest the Dog said: "Now I will dry my nose."

His companions answered: "All right, we will go for firewood."

The Palm-rat and the Hawk fetched the wood, and the Eagle went for the fire. The Dog put his nose near the fire, but every time it dried he made it wet again by licking it. They remained a long time in the forest, but the Dog's nose never became properly dry: it was an endless job. His companions became vexed, and the Hawk and the Eagle flew away, leaving the Palm-rat and the Dog alone. At last the patience of the Palm-rat was exhausted, and he, too, ran away; but the Dog chased him to kill him, and this is the reason why the Dog and the Palm-rat hate each other. He would not wait until the Dog's nose was dry.

Why the Owls and the Fowls
Never Speak to Each Other
(From the Lower Congo Basin)

AFOWL AND AN OWL became friends, but they built their houses at some distance from each other. One day the Owl heard that his friend was very sick, so he gathered some

money together and went to pay a visit to the Fowl. When he arrived he enquired after the health of his friend, and finding he was still very ill he sent for a "medicine man," and in due time his friend the Fowl recovered, and the Owl returned to his town.

By and by the Owl fell ill with a very bad illness, and the news reached the Fowl that his friend was on the point of death. He gathered some money and went to visit his friend and give him the best advice about getting better. He said to the wives of the Owl: "Get ready some very hot water, and pound up some red peppers."

The wives did as they were told, and then the Fowl said to the Owl: "Take off your clothes and get into the saucepan."

"Won't it burn me?" asked the Owl.

"No, my friend, it will not hurt you," deceivingly replied the Fowl.

So he did as his friend bade him, and put himself carefully into the saucepan of hot water. In a short time the Fowl said to the Owl's wives: "Take him out, and pluck his feathers, rub him well with the red pepper, and put him on a line to dry, and be sure and not take him down until he is thoroughly dry." Leaving these directions with them, the Fowl went home. After he had left, the Owl died, and the family was so angry at the outrage the Fowl had committed that they desired to punish him.

The family sent word to the Fowl that on a certain day the funeral would take place, and they invited him to attend it. On the appointed day the Fowl went with his band and his followers, who were the Leopard, the Lion, the Dog and the Shrew-mole.

Now the Owl's family had collected some strong followers who were called the Fox, the Viper, the Boa, the Elephant, the Antelope and the Palm-rat, all of whom were friends of the Owl. By and by they heard the Fowl's band playing "The tail of the Owl is very powerful." This insult to his dead friend made the Owl's family very angry, so they arranged their followers in ambush, and told them to be sure and "catch that rascal the Fowl."

As the Fowl's party drew near to the town, out came the Boa from his hiding place to catch the Fowl, but the Shrew-mole squeaked, and the Boa split all down one side and had to retreat; then came the Fox, but the Dog fought him and made him run away; then came the Elephant, but the Lion bit his trunk, and he fled; and the Antelope caught sight of the Leopard's marks and bolted. The Fowl at last arrived in the town, and played at the funeral of the Owl "The tail of the Owl is very powerful," and after ridiculing his late friend in this manner, he returned home with his band and followers. The Owls never speak now to the Fowls.

Why the Congo Robin has a Red Breast
(From the Lower Congo Basin)

"KINSIDIKITI" is a small bird with red round its mouth and red spots on its breast. The female has no red spots on the breast, and the following is the legend accounting for the difference:

One day the Robin and his wife found that they had no red-camwood powder with which to beautify themselves, so the husband made preparations for a journey to Stanley Pool to buy some redwood from those who brought it from the Upper Congo towns to sell at the Pool markets.

He was a long time on the road, but at last reached the place only to find that all the redwood for making the powder had been sold to others, who were before him. He tried one trader after another with no success, for all had sold out, but one said: "I have none to sell, but I can give you a small piece, enough for yourself."

He gave him a small piece, and for safety the Robin put it in his throat, as he wanted to take it home to his wife. As he travelled homeward the redwood melted in his mouth and throat, and came out round his beak and through his chest to his feathers, and ever since then he has had a red mouth and breast.

The Fight Between the Two Fetishes, Lifuma and Chimpukela
(From the Kongo people, Congo)

Now this is a sad but true story, for it is of recent occurrence, and many living witnesses can vouch for its truth.

Poor King Jack, late of Cabinda, now retired a little into the interior of KaCongo, known to all who visit this part of Africa, either in whaler, steamer, or man of war, owns the fetish called Lifuma. Lifuma had all his life sniffed the fresh sea breezes, and rejoiced with his people when they returned from the deep sea in their canoes laden with fish. But now circumstances (namely, the occupation of Cabinda by the Portuguese) forced him to retire to the interior, behind the coastline between Futilla and Cabinda.

How he longed to see his people happy yet again is proved by the trouble he put himself to in trying to gain possession of a part of the seabeach that he thought should belong to his 'hinterland'. He left the sweet waters of Lake Chinganga Miyengela (waters that have travelled even to the white man's country, and returned without being corrupted) and quietly travelled down to the seabeach, near to a place called Kaia. Once there, he picked up a few shells and pebbles, and filled a pint mug with salt water, meaning to carry them back to his sweetwater home, and to place them on the holy ground beside him as a sign of his ownership of the seabeach, and as a means whereby his people might once more play on the seabeach by the salt water, and once again occupy themselves in fishing in the deep blue sea.

Peaceful and benevolent was indeed his mission, and perhaps, as he passed the town of Kaia and Subantanu unmolested, he at last thought that his object was secured. Alas! The bird Ngundu espied him, and rushed to town to acquaint the Kaia people's fetish, called Chimpukela. Then Chimpukela, ran after Lifuma, and caught him up, and roughly asked him what he had there, bidden under his cloth.

"Go away," cried the anxious Lifuma, as he pushed Chimpukela aside.

Chimpukela stumbled over an ant hill and fell, so that when he got up again he was very angry with Lifuma, and knocked him down. Poor Lifuma fell upon a thorn of the Minyundu tree and broke his leg. The mug of salt water was also spilt, and Chimpukela took from him all the relies he had gathered upon his seabeach.

Then Chimpukela swore that ant hills should no longer exist in his country, and that is why you never see one there now as you travel through his country.

And Lifuma cursed the bird Ngundu, and the tree Minyundu, and canoes, and salt water and everything pertaining to the beach. And that is why all these things do not now exist in his country, or on his sweetwater lake.

The Fetish of Chilunga
(From the Kongo people, Congo)

A T A PLACE called Chilunga, north of Loango, there is a fetish called Boio, who by his representative in the flesh, a princess, rules the country with a rod of iron. His dwelling place is the earth; and as people pass that part which is dedicated to him, they bear his voice. People place their offerings here, and while yet they are looking at them they disappear. The spirit, or fetish, has, besides this human voice, the voice of a certain bird.

The sister of my cook, married to a man in Chilunga, was one day gathering sticks in a wood, when she heard a bird singing very loudly. Half in fun, half seriously, she spoke roughly to it, telling it to keep quiet; when to her astonishment her hands were roughly tied behind her back by some invisible force. She stood rooted to the place, as it were, by fear, and was found there by her husband who, wondering at her delay, had come to look for her.

"How have you angered Boio?" he asked.

She told him what had happened, and said that she did not know that the voice of the bird was that of Boio. The husband ran to the princess, and, having explained the matter, made her a peace offering. The princess then gave the woman her liberty.

On another occasion some natives laughed at two men who were carrying a hammock pole as if a hammock was hanging from it. Immediately they were made prisoners by invisible bands, and only released upon a heavy payment being made to the princess by their relations. The men, you see, were carrying the fetish in his hammock, although both it and the hammock were invisible to the passersby.

Girls who are given in marriage by their parents to ugly men, and who object to them on that account, are taken to the holy ground. Then they hear a voice speaking to them, saying: "Are you then so beautiful that you can afford to despise these good men on account of their ugliness?" Then their hands are tied behind them; and there they remain prisoners until such time as they are willing to marry the men. When the whole town, men, women, and children, go to the holy ground to praise this fetish, it takes a great delight in those who dance well, and punishes those who dance badly.

A certain white man would not believe in the sudden disappearance of the offerings made to this spirit. So he was asked by the princess to come to the holy ground and bring some presents for the spirit. The white man immediately set out with many presents, laughing at the whole matter as if it were a huge joke. His servants placed the gifts upon the ground, while he looked sharply after them. Then they cleared the ground and left him there. And lo! While he was yet looking, the presents disappeared. Then he said he believed in that spirit.

Only two men have the power of seeing this fetish in his earthly home; and they are the men appointed to carry food to him.

Why Some Men Are White and Others Black
(From the Kongo people, Congo)

I
T WAS IN THE BEGINNING, and four men were walking through a wood. They came to a place where there were two rivers. One river was of water, clear as crystal and of great purity; the other was black and foul and horrible to the taste.

And the four men were puzzled as to which river they should cross; for, whereas the dirty river seemed more directly in their way, the clear river was the most pleasant to cross, and perhaps after they had crossed it they might regain the proper path. The men, after some consultation, thought that they ought to cross the black river, and two of them straightway crossed it. The other two, however, scarce touched and tasted the water than they hesitated and returned.

The two that had now nearly crossed the river called to them and urged them to come, but in vain. The other two had determined to leave their companions, and to cross the beautiful and clear river. They crossed it, and were astonished to find that they had become black, except just those parts of them that had touched the black river, namely, their mouths, the soles of their feet and the palms of their hands. The two who had crossed the black river, however, were of a pure white colour.

The two parties now travelled in different directions, and when they had gone some way, the white men were agreeably surprised to come across a large house containing white wives for them to marry; while the black men also found huts, or shimbecs, with black women whom they married. And this is why some people are white and some black.

The Three Brothers
(From the Kongo people, Congo)

IN THE BEGINNING, when KaCongo had still one mother, and the whole family yet lived on grass and roots, and knew not how to plant, a woman brought forth three babes at one birth.

"Oh, what am I to do with them?" she cried. "I do not want them; I will leave them here in the grass." And the three little ones were very hungry, and looked about them for food. They walked and walked a long long way, until at last they came to a river, which they crossed.

They saw bananas, and palm trees and mandioca, growing in great quantities, but dared not eat the fruit thereof. Then the river spirit called to them, and told them to eat of these good things. And the tiniest of the three tried a banana and found it very sweet. Then the other two ate them, and found them very good. And after this they ate of the other trees, and so grew up well nurtured and strong; and they learnt how to become carpenters and blacksmiths, and built themselves houses. The river spirit supplied them with women for wives; and soon they multiplied and created a town of their own.

A man who had wandered far from his town came near to where the three brothers had built their home, and was astonished as he approached it, to bear voices. This man happened to be the father of the three brothers. So he returned to his town, without having entered the village, to tell his wife that he had found her children. Then the old woman set out with her husband to seek for her children, and wandered and wandered on, until she was too tired to go any further, when she sank down by the wayside to rest.

Now one of the children of the three brothers came across the old woman, and was afraid, and ran back to tell his father.

Then the three brothers set out with the intention of killing the intruder; but the river spirit called out to them, and told them not to kill her, but to take her to their home, and feed her, for she was their mother. And they did so.

Death And Burial of the Fjort
(From the Kongo people, Congo)

ONE OF MY COOK'S many fathers having died (this time, his real father), he came to me with tears in his eyes to ask me for a little rum to take to town, where he said his family were waiting for him. Some days previously the cook had told me that his father was suffering from the sleeping sickness, and was nearing his end, so that when I heard the cry of "Chibai-I" floating across the valley from a little town close to that in which the cook

lived, I guessed who the dead one was, and was prepared to lose the cook's services for a certain number of days.

The death of the father of a family is always a very sad event, but the death of the father of a Fjort family seems to me to be peculiarly pathetic. His little village at once assumes a deserted appearance; his wives and sisters, stripped of their gay cloths, wander aimlessly around and about the silent corpse, crying and wringing their hands, their tears coursing down their cheeks along little channels washed in the thick coating of oil and ashes with which they have besmeared their dusky faces. Naked children, bereft for the time being of their mother's care, cry piteously; and the men, with a blue band of cloth (*ntanta mabundi*) tied tightly round their heads, sit apart and in silence, already wondering what evil person or fetish has caused them this overwhelming loss.

The first sharp burst of grief being over, loving bands shave and wash the body, and, if the family be rich enough, palm wine or rum is used instead of water. Then the heavy body is placed upon mats of rushes and covered with a cloth. After resting in this position for a day, the body is wrapped in long pieces of cloth and placed upon a kind of rack or framework bed, underneath which a hole has been dug to receive the water, etc, that comes from the corpse. A fire is lighted both at the head and foot of the rack, and the body is covered each day with the leaves of the Acaju, so that the smoke that hangs about it will keep off the flies. More cloth is from time to time wrapped around the body; but, unless there are many palavers which cannot be quickly settled, it is generally buried after two or three wrappings. The more important the person, the longer, of course, it takes to settle these palavers and their many complications; and as the body cannot be buried until they are settled, one can understand how the heirs of a great king sometimes come to give up the hope of burying their relation, and leave him unburied for years. On the other hand, the slave, however rich he may be, is quickly buried.

The family being all present, a day is appointed upon which the cause of the death shall be divined. Upon this day the family, and the family in which the deceased was brought up, collect what cloth they can and send it to some well-known Nganga, a long way off. The Nganga meets the messengers and describes to them exactly all the circumstances connected with the life, sickness and death of the deceased; and if they conclude that this information agrees with what they know to be the facts of the case, they place the cloth before him and beseech him to inform them the cause of their relation's death. This the Nganga sets himself to divine. After some delay he informs the relations (1) that the father has died because someone (perhaps now dead) knocked a certain nail into a certain fetish, with his death as the end in view, or (2) that so-and-so has bewitched him, or (3) that he died because his time had come.

The relations then go to the Nganga of the fetish or Nkissi mentioned, and ask him if he remembers so-and-so knocking a nail into it? And if so, will be kindly point out the nail to them? He may say yes. Then they will pay him to draw it out, so that the rest of the family may not die. Or the relations give the person indicated by the Nganga as having bewitched the dead man, the so-called Ndotchi (witch), a powdered bark, which he must swallow and vomit if he be really innocent. The bark named *Mbundu* is given to the man who owns to being a witch, but denies having killed the person in question. That of *Nkassa* is given to those who deny the charge of being witches altogether. The witches or other persons who, having taken the bark, do not vomit are either killed or die from the effects of the poison, and their bodies used to be burnt. Since civilized government have occupied the country a slight improvement has taken place, in that the relations of the witch are allowed to bury the body. If events turns out as divined by the Nganga, he retains the cloth given to him by the relations or their messengers: otherwise he must return it to the family, who take it to another Nganga.

While all this is going on, a carpenter is called in to build the coffin; and he is paid one fowl, one mat of rushes and one closely woven mat per day. Rum and a piece of blue cloth are given to him on the day he covers the case with red cloth. Palm wine, rum and cloth are given to him as payment on its completion. And now that all palavers are finished, and the coffin ready, the family are once more called together; and the prince of the land and strangers are invited to come and bear how all the palavers have been settled. A square in front of the shimbec containing the coffin is cleared of herbs and grass, and carefully swept; and here, during the whole night previous to the official meeting, women and children dance. Mats are placed immediately in front of the shimbec for the family and their fetishes (Poomba): the side opposite is prepared for the prince and his followers; and the other two sides are kept for those strangers and guests who care to come. At about three o'clock guns are fired off as a signal that all is ready. The family headed by their elder and spokesman then seat themselves ready to receive their guests. Then the guests glide into the village and make their way to the elder, present themselves, and then take their allotted seats.

When all are assembled, the elder addresses the two family fetishes held by two of the family. Pointing and shaking his hand at them, he tells them how the deceased died, and all the family has done to settle the matter; he tells them how they have allowed the father to be taken, and prays them to protect the rest of the family; and when he has finished his address, the two who hold the fetishes, or wooden figures, pick up a little earth and throw it on the beads of the fetishes, then, lifting them up, rub their heads in the earth in front of them.

Then the elder addresses the prince and his people, and the strangers who have come to bear how the deceased has died, and offers them each a drink. When they have finished drinking, he turns to the fetishes and tells them that they have allowed evil to overtake the deceased, but prays them to protect his guests from the same. Then the fetishes again have earth thrown at them, and their heads are once more rubbed in the earth.

And now the elder addresses the wives and tells them that their husband has been cruelly taken from them, and that they are now free to marry another; and then, turning to the fetishes, he trusts that they will guard the wives from the evil that killed their husband; and the fetishes are again dusted and rubbed in the earth.

On the occasion that I watched these proceedings, the elder got up and addressed me, telling me that my cook, who had served me so well and whom I had sent to town when he was sick, etc., etc., had now lost his father; and once more turning to his fetishes, the poor creatures were again made to kiss old mother earth, this time for my benefit.

If a witch has to undergo the bark test, rum is given to the prince, and he is told that if he hears that the Ndotchi has been killed he is to take no official notice of the fact.

Then the men dance all through the night; and the next day the body is placed in the coffin and buried. In KaCongo the coffin is much larger than that made in Loango; and it is placed upon a huge car on four or six solid wheels. This car remains over the grave, ornamented in different ways with stuffed animals and empty demijohns, animal boxes and other earthenware goods, in accordance with the wealth of the deceased. I can remember when slaves and wives were buried together with the prince; but this custom has now died out in Loango and KaCongo, and we only bear of its taking place far away inland.

The "fetish cbibinga" sometimes will not allow the corpse to close its eyes. This is a sure sign that the deceased is annoyed about something, and does not wish to be buried. In such a case no coffin is made, the body is wrapped in mats and placed in the woods near to an Nlomba tree. Should he be buried in the ordinary way, all the family would fall sick and die. Should his chimyumba (KaCongo *chimbindi*) appear to one of his family, that person would surely die. But others not of the family may see it and not die.

The deceased will often not rest quiet until his *nkulu* (soul? spirit?) is placed in the head of one of his relations, so that he can communicate with the family. This is done by the Nganga picking up some of the earth from the grave of the deceased, and, after mixing it with other medicine, placing it in either the born of an antelope (*lekorla*) or else a little tin box (*nkobbi*). Then seating himself upon a mat within a circle drawn in chalk on the ground, he shakes a little rattle (*nquanga*) at the patient, and goes through some form of incantation, until the patient trembles and cries out with the voice of the deceased, when they all know that the *nkulu* has taken up its residence in his head. The medicine and earth together with the *nkobbi* is called *nkulu mpemba*, and shows that the deceased died of some ordinary disease; but when the medicine and earth are put into the *lekorla* it shows that the deceased died of some sickness of the bead, and this is called *nkulu mabiali*.

The Fjort say the "shadow" ceases at the death of the person. I asked if that was because they kept the corpse in the shade; what if they put the corpse in the sun? The young man asked turned to his elderly aunt and re-asked her this question. "No," she said emphatically, "certainly not!"

Animal Stories & Fables

IN THIS SECTION, stories about human action are common. They often involve the ordinary tensions of social existence, especially those relating to questions of marriage partners, the rivalry of co-wives and the position of children. Most of these stories involve animals and fables. The stories are centred around animal characters involving the major character (the trickster) and the other animals (the dupes). In the stories the trickster is usually a relatively small animal, for example a hare, squirrel, spider, tortoise, etc. The dupes – those who are fooled by the tricksters – are usually bigger animals such as the hyena, leopard, elephant or lion.

Sometimes the trickster is also tricked (see the story of 'How the Tortoise was Punished for his Deceit'). In other stories the cunning animal may also be tricked by slothful animals, for instance the tortoise. You will find in this section how a typical trickster story involves the making of friendship, the trickster's double dealing or trickery and the final escape of the trickster or suffering of the foolish character.

It should be noted that in most of the stories in this category the trickster does escape – probably because the storyteller's intention is to teach the audience the necessity of wisdom. The foolish character suffers for no mistake of his own. One common theme in this section is that of generosity. Most people in the central African sub-region are naturally generous, but a few people misuse the generosity of their friends for their own benefit. Through such stories the audience are reminded that evil forces are always at work in society; people must be wise and vigilant if they are to avoid being tricked.

Meusep Nforpeyam
(From the Bamoun people, Cameroon, told by Mama Asanatou, storyteller)

ALONG TIME AGO in a big village there lived a king called Nfordoboh, who had an only daughter and many people came from far and near for her hand in marriage. Nfordoboh gave two conditions. First, the person that would bring a big bundle of grass that would be used to roof his house would marry his daughter. He further added that this bundle of grass would not be like any other one; it had to produce a sound when thrown on the ground. The second condition was that the person should also climb the tallest palm tree in the village, and bring down one palm nut.

All the animals who were suitors for the daughter of Nfordoboh gathered and set out to fulfill these conditions. First, they all brought their bundle of grass; and all of them failed the first test, except for Meusep Nforpeyam (this literally means a small animal which is more sensible than all others, in the local language of Bamoun), who had actually buried a huge stone in the middle of his own bundle of grass, such that when thrown down on the bare floor, it produced a loud sound. Condition number two – to climb the tallest palm tree and bring down a nut. Meusep Nforpeyam had gone down to the stream and had been fortunate to see a palm nut, which he collected and hid in his dress. Upon seeing the height of the palm tree, and imagining the task of harvesting a single nut, all the other animals desisted from the contest. Meusep Nforpeyam prepared himself for the task. Armed with a climbing rope and a song that he would sing while climbing he moved forward to the view of the entire village. Here is the song Meusep Nforpeyam sang on climbing:

> *"akwo meteum ndamo banga, kpong"*
> *"mela para mohmibanga, kpong"*
> *"foumbiiere shinda malong, kpong"*

Roughly the song can be translated as follows: "If I climb this tree successfully, I will marry the daughter of the king, and the king will build a beautiful house for me, full of treasure".

When he successfully climbed and "harvested" the nut, on his way down he sang the following song:

> *"osib meteum ndanmo banga, kpong"*
> *"mela para mohmibanga, kponga, kpong"*
> *"foumbiiere shinda malong, kpong"*

Roughly the song can be translated as follows: "If I climb down this and marry the daughter of the king, what he will do for me is yet to be imagined."

When Meusep Nforpeyam climbed down, he was applauded by the entire people who had gathered to watch him, including all the animals who could not believe that he could do that. The thought that Meusep Nforpeyam would then marry the king's daughter did not go down well with the other animals, who concluded that he was too small and unimportant to have such an honour. They conspired to position themselves in several road junctions where Meusep Nforpeyam was supposed to pass with his new wife to his own village, across the big river. To counter their conspiracy, Meusep Nforpeyam changed his name to Teta Mekepeuh ('Teta Mekepeuh' is actually a name for a particular type of calabash in the local Bamoun language) and entered inside a calabash with his wife. The calabash began to roll with them through the roads where the other animals were standing guards. At each roadblock, the animals asked: "Who are you?" Meusep Nforpeyam replied: "My name is Teta Mekepeuh. I came here to see my father who was sick, and I am going back. I chose to come this time so that Meusep Nforpeyam, who is coming behind with his beautiful wife, should not crush me, since I am too tiny."

At the last roadblock Meusep Nforpeyam, now known as Teta Mekepeuh, met a huge animal, who asked him: "Who are you and where are you going?" Again Teta Mekepeuh said: "My name is Teta Mekepeuh. I came here to see my father who was sick, and I am going back. I chose to come this time so that Meusep Nforpeyam, who is coming behind with his beautiful wife, should not crush me, since I am too tiny." After narrating this story, the big animal was very sympathetic for him, and offered to help him cross the big river. Since this big animal himself couldn't swim across the big river, he rather carried him and threw on the other side of the river. When Teta Mekepeuh (in a calabash) fell on the other side, it broke and he and his wife emerged from the calabash to an applause by his own people. When all the other animals heard and saw from across the river, they were very disappointed with themselves. They picked up quarrels, each accusing the other for failing to do one thing or the other.

Do Not Trust Your Friend
(From the Mpongwe people, Gabon)

A TIME LONG AGO, the Animals were living in the Forest together. Most of them were at peace with each other. But Leopard was discovered to be a bad person. All the other animals refused to be friendly with him. Also, Wild Rat, a small animal, was found out to be a deceiver.

One day, Rat went to visit Leopard, who politely gave him a chair, and Rat sat down. "Mbolo!" "Ai, Mbolo!" each saluted to the other. Leopard said to his visitor, "What's the news?" Rat replied, "Njĕgâ! News is bad. In all the villages I passed through, in coming today, your name is only ill-spoken of, people saying, 'Njĕgâ is bad! Njĕgâ is bad!'"

Leopard replies, "Yes, you do not lie. People say truly that Njĕgâ is bad. But, look you, Ntori, I, Njĕgâ, am an evil one: but my badness comes from other animals. Because, when I go out to visit, there is no one who salutes me. When anyone sees me, he flees with fear. But, for what does he fear me? I have not vexed him. So, I pursue the one that fears me. I want to ask him, 'Why do you fear me?' But, when I pursue it, it goes on fleeing more rapidly. So, I become angry, wrath rises in my heart, and if I overtake it, I kill it on the spot. One reason why I am bad is that. If the animals would speak to me properly, and did not flee from me, then, Ntori, I would not kill them.

See! You, Ntori, have I seized you?" Rat replied, "No." Then Leopard said, "Then, Ntori, come near to this table, that we may talk well."

Rat, because of his subtlety and caution, when he took the chair given him on his arrival, had placed it near the door.

Leopard repeated, "Come near to the table." Rat excused himself: "Never mind; I am comfortable here; and I came here today to tell you that it is not well for a person to be without friends; and, I, Ntori, I say to you, let us be friends." Leopard said, "Very good!"

But now, even after this compact of friendship, Rat told falsehoods about Leopard, who, not knowing this, often had conversations with him, and would confide to him all the thoughts of his heart. For example, Leopard would tell to Rat, "Tomorrow I am going to hunt Ngowa, and next day I will go to hunt Nkambi," or whatever the animal was. And Rat, at night, would go to Hog or to Antelope or the other animal, and say, "Give me pay, and I will tell you a secret." They would lay down to him his price. And then he would tell them, "Be careful tomorrow. I heard that Njĕgâ was coming to kill you." The same night, Rat would secretly return to his own house, and lie down as if he had not been out.

Then, next day, when Leopard would go out hunting, the Animals were prepared and full of caution, to watch his coming. There was none of them that he could find; they were all hidden. Leopard thus often went to the forest, and came back empty handed. There was no meat for him to eat, and he had to eat only leaves of the trees. He said to himself, "I will not sit down and look for explanation to come to me. I will myself find out the reason of this. For, I, Njĕgâ, I should eat flesh and drink blood; and here I have come down to eating the food of goats, grass and leaves."

So, in the morning, Leopard went to the great doctor Ra-Marânge, and said, "I have come to you, I, Njĕgâ. For these five or six months I have been unable to kill an animal. But, cause me to know the reason of this." Ra-Marânge took his looking glass and his harp, and struck the harp, and looked at the glass. Then he laughed aloud, "Kĕ, kĕ, kĕ—"

Leopard asked, "Ra-Marânge, for what reason do you laugh?" He replied, "I laugh because this matter is a small affair. You, Njĕgâ, so big and strong, you do not know this little thing!" Leopard acknowledged, "Yes; I have not been able to find it out." Ra-Marânge said, "Tell me the names of your friends." Leopard answered "I have no friends. Nkambi dislikes me, Nyare refuses me, Ngowa the same. Of all animals, none are friendly to me." Ra-Marânge said, "Not so; think exactly; think again." Leopard was silent and thought; and then said, "Yes, truly, I have one friend, Ntori." The Doctor said, "But, look! If you find a friend, it is not well to tell him all the thoughts of your heart. If you tell him two or three, leave the rest. Do not tell him all. But, you, Njĕgâ, you consider that Ntori is your friend, and you show him all the thoughts of your heart. But, do you know the heart of Ntori, how it is inside? Look what he does! If you let him know that you are going next day to kill this and that, then he starts out at night, and goes to inform those animals, 'So-and-so, said Njĕgâ; but, be you on your guard.' Now, look! If you wish to be able to kill other animals, first kill Ntori." Leopard was surprised, "Ngâ! (actually) Ntori lies to me?" Ra-Marânge said, "Yes."

So, Leopard returned to his town. And he sent a child to call Rat. Rat came.

Leopard said, "Ntori! These days you have not come to see me. Where have you been?" Rat replies, "I was sick." Leopard says, "I called you today to sit at my table to eat." Rat excused himself, "Thanks! But the sickness is still in my body; I will not be able to eat." And he went away.

Whenever Rat visited or spoke to Leopard, he did not enter the house, but sat on a chair by the door. Leopard daily sent for him; he came, but constantly refrained from entering the house.

Leopard said in his heart, "Ntori does not approach near to me, but sits by the door. How shall I catch him?" Thinking and thinking, he called his wife, and said, "I have found a plan by which to kill Ntori. Tomorrow, I will lie down in the street, and you cover my body with a cloth as corpses are covered. Wear an old, ragged cloth, and take ashes and mark your body, as in mourning; and go you out on the road wailing, 'Njĕgâ is dead! Njĕgâ, the friend of Ntori is dead!' And, for Ntori, when he shall come as a friend to the mourning, put his chair by me, and say, 'Sit there near your friend.' When he sits on that chair, I will jump up and kill him there." His wife replied, "Very good!"

Next morning, Leopard, lying down in the street, pretended that he was dead. His wife dressed herself in worn-out clothes, and smeared her face, and went clear on to Rat's village, wailing "Ah! Njĕgâ is dead! Ntori's friend is dead!" Rat asked her, "But, Njĕgâ died of what disease? Yesterday, I saw him looking well, and today comes word that he is dead!" The wife answered, "Yes: Njĕgâ died without disease; just cut off! I wonder at the matter – I came to call you; for you were his friend. So, as is your duty as a man, go there and help bury the corpse in the jungle." Rat went, he and Leopard's wife together. And, behold, there was Leopard stretched out as a corpse! Rat asked the wife, "What is this matter? Njĕgâ! Is he really dead?" She replied, "Yes: I told you so. Here is a chair for you to sit near your friend."

Rat, having his caution, had not sat on the chair, but stood off, as he wailed, "Ah! Njĕgâ is dead! Ah! My friend is dead!"

Rat called out, "Wife of Njĕgâ! Njĕgâ, he was a great person: but did he not tell you any sign by which it might be known, according to custom, that he was really dead?" She replied, "No, he did not tell me." (Rat, when he thus spoke, was deceiving the woman.) Rat went on to speak, "You, Njĕgâ, when you were living and we were friends, you told me in confidence, saying, 'When I, Njĕgâ, shall die, I will lift my arm upward, and you will know that I am really dead.' But, let us cease the wailing and stop crying. I will try the test on Njĕgâ, whether he is dead! Lift your arm!"

Leopard lifted his arm. Rat, in his heart, laughed, "Ah! Njĕgâ is not dead!" But, he proceeded, "Njĕgâ! Njĕgâ! You said, if really dead, you would shake your body. Shake! If it is so!" Leopard shook his whole body. Rat said openly, "Ah! Njĕgâ is dead indeed! He shook his body!" The wife said, "But, as you say he is dead, here is the chair for you, as chief friend, to sit on by him." Rat said, "Yes: wait for me; I will go off a little while, and will come." Leopard, lying on the ground, and hearing this, knew in his heart, "Ah! Ntori wants to flee from me! I will wait no longer!" Up he jumps to seize Rat, who, being too quick for him, fled away. Leopard pursued him with leaps and jumps so rapidly that he almost caught him. Rat got to his hole in the ground just in time to rush into it. But his tail was sticking out; and Leopard, looking down the hole, seized the tail.

Rat called out, "You have not caught me, as you think! What you are holding is a rootlet of a tree." Leopard let go of the tail. Rat switched it in after him, and jeered at Leopard, "You had hold of my tail! And you have let it go! You will not catch me again!" Leopard, in a rage, said, "You will have to show me the way by which you will emerge from this hole; for, you will never come out of it alive!"

Tests of Death
(From the Mpongwe people, Gabon)

ON ANOTHER DAY, Leopard said to Jackal, "My friend! Let us arrange some plan, by which we can kill some animal. For, I've wandered into the forest again and again, and have found nothing." Leopard made these remarks to his friend in the dark of the evening. So they sat that night and planned and, after their conversation, they went to lie down in their houses. And they slept their sleep.

Then soon, the daylight broke. And Leopard, carrying out their plan, said to Jackal, "Take up your bedding, and put it out in the open air of the street." Jackal did so. Leopard laid down on that mattress, in accordance with their plan, and stretched out like a corpse lying still, as if he could not move a muscle. He said to Jackal, "Call Ngomba, and let him come to me." So Jackal shouted, "Come! Ngomba, come! That Beast that kills animals is dead! Come!"

So Porcupine came to the mourning, weeping and wailing, as if he was really sorry for the death of his enemy. He approached near the supposed corpse. And he jeered at it. "This was the person who wasted us people; and this is his body!" Leopard heard this derision. Suddenly he leaped up. And Porcupine went down under his paw, dead. Then Leopard said to his friend Jackal, "Well! Cut it up! And let us eat it." And they finished eating it.

On another day, Leopard, again in the street, stretched himself on the bedding. At his direction, Jackal called for Antelope. Antelope came; and Leopard killed him, as he had done to Porcupine.

On another day, Ox was called. And Leopard did to Ox the same as he had done to the others.

On another day, Elephant was called in the same way; and he died in the same way.

In the same way, Leopard killed some of almost all the other beasts one after another, until there were left only two.

Then Jackal said, "Njĕgâ! My friend! There are left, of all the beasts, only two, Ihĕli and Ekaga. But, what can you do with Ihĕli? For, he has many artifices. What, also, can you do against Ekaga? For he too has many devices." Leopard replied, "I will do as I usually have done; so, tomorrow, I will lie down again, as if I were a corpse."

That day darkened into night.

And another daylight broke.

And Leopard went out of the house to lie down on the bedding in the street. Each limb was extended out as if dead; and his mouth open, with lower jaw fallen, like that of a dead person.

Then Jackal called, "Ihĕli! Come here! That person who wastes the lives of the beasts is dead! He's dead!"

Gazelle said to himself, "I hear! So! Njĕgâ is dead? I go to the mourning!" Gazelle lived in a town distant about three miles. He started on the journey, taking with him his spear and bag; but, he said to himself, "Before I go to the mourning, I will stop on the way at the town of Ekaga."

He came to the town of Tortoise, and he said to him, "Chum! Have you heard the news? That person who kills Beasts and Mankind is dead!" But Tortoise answered, "No! Go back to your town! That person is not dead. Go back!" Gazelle said, "No! For, before I go back to my town, I will first go to Njĕgâ's to see." So Tortoise said, "If you are determined to go there, I will tell you something." Gazelle exclaimed, "Yes! Uncle, speak!"

Then Tortoise directed him, "Take Ndongo (Pepper)." Gazelle took some. Tortoise said, "Take also Hako (Ants), and take also Nyoi (Bees). Tie them all up in a bundle of plantain leaves." (He told Gazelle to do all these things, as a warning.) And Tortoise added, "You will find Njĕgâ with limbs stretched out like a corpse. Take a machete with you in your hands. When you arrive there, begin to cut down the plantain stalks. And you must cry out 'Who killed my Uncle? Who killed my uncle?' If he does not move, then you sit down and watch him."

So Gazelle went, journeyed and came to that town of mourning. He asked Jackal, "Ibâbâ! This person, how did he die?" Jackal replied, "Yesterday afternoon this person was seized with a fever; and today, he is a corpse." Gazelle looked at Leopard from a distance, his eyes fixed on him, even while he was slashing down the plantains, as he was told to do.

But, Leopard made no sign, though he heard the noise of the plantain stalk falling to the ground. Presently, Jackal said to Gazelle, "Go near to your Uncle's bed, and look at the corpse."

Leopard began in his heart to arrange for a spring, being ready to fight, and thinking, "What time Ihĕli shall be near me, I will kill him."

Gazelle approached, but carefully stood off a rod distant from the body of Leopard. Then Gazelle drew the bundle of Ants out of his bag, and said to himself, "Is this person, really dead? I will test him!" But, Gazelle stood warily ready to flee at the slightest sign. He quickly opened the bundle of insects; and he joined the three, the Ants, the Bees and the Pepper, all in one hand; and, standing with care, he threw them at Leopard.

The bundle of leaves, as it struck Leopard, flew open. Being released, the Bees rejoiced, saying, "So! I sting Njĕgâ!" Pepper also was glad, saying, "So! I will make him perspire!" Ants also spitefully exclaimed, "I've bitten you!"

The pain of all these made Leopard jump up in wrath; and he leaped toward Gazelle. But he dashed away into the forest, shouting as he disappeared, "I'm not an Ihĕli of the open prairie, but of the forest wilderness!"

So, he fled and came to the town of Tortoise. There he told Tortoise, "You are justified! Njĕgâ indeed is not dead! He was only pretending, in order to kill."

And Tortoise, remarked, "I am the doyen of Beasts. Being the eldest, if I tell anyone a thing, he should not contradict me."

A Tug-of-War
(From the Mpongwe people, Gabon
and analogous to stories from Cameroon)

LEOPARD WAS DEAD, after the accusation against him by Tortoise for killing the great Goat. The children of Leopard were still young; they had not grown to take their father's power and place. And Tortoise considered himself now a great personage. He said to people, "We three who are left, I and Njâgu

and Ngubu, are of equal power; we eat at the same table, and have the same authority." Every day he made these boasts; and people went to Elephant and Hippopotamus, reporting, "So-and-so says Ekaga." Elephant and Hippopotamus laughed, and disregarded the report, and said, "That's nothing, he's only to be despised."

One day Hippopotamus met Elephant in the forest; salutations were made, "Mbolo!" "Ai, mbolo!" each to the other. Hippopotamus asked Elephant about a new boast that Tortoise had been making, "Have you, or have you not heard?" Elephant answered, "Yes, I have heard. But I look on it with contempt. For, I am Njâgu. I am big. My foot is as big as Ekaga's body. And he says he is equal to me! But, I have not spoken of the matter, and will not speak, unless I hear Ekaga himself make his boast. And then I shall know what I will do." And Hippopotamus also said, "I am doing so too, in silence. I wait to hear Ekaga myself."

Tortoise heard of what Elephant and Hippopotamus had been threatening, and he asked his informant just the exact words that they had used, "They said that they waited to hear you dare to speak to them; and that, in the meanwhile, they despised you."

Tortoise asked, "So! They despise me, do they?" "Yes," was the reply. Then he said, "So! Indeed, I will go to them." He told his wife, "Give me my coat to cover my body." He dressed; and started to the forest. He found Elephant lying down; his trunk was eight miles long; his ears as big as a house, and his four feet beyond measure.

Tortoise audaciously called to him, "Mwĕra! I have come! You don't rise to salute me? Mwĕra has come!" Elephant looked, rose up and stared at Tortoise, and indignantly asked, "Ekaga! Whom do you call 'Mwĕra'?" Tortoise replied, "You! I call you 'Mwĕra'. Are you not, Njâgu?" Elephant, with great wrath, asked, "Ekaga! I have heard you said certain words. It is true that you said them?"

Tortoise answered, "Njâgu, don't get angry! Wait, let us first have a conversation." Then he said to Elephant, "I did call you, just now, 'Mwĕra'; but, you, Njâgu, why do you condemn me? You think that, because you are of great expanse of flesh, you can surpass Ekaga, just because I am small? Let us have a test. Tomorrow, sometime in the morning, we will have a lurelure (tug-of-war)." Said Elephant, "Of what use? I can mash you with one foot."

Tortoise said, "Be patient. At least try the test." So, Elephant, unwilling, consented. Tortoise added, "But, when we tug, if one overpulls the other, he shall be considered the greater; but, if neither, then we are Mwĕra."

Then Tortoise went to the forest, and cut a very long vine, and coming back to Elephant, said "This end is yours. I go off into the forest with my end to a certain spot, and tomorrow I return to that spot; and we will have our tug, and neither of us will stop, to eat or sleep until either you pull me over or the vine breaks." Tortoise went far off with his end of the vine to the town of Hippopotamus, and hid the vine's end at the outskirts of the town. He went to Hippopotamus and found him bathing, and going ashore, back and forth, to and from the water. Tortoise shouted to him, "Mwĕra! I have come! You! Come ashore! I am visiting you!" Hippopotamus came bellowing in great wrath with wide open jaws, ready to fight, and said, "I will fight you today! For, whom do you call 'Mwĕra'?"

Tortoise replied, "Why! *You!* I do not fear your size. Our hearts are the same. But, don't fight yet! Let us first talk." Hippopotamus grunted, and sat down; and Tortoise said, "I, Ekaga, I say that you and I and Njâgu are equal, we are Mwĕra. Even though you are great and I small, I don't care. But if you doubt me, let us have a trial. Tomorrow morning let us have a lurelure. He who shall overcome, shall be the superior. But, if neither is found superior, then we are equals." Hippopotamus exclaimed that the plan was absurd; but, finally he consented.

Tortoise then stood up, and went out, and got his end of the vine, and brought it to Hippopotamus, and said, "This end is yours. And I now go. Tomorrow, when you feel the vine shaken, know that I am ready at the other end; and then you begin, and we will not stop to eat or sleep until this test is ended."

Hippopotamus then went to the forest to gather leaves of Medicine with which to strengthen his body. And Elephant, at the other end, was doing the same, making medicine to give himself strength; and at night they were both asleep.

In the morning, Tortoise went to the middle of the vine, where at its halfway, he had made on the ground a mark; and he shook it towards one end, and then towards the other. Elephant caught his end, as he saw it shake, and Hippopotamus did the same at his end. "Orindi went back and forth" (a proverb of a fish of that name that swims in that way), Elephant and Hippopotamus alternately pulling. "Nkĕndinli was born of his father and mother" (a proverb, meaning distinctions in individualities). Each one, Hippopotamus and Elephant, doing in his own way. Tortoise smiled at his arrangement with each, that, in the tug, if one overcame, it would be proved by his dragging the other; but, if neither overcame, they were not to cease, until the vine broke.

Elephant holding the vine taut, and Hippopotamus also holding it taut, Tortoise was laughing in his heart as he watched the quivering vine.

He went away to seek for food, leaving those two at their tug, in hunger. He went off into the forest and found his usual food, mushrooms. He ate his belly full, and then took his drink; and then went to his town to sleep.

He rose in late afternoon, and said to himself, "I'll go and see about the tug, whether those fools are still pulling." When he went there, the vine was still stretched taut; and he thought, "Asai! Shame! Let them die with hunger!" He sat there, the vine trembling with tensity, and he in his heart mocking the two tired beasts. The one drew the other toward himself; and then, a slight gain brought the mark back; but neither was overcoming.

At last Tortoise nicked the vine with his knife; the vine parted; and, at their ends, Elephant and Hippopotamus fell violently back onto the ground. Tortoise said to himself, "So! That's done! Now I go to Elephant with one end of the broken vine; tomorrow to Hippopotamus." He went, and came on to Elephant, and found him looking dolefully, and bathing his leg with medicine, and said, "Mwĕra! How do you feel? Do you consent that we are Mwĕra?" Elephant admitted, "Ekaga, I did not know you were so strong! When the vine broke, I fell over and hurt my leg. Yes, we are really equal. Really! Strength is not because the body is large. I despised you because your body was small. But actually, we are equal in strength!"

So they ate and drank and played as chums; and Tortoise returned to his town.

Early the next morning, with the other end of the broken vine, he went to visit Hippopotamus, who looked sick, and was rubbing his head, and asked, "Ngubu! How do you feel, Mwĕra?" Hippopotamus answered, "Really! Ekaga! So we are equals! I, Ngubu, so great! And you, Ekaga, so small! We pulled and pulled. I could not surpass you, nor you me. And when the vine broke, I fell and hurt my head. So, indeed strength has no greatness of body." Tortoise and Hippopotamus ate and drank and played; and Tortoise returned to his town.

After that, whenever they three and others met to talk in palaver (council) the three sat together on the highest seats. Were they equal? Yes, they were equal.

"Nuts Are Eaten Because of Angângwe"; A Proverb
(From the Mpongwe people, Gabon)

THE HOGS (Ingowa; singular Ngowa) had cleared a space in the forest, for the building of their town. They were many men and women and children.

In another place, a Hunter was sitting in his town. Every day, at daybreak, he went out to hunt. When he returned in the afternoons with his prey, he left it a short distance from the town, and entering his house, would say to his women and children, "Go to the outskirts of the town, and bring what animal you find I have left there."

One day, having gone hunting, he killed Elephant (Njâgu). The children went out to cut it up and bring it in.

Another day, he killed Gorilla (Njina).

And so, each day, he killed some animal. He never failed of obtaining something.

One day, his children said to him, "You always return with some animal; but you never have brought us Ngowa." He replied, "I saw many Ingowa today, when I was out there. But, I wonder at one thing; that, when they are all together eating, and I approach, they run away. As to Ingowa, they eat nkula nuts and I know where the trees are. Well, then, I ambush them; but, when I go nearer, I see one big Ngowa not eating, but going around and around the herd. Whether it sees me or does not see, sure when I get ready to aim my gun, then they all scatter. The reason that Ingowa escape me, I do not know."

The Hogs, when they had finished eating, and were returning to their own town, as they passed the town of Elephant, heard mourning; and they asked, "Who is dead?" The answer was, "Njâgu is dead! Njâgu is dead!" They enquired, "He died of what disease?" They were told, "Not disease; Hunter killed him." Then another day, when Ox (Nyare) was killed, his people were heard mourning for him. Another day, Antelope (Nkambi) was killed; and his people were mourning for him. All these animals were dying because of Hunter killing them.

At first, the Hogs felt pity for all these other Beasts. But, when they saw how they were dying, they began to mock at them, "These are not people! They only die! But, as to us Ingowa, Hunter is not able to kill us. We hear only the report that there is such a person as Hunter, but he is not able to kill us."

When Hogs were thus boasting, their King, Angângwe, laughed at them, saying, "You don't know, you Ingowa! You mock others, that Hunter kills them?" They answered, "Yes, we mock at them; for, we go to the forest as they do, but Hunter does not touch us." Angângwe asked, "When you thus in the forest eat your inkula nuts, you each one eat them by his own strength and skill?" They answered, "Yes; ourselves we go to the forest on our own feet; we ourselves pick up and eat the inkula. No one feeds us." Angângwe said, "It is not so. Those inkula you eat si nyo o'kângâ wa oma (they are eaten because of a person)." They insisted, "No, it is not so. Inkula have no person in particular to do anything about them." Thus they had this long discussion, the Hogs and their King; and they got tired of it, and lay down to sleep.

In the morning, when daylight came, the King said, "A journey for nuts! But, today, I am sick. I am not able to go to gather nuts with you. I will stay in town." The Hogs said, "Well! We do not mistake the way. It is not necessary for you to go."

When they went, they were jeering about their King, "Angângwe said, 'Inkula si nyo o'kângâ w' oma'; but we will see today without him." They went to the inkula trees, and found great abundance fallen to the ground during the night. The herd of Hogs, when they saw all these inkula, jumped about in joy. They stooped down to pick up the nuts, their eyes busy with the ground. They ate and ate. No one of them thought of Hunter, whether he was out in the forest.

But, that very morning, Hunter had risen, taken his gun and ammunition box, and had gone to hunt. And, after a while, he had seen the Hogs in the distance. They were only eating and eating, not looking at anything but nuts.

Hunter said in his heart, "These Hogs, I see them often, but why have I not been able to kill them?" He crept softly nearer and nearer. Creeping awhile then he stood up to spy; and again stooping, and again standing up to spy. He did not see the big Hog which, on other days, he had always observed going around and around the herd. Hunter stooped close to the ground, and crept onward. Then, as he approached closer, the Hogs still went on eating. He bent his knee to the earth, and he aimed his gun! Ingowa still eating! His gun flashed! And ten Hogs died!

The Hogs fled; some of them wounded. Those who were not wounded, stopped before they reached their town, and said, "Let us wait for the wounded." They waited. When the hindmost caught up and joined the others, they showed them their wounds, some in the head, some in the legs. These wounded ones said, "As we came, we saw none others behind us. There are ten of us missing; we think they are dead." So, they all returned toward their Town; and, on their way, began to mourn.

When they had come clear on to the town, Angângwe asked, "What news, from where you come?" They answered, "Angângwe! Evil news! But we do not know what is the matter. Only we know that the words you said are not really so, that 'nuts are eaten because of a certain person.' Because, when we went, each one of us gathered by his own skill, and ate by his own strength, and no one trusted to anyone else. And when we went, we ate abundantly, and everything was good. Except that, Hunter has killed ten of us. And many others are wounded."

The King enquired, "Well! Have you brought nuts for me who was left in Town?" They replied, "No; when Hunter shot us, we feared, and could no longer wait." Then Angângwe said, "I told you that inkula are eaten because of a person, and you said, 'not so.' And you still doubt me."

Another day, the Hogs went for inkula; and the King, remained in town. And, as on the other day, Hunter killed them. So, for five successive days, they went, the King staying in town; and Hunter killing them.

Finally, Angângwe said to himself, "Ingowa have become great fools. They do not consent to admit that nuts are eaten by reason of a certain person. They see how Hunter kills them; and they still doubt my words. But, I pity them. Tomorrow, I will go with them to the nuts. I will explain to them how Hunter kills them."

So, in the morning, the King ordered, "Come all to nuts! But when we go for the nuts, if I say, 'Ngh-o-o!' then every one of you who are eating them must start to town, and not come back, because then I have seen or smelt Hunter; and I grunt to let you know." All the Hogs agreed. They went on clear to the nkula trees, and ate, they stooping with eyes to the ground. But Angângwe, not eating, kept looking here and there. He sniffed wind from south to north, and assured them, "Eat you all! I am here!" He watched and watched; and presently he saw a speck far away. He passed around to sniff the wind. His nose uplifted, he caught the odor of Hunter. He returned to the herd, grunted "Ngh-o-o." And he and they all fled. They arrived safely at town.

Then he asked them, "Who is dead? who is wounded?" They assured, "None." He said, "Good!"

Thus they went nutting, for five consecutive days, they and their King, Angângwe only keeping watch. And none of them died by Hunter.

Then Angângwe said to them, "Today let us have a conversation." And he began, "I told you, inkula si nyo o'kângâ w' oma; you said, 'Not so!' But, when you went by yourselves to eat nuts, did not Hunter kill you? And these five days that we have gone, you and I together, and you obeyed my voice, who has died?"

They then replied, "No one! No one! Indeed, you spoke truly. You are justified. Inkula si nyo o'kângâ wa 'Ngângwe. It is so!"

Who Are Crocodile's Relatives?
(From the Mpongwe people, Gabon)

CROCODILE WAS VERY OLD. Finally he died. News of his death spread abroad among the Beasts; and his relatives and friends came to the Mourning. After a proper number of days had passed, the matter of the division of the property was mentioned. At once a quarrel was developed, on the question as to who were his nearest relatives.

The tribe of Birds said, "He is ours and we will be the ones to divide the property." Their claim was disputed, others asking, "On what ground do you claim relationship? You wear feathers; you do not wear plates of armour as he." The Birds replied, "True, he did not wear our feathers. But, you are not to judge by what he put on during his life. Judge by what he was in his life's beginning. Look you! In his beginning, he began with us as an egg. We believe in eggs. His mother bore him as an egg. He is our relative, and we are his heirs."

But the Beasts said, "Not so! We are his relatives, and by us shall his property be divided."

Then the Council of Animals demanded of the Beasts on what ground they based their claim for relationship, and what answer they could make to the argument of the birds as to Crocodile's egg-origin.

The Beasts said, "It may be true that the mark of tribe must be found, in a *beginning*, but not in an egg. For, all Beings began as eggs. *Life* is the original beginning. Look you! When life really begins in the egg, then the mark of tribe is shown. When Ngando's life began, he had four legs as we have. We judge by legs. So we claim him as our relative. And we will take his property."

But, the Birds answered, "You Beasts said we were not relatives because we wear feathers, and not ngando-plates. But, you, look you! Judge by your own words. Neither do you wear ngando-plates, you with your hair and fur! Your words are not correct. The *beginning* of his life was not, as you say, when little Ngando sprouted some legs. There was *life* in the egg before that. And his egg was like ours, not like what you call your eggs. You are not his relatives. He is ours."

But the Beasts disputed still. So the quarrel went back and forth. And they never settled it.

Who is King of Birds?
(From the Mpongwe people, Gabon)

ALL THE BIRDS had their dwelling place in a certain country of Njambi's Kingdom. The pelicans, chickens, eagles, parrots and all other winged kinds all lived together,

separated from other animals, in that country under the Great Lord Njambi.

One day, they were discussing together on the question, "Who is King of the Birds?" They all, each one, named himself, e.g., the Chicken said, "I!" the Parrot, "I!" the Eagle "I!" and so on. Every day they had this same discussion. They were not able to settle it, or to agree to choose any one of their number. So, they said, "Let us go to Ra-Njambi, and refer the question to him." They agreed; and all went to him so that he might name who was the superior among them. When they all had arrived at Njambi's Town, he asked, "What is the affair on which you have come?" They replied, "We have come together here, not to visit, but for a purpose. We have a discussion and a doubt among ourselves. We wish to know, of all the Birds, who is Head or Chief. Each one says for himself that he is the superior. This one, because he knows how to fly well; that one because he can speak well; and another one, because he is strong. But, of these three things – flight, speech and strength – we ask you, which is the greatest?"

Immediately all the Birds began a competition, each one saying, "Choose me; I know how to speak!" Njambi silenced them, and bade them, "Well, then, come here! I know that you all speak. But, show me, each one of you, your manner of speaking."

So Eagle stood up to be examined. Njambi asked him, "How do you speak? What is your manner of talking?" Eagle began to scream, "So-o-we! So-o-we! So-o-we!" Njambi said, "Good! Now call me your wife!" The wife of Eagle came, and Njambi said to her, "You are the wife of Ngwanyâni, how do you talk?" The wife replied, "I say, 'So-o-we! So-o-we! So-o-we!'" Ra-Njambi said to Eagle, "Indeed! You and your wife speak the same kind of language." Eagle answered, "Yes; I and my wife, we speak alike." They were ordered, "Sit you aside."

Then Ra-Njambi directed, "Bring me here Ngozo." And he asked, "Ngozo, how do you talk? What is your way of speaking?" Parrot squawked, "I say, 'Ko-do-ko!'" Ra-Njambi ordered, "Well, call me your wife!" She came; and he asked her, "How do you talk? Talk now!" The wife replied, "I say, 'Ko-do-ko!'" Njambi asked Parrot, "So! Your wife says, 'Ko-do-ko?'" Parrot answered "Yes; my wife and I both say, 'Ko-do-ko.'"

Njambi then ordered, "Call me here, Ugulungu." He came, and was asked, "And how do you talk?" He shouted, "I say, 'Mbru-kâ-kâ! Mbru-kâ-kâ! Mbru!'" Njambi told him, "Call me your wife!" She came, and, when asked, spoke in the same way as her husband. Njambi dismissed them, "Good! You and your wife say the same thing. Good!"

So, all the Birds, in succession, were summoned; and they all, husband and wife, had the same mode of speaking, except one who had not hitherto been called.

Njambi finally said, "Call Njâgâni here!" The Cock stood up, and strutted forward. Njambi asked him, "What is your speech? Show me your mode of talking!" Cock threw up his head, stretched his throat, and crowed, "Kâ-kâ-re-kââ." Njambi said, "Good! Summon your wife hither." The wife came; and, of her, Njambi asked, "And, what do you say?" She demurely replied, "My husband told me that I might talk only if I bore children. So, when I lay an egg, I say 'Kwa-ka! Kwa-ka!'" Njambi exclaimed, "So! You don't say, 'Kâ-kâ-re-kââ,' like your husband?" She replied, "No, I do not talk as he."

Then Njambi said to Cock, "For what reason do you not allow your wife to say, 'Kâ-kâ-re-kââ?'" Cock replied, "I am Njâgâni, I respect myself. I jeer at all these other birds. Their wives and themselves speak only in the same way. A visitor, if he comes to their towns, is not able to know, when one of them speaks, which is husband and which is wife, because they both speak alike. But I, Njâgâni, as to my wife, she is unable to speak as I do. I do not allow it. A husband should be at the head; and in his wife it is not becoming for her to be equal with him or to talk as well as he does."

Njambi listened to this long speech; and then enquired, "Have you finished?" Chicken answered, "Yes."

Njambi summoned all the Birds to stand together in one place near him, and he said, "The affair which you brought to me, I settle it thus: Njâgâni is your Head; because you others all speak, husband and wife, each alike. But, he speaks for himself in his own way, and his wife in her way; to show that a husband has priority and superiority over a wife. Therefore, as he knows how to be Head of his family, it is settled that Njâgâni is Head also of your Tribe."

But, Njambi went on to say, "Though this is true, you, Njâgâni, don't you go back again into the Forest, to your Kingship of the Birds. For the other birds will be jealous of you. You are not strong, you cannot fight them all. Lest they kill you, stay with me in my Town."

Cock went to get his wife and children, and returned and remained there with Ra-Njambi. Therefore, the original bird to dwell among Mankind was the chicken.

When the other Birds scattered and went back to their own forest country without their king, they said, "Let it be so! We will not choose another King. Our King has left us, and has emigrated to another country, and has sat down in Njambi's Town."

So, the Birds have lived in the forest without any King.

* * *

There is another story which gives a different explanation of chickens being the first of birds to dwell among Mankind.

The Birds had no fire. They had to eat their food raw, and to shiver on cold days. In flying over the other countries, they saw Mankind using, in the preparation of their food, a thing which birds did not have. They observed that that thing seemed to add much to the comfort of Mankind. So, they chose Chicken, not as their King, but, because he knew so well how to speak, to go as their messenger, to ask Mankind to share that thing with them. Chicken left the Forest, and started on his journey, and came to the towns of Men.

He found so much food lying around, and it tasted so good because it had been touched by that bright thing which he heard people call "Fire," that he delayed the delivery of his message. And Men were pleased with his usefulness in awaking them in the morning, as he called them to get up and make their fires. The situation was so comfortable, as Mankind allowed him to walk in and out of their houses at will, that he forgot his errand, and chose to stay with Men, and never went back to the Forest.

The Birds, having no one else who united both audacity to act and ability to speak, never sent another messenger on that errand, and they remain without fire to this day.

Which is the Fattest?
(From the Mpongwe people, Gabon)

RA-MBORAKINDA WAS DWELLING in his Town, with his people and the glory of his Kingdom. There were gathered there the Manatus, the Oyster and the Hog, waiting to be assigned their kingdoms. To pass the time, while waiting until the King should summon them for their assignments, Oyster said, "You, Manga and Ngowa, let us have a dance!" And they went to exhibit before the King. They danced and danced, each one dancing his own special dance.

After that they made a fire, each one at his own fireplace, and sat down to rest. Then Hog proposed a new entertainment. He said, "You, Arandi, and Manga, we all three shall test ourselves by fire, to see who has the most fat." And they all three went into their respective fireplaces, Hog into his, and Manatus into his, and Oyster into its. Under the influence of the heat, the fat in their bodies began to melt.

Then the King announced, "To the one who shall prove to have the most fat, I will give a great extent of country as its kingdom." So, they all three tried to show much fat, in their effort to win the prize.

Presently, the fat of Hog began to cease exuding, for he had not a great deal. As to Oyster, it had no fat. What it produced was not fat at all, but water; and that was in such quantity that it put out its fire.

These facts about the Hog and Oyster were reported to the King, and when he enquired how Manatus was getting on, lo!, it was found that she had such abundance of fat, that the oil flowing from her had burst into flame and had set the town on fire.

At this, the King wondered, and exclaimed, "This Manga, that lives in the water, has yet enough fat to set the town afire!"

Then Manatus with Hog and Oyster went and sat together in the open court before the King's house, to await what would be his decision. When he was ready, he sent two heralds to summon not only those three, but all the

Tribes of the Beasts of the Forest, and of the Fishes of the Sea; and the town was full of these visitors. But, Hog and all his tribe had become impatient of waiting, and had gone off for a walk. All the other animals that had been summoned, came into the King's presence, and he, having ascended his throne, said, "I am ready now to speak with these three persons; but, I see that the Ingowa are not here. So, because of their disrespect in going off to amuse themselves with a walk instead of waiting for me, I condemn that they shall no longer wear any horns."

Then the King announced that, as Manatus had the most fat, her promised territory should be the Sea, and of it she should be ruler. But, Manatus said, "I do not want to live in the Sea, lest I be killed there." The King asked, "Then, where will you prefer to live?" She answered, "In such rivers as I shall like."

That is the reason that the Manatus lives only in rivers and bays. For one day she and her children had floated with the tide to the mouth of a river and into the Sea; and some of them had been killed there by sharks and other big fish. So, the Manatus is never now found near the Sea on ordinary tides, but only when high tides have swept it down.

Just as the King had made his announcement, the company of Hogs returned and entered the Assembly. They explained, "We have just come back from our walk, and we wish to resume our horns which we left here." But the King refused, and kept possession of the horns. Hog begged, "Please! Let me have my horns!" But the King swore an oath, saying, "O savi! (By the Blessing!) Wherever you go, and whatever you be, you shall have no horns." So the Hogs departed.

Now Oyster stood up, and said, "I wish to go to my place. Where shall it be?" The King said, "I will give you no other place than what you already have had. I do not wish to put you into the freshwater springs and brooks with Manga. You shall go into the salty waters." So Oyster went; and its race lives on the edge of the rivers, near the Sea, in brackish waters. And the King said to Oyster, "All the tribes of Mankind, by the Sea, when they fail to obtain other fish, shall be allowed to eat you."

All knew that this was a punishment given by the King to Oyster, for having dared the test by fire, pretending that it had fat, the while it had none.

Why Mosquitoes Buzz
(From the Mpongwe people, Gabon)

IN THE TIME of Long-ago, in Njambi's Town, Mosquito and Ear
went out to take a bath together. After taking her bath, Ear
began to rub an oily substance over herself, while Mosquito
did not. So Ear said to Mosquito, "Why do you leave your skin so
rough? It is better to rub on a little oil." Mosquito replied, "I have
none." So Ear said, "Indeed! I did not know that. I will give you
part of mine, as I have plenty." Mosquito had to wait the while that
Ear was rubbing the soft wax over herself. But, as soon as Ear had
finished, she put back the wax into her ear where she usually kept
it, and did not fulfil her promise to Mosquito.

When Mosquito saw this, that the wax was put away, he came near to the
door, and said, "I want the oil you promised for rubbing on my body." But
Ear took no notice of him, except to call on Hands to drive Mosquito away.

So, to this day, Mosquito is not willing to cease making his claim for the
unfulfilled promise; and is always coming to our ears, and buzzing and
crying. Always Mosquito comes and says, "I want my oil, Bz-z-z-z." But Ear
remains silent, and gives no answer. And Mosquito keeps on grumbling and
complaining, and gets angry and bites.

Unkind Criticism
(From the Mpongwe people, Gabon)

THE BLACK MONKEY, up a tree, saw Tortoise passing beneath,
slowly and awkwardly moving step by step. Monkey laughed
at the dull manner and appearance of Tortoise; and, to tease
one whom he thought stupid and unable to resent insult, he

jumped down onto the back of Tortoise. There, safely perched, he jeered at Tortoise, saying many unkind things. Tortoise was unable to throw off his tormentor; nor could he reach him. His short hands and feet could not touch Monkey. So, Tortoise was compelled to carry Monkey on the way, the while that the latter was taunting him. Finally, the patience of Tortoise was exhausted, and, his indignation being aroused, he stopped, and said angrily, "Get off of my back, you black monkey!"

Monkey was sensitive about his colour; and, at that word "black", he slipped off, and went away ashamed. But he was angry also, and determined to have some revenge.

Sometime after this, Monkey made a feast, and invited a number of beasts, among the rest Tortoise. But Monkey purposely placed all the dishes up high, so that Tortoise, unable to reach to them, could get no food, as he vainly went around and around the table. All the while, Monkey was sarcastically urging him to come and help himself and eat. Tortoise bore it without complaint; and at the end of the feast, he went away hungry. But he also determined to have his revenge.

On another day, Tortoise made a feast, and invited the same persons who had seen his humiliation at the house of Monkey. Monkey came to the feast. But Tortoise had prepared the food in only one dish, around which the company were to sit on the ground, and from which they were to eat with their hands. Before calling them to eat, Tortoise had provided water and soap for them to wash their hands previous to their putting them into the same dish. As Monkey was about to put his, Tortoise reminded him that it was black, and that he should first wash it. He said, "Here is water, and the soap by which white people keep their hands from getting black."

Monkey was ashamed, and lathered the soap over his hands until they were white with foam. "Now," said Tortoise, "put your hand into the water to remove the foam." Monkey did so; and his hands were still black.

The rest of the company objected to his black hand going into their food. And he went away ashamed and hungry.

The Suitors of Princess Gorilla
(From the Mpongwe people, Gabon)

KING GORILLA HAD a daughter, whose beauty had been much praised. She being of marriageable age, he announced to all the tribes that he would give her in marriage to anyone who could accomplish a certain task. He said he would not take any of the goods usually given in payment for a wife, as dowry. But, that he had a new kind of water [rum], such as had never before been seen; and, whoever could drink an entire barrelful of it, should have the prize that had been coveted by many.

So, all the tribes came together one day in the forest country of the King, to compete for the young woman, and the paths were crowded with the expectant suitors on their way to the King's Court.

First, because of his size, Elephant stepped forward. He walked with his solemn dignity, his ponderous feet sounding, tubu, tubu, as he strode toward where the barrel stood. He could, however, scarcely suppress his indignation, in the presence of the King, at what he considered the insultingly small test to which he was about to be subjected. He thought in his heart, "That barrelful of water! Why! I, Njâgu, when I take my daily bath, I spurt from my trunk many barrelfuls over my whole body, and I drink half a barrelful at every meal. And this! Why! I'll swallow it down in two gulps!" He thrust his proboscis into the barrel to draw up a big mouthful. But, he instantly withdrew it, before he began to suck up any of it. "The new water" stung him. He lifted his trunk, and trumpeting with rage, declared that the task was impossible.

Many in the company, who had feared that the big elephant would leave no chance for them, secretly rejoiced at his failure; and began to hope for themselves.

Then Hippopotamus blundered forward. He was in haste, for he was sure he would succeed. He was not as big or heavy as Elephant, though he was more awkward. But he did not hesitate to boast aloud what he could do. "You, Njâgu, with your big body, afraid of that little barrel of water! Why!

I live in water half of the time. And when I begin to drink in a river, I cause the Bejaka to be frightened." So he came bellowing and roaring, in order to impress the young woman with his importance. But his mouth had not sunk into the barrel as he thrust his nose in, before he jerked his head up with a bigger bellow of pain and disgust at the new water. Without making even a bow to the King, he shambled off to a river to wash his mouth.

Next came Hog. He said to Gorilla, "King Gorilla, I do not boast like those two other fellows, nor will I insult you as they have done, even if I fail. But, I do not think I shall fail. I am accustomed to putting my nose into all sorts of dirty places; so I shall try." He did try, slowly and carefully. But, even he, used to all sorts of filth and bad smells, turned from the barrel in disgust, and went away grunting.

Then Leopard came bounding forward, boasting and jumping from side to side to show his beautiful skin to the young woman. He derided the other three who had preceded him. "O! You fellows! You had no chance at all, even if you had drunk up that water. The woman would not look at you, nor live with such blundering, awkward gawks as you. Look at my graceful body and tail! These strong but soft paws of mine! And, as to that barrel, you shall see in a few minutes. Though we of the Cat Tribe do not like to wet our feet, I will do it for the sake of the woman. I'm the dandy of the Forest, and I shall go at it more gracefully than you." He leaped on to the barrel. But, its very fumes sickened him. He made one vain effort. And with limp tail between his legs he crawled away to hide his shame.

One after another of the various Beasts attempted. And all failed. Finally, there crept forward the little Telinga. He had left the hundreds of his Tribe of little Monkeys hidden out in the grass field. As he advanced, there was a murmur of surprise from the unsuccessful spectators. Even King Gorilla could not refrain from saying, "Well! My little fellow! What do you want?" Telinga replied, "Your Majesty, did not you send word to all the Tribes that anyone might compete?" "Yes, I did," he answered. And Telinga said, "Then I, Telinga, small as I am, I shall try." The King replied, "I will keep my royal word. You may try." "But, Your Majesty," asked Telinga, "is it required that the barrel must be drank at one draught? May I not, between each mouthful, take a very short rest out in the grass?" Said Gorilla, "Certainly, just so you drink it today."

So Telinga took a sip, and leaped off into the grass. And, apparently, he immediately returned, and took another sip and leaped back into the grass; and, apparently, immediately returned again. And apparently (they were his companions who had come one by one to help him!), thus the barrelful of firewater was rapidly sipped away.

King Gorilla announced Telinga as the winner of the prize.

What the young woman thought of the loss of her graceful lovers, the Antelopes and others, is not known. For, when Telinga advanced to take her, Leopard and others dashed at him, shouting, "You miserable little snip of a fellow! You've won her; but if we can't have her you shan't. There! Take that! And that! And that!" as they began to beat and kick and bite him.

In terror, he jumped into the trees, abandoning his bride.

And he and his tribe have remained in the trees ever since, afraid to come down to the ground.

Leopard of the Fine Skin
(From the Mpongwe people, Gabon)

AT THE TOWN of King Ra-Mborakinda, where he lived with his wives and his children and his glory, this occurred.

He had a beloved daughter, by name Ilâmbe. He loved her much; and sought to please her in many ways, and gave her many servants to serve her. When she grew up to womanhood, she said that she did not wish any one to come to ask her in marriage; that she herself would choose a husband. "Moreover, I will never marry any man who has any, even a little bit of, blotch on his skin."

Her father did not like her to speak in that way; nevertheless, he did not forbid her.

When men began to come to the father and say, "I desire your daughter Ilâmbe for a wife," he would say, "Go, and ask herself." Then when the man went to Ilâmbe's house, and would say, "I have come to ask you in marriage," her only reply was a question, "Have you a clear skin, and no blotches on your body?" If he answered, "Yes," Ilâmbe would say, "But, I must see for myself; come into my room." There she required the man to take off all his clothing. And if, on examination, she saw the slightest pimple or scar, she would point toward it, and say, "That! I do not want you." Then perhaps he would begin to plead, "All my skin is right, except—" But she would interrupt him, "No! For even that little mark I do not want you."

So it went on with all who came, she finding fault with even a small pimple or scar. And all suitors were rejected. The news spread abroad that Ra-Mborakinda had a beautiful daughter, but that no one was able to obtain her, because of what she said about diseases of the skin.

Still, many tried to obtain her. Even animals changed themselves to human form, and sought her, in vain.

At last, Leopard said, "Ah! This beautiful woman! I hear about her beauty, and that no one is able to get her. I think I better take my turn, and try. But, first I will go to Ra-Marânge." He went to that magic-doctor, and told his story about Ra-Mborakinda's fine daughter, and how no man could get her because of her fastidiousness about skins. Ra-Marânge told him, "I am too old. I do not now do those things about medicines. Go to Ogula-ya-mpazya-vazya."

So, Leopard went to him. As usual, the sorcerer Ogula jumped into his fire; and coming out with power, directed Leopard to tell what he wanted. So he told the whole story again, and asked how he should obtain the clean body of a man. The sorcerer prepared for him a great "medicine" by which to give him a human body, tall, graceful, strong and clean. Leopard then went back to his town, told his people his plans, and prepared their bodies also for a change if needed. Having taken also a human name, Ogula, he then went to Ra-Mborakinda, saying, "I wish your daughter Ilâmbe for wife."

On his arrival, at Ra-Mborakinda's, the people admired the stranger, and felt sure that Ilâmbe would accept this suitor, exclaiming, "This fine-looking man! His face! And his gait! And his body!" When he had made his request of Ra-Mborakinda, he was told, as usual, to go to Ilâmbe and see whether she would like him. When he went to her house, he looked so handsomely, that Ilâmbe was at once pleased with him. He told her, "I love you; and I come to marry you. You have refused many. I know the reason why, but I think you will be satisfied with me." She replied, "I think you have heard from others the reason for which I refuse men. I will see whether you have what I want." And she added, "Let us go into the room; and let me see your skin."

They entered the room; and Ogula-Njĕgâ removed his fine clothing. Ilâmbe examined with close scrutiny from his head to his feet. She found not the slightest scratch or mark; his skin was like a babe's. Then she said, "Yes! This is my man! Truly! I love you, and will marry you!" She was so pleased with her acquisition, that she remained in the room enjoying again a minute examination of her husband's beautiful skin. Then she went out, and ordered her servants to cook food, prepare water, etc., for him; and he did not go out of the house, nor have a longing to go back to his town, for he found that he was loved.

On the third day, he went to tell the father, Ra-Mborakinda, that he was ready to take his wife off to his town. Ra-Mborakinda consented. All that day, they prepared food for the marriage-feast. But, all the while that this man-beast, Ogula-Njĕgâ was there, Ra-Mborakinda, by his okove (a magic fetish) knew that some evil would come out of this marriage. However, as Ilâmbe had insisted on choosing her own way, he did not interfere.

After the marriage was over, and the feast eaten, Ra-Mborakinda called his daughter, and said, "Ilâmbe, mine, now you are going off on your journey." She said, "Yes; for I love my husband." The father asked, "Do you love him truly?" She answered "Yes." Then he told her, "As you are married now, you need a present from me, as your ozendo (bridal gift)." So, he gave her a few presents, and told her, "Go to that house," indicating a certain house in the town; and he gave her the key of the house, and told her to go and open the door. That was the house where he kept all his charms for war, and fetishes of all kinds. He told her, "When you go in, you will see two Kabala, standing side by side. The one that will look a little dull, with its eyes directed to the ground, take it; and leave the brighter looking one. When you are coming with it, you will see that it walks a little lame. Nevertheless, take it." She objected, "But, father, why do you not give me the finer one, and not the weak one?" But he said, "No!" and made a knowing smile, as he repeated, "Go, and take the one I tell you." He had reason for giving this one. The finer-looking one had only fine looks; but this other one would someday save her by its intelligence.

She went and took Horse, and returned to her father; and the journey was prepared. The father sent with her, servants to carry the baggage, and to remain with and work for her at the town of her marriage. She and her husband arranged all their things, and said goodbye, and off they went, both of them sitting on Horse's back.

They journeyed and they journeyed. On the way, Ogula-Njĕgâ, though changed as to his form and skin, possessed all his old tastes. Having been so many days without tasting blood or uncooked meats, as they passed through the forest of wild beasts, the longing came on him. They emerged onto a great prairie, and journeyed across it toward another forest. Before they had entirely crossed the prairie, the longing for his prey so overcame him that he said, "Wife, you with your Kabala and the servants stay here while I go rapidly ahead; and wait for me until I come again." So he went off, entered the forest, and changed himself back to Leopard. He hunted for prey, caught a small animal and ate it; and another, and ate it. After being satisfied, he washed his hands and mouth in a brook; and, changing again to human form, he returned on the prairie to his wife.

She observed him closely, and saw a hard, strange look on his face. She said, "But, all this while! What have you been doing?" He made an excuse. They went on.

And the next day, it was the same, he leaving her, and telling her to wait till he returned; and hunting and eating as a Leopard. All this that was going on, Ilâmbe was ignorant of. But Horse knew. He would speak after a while, but was not ready yet.

So it went on, until they came to Leopard's town. Before they reached it, Ogula-Njĕgâ, by the preparations he had first made, had changed his mother into a human form in which to welcome his wife. Also the few people of the town, all with human forms, welcomed her. But, they did not sit much with her. They stayed in their own houses; and Ogula-Njĕgâ and his wife stayed in theirs. For a few days, Leopard tried to be a pleasant Ogula, deceiving his wife. But his taste for blood was still in his heart. He began to say, "I am going to another town; I have business there." And off he would go, hunting as a leopard; when he returned, it would be late in the day. So he did on other days.

After a time, Ilâmbe wished to make a food plantation, and sent her menservants to clear the ground. Ogula-Njĕgâ would go around in the forest on the edge of the plantation; and catching one of the men, there would return that day one servant less.

One by one, all the menservants were thus missing; and it was not known what became of them, except that Leopard's people knew. One night Ogula-Njĕgâ was out; and, meeting one of the female servants, she too was reported missing.

Sometimes, when Ogula-Njĕgâ was away, Ilâmbe, feeling lonesome, would go and pet Horse. After the loss of this maidservant, Horse thought it was time to warn Ilâmbe of what was going on. While she was petting him, he said, "Eh! Ilâmbe! You do not see the trouble that is coming to you!" She asked, "What trouble?" He exclaimed, "What trouble? If your father had not sent me with you, what would have become of you? Where are all your servants that you brought with you? You do not know where they go to, but I know. Do you think that they disappear without a reason? I will tell you where they go. It is your man who eats them; it is he who wastes them!" She could not believe it, and argued, "Why should he destroy them?" Horse replied, "If you doubt it, wait for the day when your last remaining servant is gone."

Two days after that, at night, another maidservant disappeared. Another day passed. On another day, Ogula-Njĕgâ went off to hunt beasts, with the intention that, if he failed to get any, at night he would eat his wife.

When he had gone, Ilâmbe, in her loneliness, went to fondle Horse. He said to her, "Did I not tell you? The last maid is gone. You yourself will be the next one. I will give you counsel. When you have opportunity this night, prepare yourself ready to run away. Get yourself a large gourd, and fill it with ground nuts; another with gourd seeds; and another with water." He told her to bring these things to him, and he would know the best time to start.

While they were talking, Leopard's mother was out in the street, and heard the two voices. She said to herself, "Ilâmbe, wife of my son, does she talk with Kabala as if it was a person?" But, she said nothing to Ilâmbe, nor asked her about it.

Night came on; and Ogula-Njĕgâ returned. He said nothing; but his face looked hard and bad. Ilâmbe was troubled and somewhat frightened at his ugly looks. So, at night, on retiring, she began to ask him, "But why? Has anything displeased you?" He answered, "No; I am not troubled about anything. Why do you ask questions?" "Because I see it in your face that your countenance is not pleasant." "No; there's no matter. Everything is right. Only, about my business, I think I must start very early." Ogula-Njĕgâ had begun to think, "Now she is suspecting me. I think I will not eat her this night, but will put it off until next night."

That night, Ilâmbe did not sleep. In the morning, Leopard said that he would go to his business, but would come back soon. When he was gone away to his hunting work, Ilâmbe felt lonesome, and went to Horse. He, thinking this a good time to run away, they started at once, without letting anyone in the village know, and taking with them the three gourds. Horse said that they must go quickly; for, Leopard, when he discovered them gone, would rapidly pursue. So they went fast and faster, Horse looking back from time to time, to see whether Leopard was pursuing.

After they had been gone quite a while, Ogula-Njĕgâ returned from his business to his village, went into his house, and did not see Ilâmbe. He called to his mother, "Where is Ilâmbe?" His mother answered, "I saw Ilâmbe with her Kabala, talking together; they have been at it for two days." Ogula-Njĕgâ began to search; and, seeing the hoofprints, he exclaimed, "Mi asaiya (shame for me). Ilâmbe has run away. I and she shall meet today!"

He instantly turned from his human form back to that of leopard, and went out, and pursued, and pursued, and pursued. But, it took some time before he came in sight of the fugitives. As Horse turned to watch, he saw Leopard, his body stretched low and long in rapid leaps. Horse said to Ilâmbe, "Did I not tell you? There he is, coming!" Horse hasted, with foam dropping from his lips. When he saw that Leopard was gaining on them, he told Ilâmbe to take the gourd of peanuts from his back, and scatter them along behind on the ground. Leopards like peanuts; and when Ogula-Njĕgâ came to these nuts, he stopped to eat them. While he was eating, Horse gained time to get ahead. As soon as Leopard had finished the nuts, he started on in pursuit again, and soon began to overtake. When he approached, Horse told Ilâmbe to throw out the gourd seeds. She did so. Leopard delayed to eat these seeds also. This gave Horse time to again get ahead. Thus they went on.

Leopard, having finished the gourd seeds, again went leaping in pursuit; and, for the third time, came near. Horse told Ilâmbe to throw the gourd of water behind, with force so that it might crash and break on the ground. As soon as she had done so, the water was turned to a stream of a deep wide river, between them and Leopard. Then he was at a loss. So, he shouted, "Ah! Ilâmbe! Mi asaiya! If I only had a chance to catch you!" So he had to turn back.

Then Horse said, "We do not know what he may do yet; perhaps he may go around and across ahead of us. As there is a town which I know near here, we had better stay there a day or two while he may be searching for us." He added to her, "Mind! This town where we are going, no woman is allowed to be there, only men. So, I will change your face and dress like a man's. Be very careful how you behave when you take your bath, lest you die." Ilâmbe promised; and Horse changed her appearance. So, a fine-looking young man was seen riding into the street of the village. There were exclamations in the street, "This is a stranger! Hail! Stranger; hail! Who showed you the way to come here?" This young man answered, "Myself; I was out riding; I saw an open path; and I came in." He entered a house, and was welcomed; and they told him their times of eating, and of play, etc. But, on the second day, as this young man went out privately, one of the men observed, and said to the other, "He acts like a woman!" The others asked, "Really? You think so?" He asserted, "Yes! I am sure!" So, that day Ilâmbe was to meet with some trouble; for, to prove her, the men had said to her, "Tomorrow we all go bathing in the river, and you shall go with us." She went to ask Horse what she should do. He rebuked her, "I warned you, and you have not been careful. But, do not be troubled; I will change you into a man."

That night, Ilâmbe went to Horse; and he changed her. He also told her, "I warn you again. Tomorrow you go to bathe with the others, and you may take off your clothes; for, you are now a man. But, it is only for a short time, because we stay here only a day and a night more, and then we must go."

The next morning all the town went to play, and after that to bathe. When they went into the water, the other men were all expecting to see a woman revealed; but they saw that their visitor was a man. They admired his wonderfully fine physique. On emerging from the water, the men said to the one who had informed on Ilâmbe, "Did you not tell us that this was a woman? See, how great a man he is!" As soon as they said that, the young man Ilâmbe was vexed with him, and began to berate him, saying, "Eh! You said I was a woman?" And she chased him and struck him. Then they all went back to the town.

In the evening, Horse told Ilâmbe, "I tell you what to do tomorrow. In the morning, you take your gun, and shoot me dead. After you have shot me, these men will find fault with you, saying 'Ah! You shoot your horse, and did not care for it?' But, do not say anything in reply. Cut me in pieces, and burn the pieces in the fire. After this, carefully gather all the black ashes; and, very early in the following morning, in the dark before any one is up, go out of the village gateway, scatter the ashes, and you will see what will happen."

The young man did all this. On scattering the ashes, he instantly found himself changed again to a woman, and sitting on Horse's back; and they were running rapidly away.

That same day, in the afternoon, they came to the town of the father Ra-Mborakinda. On their arrival there, they (but especially Horse) told their whole story. Ilâmbe was somewhat ashamed of herself; for, she had brought these troubles on herself by insisting on having a husband with a perfectly fine skin. So, her father said, "Ilâmbe, my child, you see the trouble you have brought on yourself. For you, a woman, to make such a demand was too much. Had I not sent Kabala with you, what would have become of you?" The people gave Ilâmbe a glad welcome. And she went to her house, and said nothing more about fine skins.

Swine Talking
(From the Benga people, Equatorial Guinea and Gabon)

THERE WAS A CERTAIN man in the time long ago, by name Bokona, whose family name was Bodikito. He went to the depths of the forest to do some business.

When he was about to return in the afternoon to go to his village, he heard in advance of him, a noise of conversation. He thought that perhaps they were people (of whose presence he was not aware; for, there were no villages in that part of the forest). But when he had approached the spot, he did not see people; but only a herd of Hogs speaking with the voices of people. He was thus perfectly sure that they speak the language of Mankind.

Origin of the Elephant
(From the Benga people, Equatorial Guinea and Gabon)

UHÂDWE, BOKUME and Njâku were human beings, all three born of one mother. (Afterwards Bokume was called "Njâpĕ.")

As time went on, Uhâdwe called his brethren, Bokume and Njâku, and said, "My brothers! Let us separate; myself, I am going to the Great Sea; you, Bokume go to the Forest; you, Njâku, also go to the Forest."

Bokume went to the forest and grew up there, and became the valuable mahogany tree (Okume).

Njâku departed; but he went in anger, saying, "I will not remain in the forest, I am going to build with the townspeople." He came striding back to the town. As he emerged there from the forest, his feet swelled and swelled, and became elephant feet. His ear extended halfway down. His teeth spreading, this one grew to a tusk, and that one grew to a tusk. The townspeople began to hoot at him. And he turned back to the forest. But, as he went, he said to them, "In my going now to the Forest, I and whatever plants you shall plant in the forest shall journey together," (i.e., that their plantations should be destroyed by him). So Njâku went; and their food went.

When Uhâdwe had gone thence and emerged at the Sea, from the place where he emerged there grew the stem of "bush-rope" (the

Calamus palm); and the staff he held became a mangrove forest. The footprints where he and his dog trod are there on the beach of Corisco Bay until this day. He created a sandbank from where he stood, extending through the ocean, by which he crossed over to the Land of the Great Sea. When he reached that Land, he prepared a ship. He put into it every production by which white people obtain wealth, and he said to the crew, "Go ye and take for me my brother."

The ship came to Africa and put down anchor; but, for four days the crew did not find any person coming from shore to set foot on the ship, or to go from the ship to set foot ashore, the natives being destitute of canoes.

Finally, Uhâdwe came and appeared to the townspeople in a dream, and said, "Go ye to the forest and cut down Njâpě, dig out a canoe, and go alongside the ship."

Early next morning they went to the forest, and came to the Okume trees; they cut one down, and hacked it into shape. They launched it on the sea, and said to their young men, "Go!" Four young men went into the canoe to go alongside the ship. When they had nearly reached it, looking hither and thither they feared, and they stopped and ceased paddling. The white men on the ship made repeated signs to them. Then the young men, having come close, spoke to the white men in the native language. A white man answered also in the same language. That white man said, "I have come to buy the tusks of the beast which is here in the forest with big feet and tusks and great ears, that is called Njâku." They said, "Yes! A good thing!" When they were about leaving, the white man advancing to them, deposited with them four bunches of tobacco, four bales of prints, four caps and other things.

When they reached the shore, they told the others, "The white men want Njâku's tusks; and also they have things by which to kill his tribe."

The next morning, they went to the white men; they were trusted with guns and bullets and powder; they went to the forest, and fought with the elephants. In two days the ship was loaded, and it departed.

This continues to happen so until this day, in the Ivory Trade.

Tortoise in a Race
(From the Benga people, Equatorial Guinea and Gabon)

TORTOISE HAD FORMERLY lived in the same town with several other animals. But after a while, they had decided to separate, and each built his own village.

One day, Tortoise decided to roam. So he started, and went on an excursion; leaving his wife and two children in the village. On his way, he came to the village of Antelope. The latter welcomed him, killed a fowl and prepared food for him; and they sat at the table, eating.

When they had finished eating, Antelope asked, "Kudu! My friend, what is your journey for?"

Tortoise answered, "I have come to enquire of you, as to you and me, which is the elder?" Antelope replied, "Kudu! I am older than you!" But Tortoise responded, "No! I am the elder!" Then Antelope said, "Show me the reason why you are older than I!" Tortoise said, continuing the discussion, "I will show you a sign of seniority. Let us have a race, as a test of speed." Antelope replied derisively, "Aiye! How shall I know to test speed with Kudu? Does Kudu race?" However, he agreed, and said, "Well! In three days the race shall be made."

Tortoise spoke audaciously, "You, Mbalanga, cannot surpass me in a race!" Antelope laughed, having accepted the challenge; while Tortoise pretended to sneer, and said, "I am the one who will overcome!"

The course chosen, beginning on the beach south of Batanga, was more than seventy miles from the Campo River northward to the Balimba Country.

Then Tortoise went away, going everywhere to give directions, and returned to his village. He sent word secretly to all the Tortoise Tribe to call them. When they had come very many of them together, he told them, "I have called my friend Mbalanga for a race. I know that he can surpass me in this race, unless you all help me in my plan. He will follow the seabeach. You all must line yourselves among the bushes at the top of the beach along the entire route all the way from Campo to Balimba. When Mbalanga, coming along, at any point, looks around to see whether I am following, and calls out, 'Kudu! Where are you?' the one of you who is nearest that spot must step out from his place, and answer for me, 'Here!'"

Thus he located all the other tortoises in the bushes on the entire route. Also, he placed a coloured mark on all the tortoises, making the face of everyone alike. He stationed them clear on to the place where he expected that Antelope would be exhausted. Then he ended, taking his own place there.

Antelope also arranged for himself, and said, to his wife, "My wife! Make me food; for, Kudu and I have agreed on a race; and it begins at seven o'clock in the morning."

When all was ready, Antelope said, to (the one whom he supposed was) Kudu, "Come! Let us race!" They started. Antelope ran on and on, and came as far as about ten miles to the town of Ubĕnji, among the Igara people. At various spots on the way Tortoise apparently was lost behind; but as constantly he seemed to re-appear, saying, "I'm here!"

At once, Antelope raced forward rapidly, pu!, pu!, pu!, to a town named Ipĕnyĕnyĕ. Then he looked around and said, "Where is Kudu?" A tortoise stepped out of the bushes, saying "Here I am! You haven't raced."

Antelope raced on until he reached the town of Beyâ. Again looking around, he said, "Where is Kudu?" A tortoise stepped out, replying, "I'm here!"

Antelope again raced, until he reached the town Lolabe. Again he asked, "Where is Kudu?" A tortoise saying to himself, "He hasn't heard anything," replied, "Here I am!"

Again Antelope raced on as far as from there to a rocky point by the sea named Ilale-ja-moto; and then he called, "Wherever is Kudu?" A tortoise ready answered, "Here I am!"

From thence, he came on in the race another stretch of about ten miles, clear to the town of Bongahĕli of the Batanga people. At each place on the route, when Antelope, losing sight of Tortoise, called, "Kudu! Where are you?" promptly the tortoise on guard at that spot replied, "I'm here!"

Then on he went, steadily going, going, another stretch of about twenty miles to Plantation Beach. Still the prompt reply to Antelope's call, "Kudu, where are you?" was, "I'm here!"

As he started away from Plantation, the wearied Antelope began to feel his legs tired. However, he pressed on to Small Batanga, hoping for victory over his despised contestant. But, on his reaching the edge of Balimba, the tortoise was there ready with his, "I'm here!"

Finally, on reaching the end of the Balimba settlement, Antelope fell down, dying, froth coming from his mouth, and lay dead, being utterly exhausted with running. But, when Tortoise arrived, he took a magic medicine, and restored Antelope to life; and then exulted over him by beating him, and saying, "Don't you show me your audacity another day by daring to run with me! I have surpassed you!"

So, they returned separately to their homes on the Campo River. Tortoise called together the Tortoise Tribe; and Antelope called all the Antelope Tribe. And they met in a Council of all the Animals. Then Tortoise rose and spoke: "All you Kudu Tribe! Mbalanga said I would not surpass him in a race. But this day I have surpassed!"

So the Antelope Tribe had to acknowledge, "Yes, you, Kudu, have surpassed our champion. It's a great shame to us; for we had not supposed that a slow fellow such as we thought you to be, could possibly do it, or be able to outrun a Mbalanga."

So the Council decided that, of all the tribes of animals, Tortoise was to be held as greatest; for that it had outrun Antelope. And the Animals gave Tortoise the power to rule.

Goat's Tournament
(From the Benga people, Equatorial Guinea and Gabon)

THE TRIBE OF GOATS sent a message to the Tribe of Leopards, saying, "Let us have a wrestling match, in an effort to see which is the stronger." Then Leopard took counsel with his Tribe. "This Tribe of Goats! I do not see that they have any strength. Let us agree to the contest; for, they can do nothing to me."

So, the Goat Tribe gathered all together; and the Leopard Tribe all together; and they met in a street of a town, to engage in the drumming and dancing and singing usually preceding such contests.

For the wrestling, they joined in thirty pairs, one from each tribe. The first pair wrestled; and the representative of the Leopards was overcome and thrown to the ground. Another pair joined; and again the Leopard champion was overcome. A third pair joined and wrestled, contesting desperately; the Leopard in shame, and the Goat in exultation. Again the Leopard was overcome.

There was, during all this time, drumming by the adherents of both parties. The Leopard drum was now beaten fiercely to encourage their side, as they had already been overcome three times in succession.

Then, on the fourth effort, the Leopard succeeded in overcoming. Again a pair fought; and Leopard overcame a second time. The sixth pair joined; and Leopard said, "Today we wrestle to settle that doubt as to which of us is the stronger."

So, pair after pair wrestled, until all of the thirty arranged pairs had contested. Of these, the Leopard Tribe were victors ten times; and the Goat Tribe twenty times.

Then the Leopard Tribe said, "We are ashamed that the report should go out among all the animals that we beat only ten times, and the Tomba twenty times. So, we will not stay any longer here, with their and our towns near together," for they knew that their Leopard Tribe would always be angry when they should see a company of Goats passing, remembering how often they were beaten.

So, the Leopard Tribe moved away into the forest distant from their hated rivals. In their cherished anger at being beaten, and to cover their shame, Leopard attacks a Goat when he meets him alone, or any other single beast known to be friendly to the Goats, e.g., Oxen or Antelopes.

Iguana's Forked Tongue
(From the Benga people, Equatorial Guinea and Gabon)

THERE WERE TWO FRIENDS, Iguana (Ngâmbi) and Leopard (Njâ), living in the same village, one at each end. Iguana had six wives; Leopard also had six. Leopard begot twenty children; Iguana had eight. One time, at night, they were sitting with their wives and children in the street, in a conversation. Leopard said to Iguana, "Ngâmbi! I have a word to say to you." Iguana said, "Speak."

Then Leopard said, "I wish you and me to have our food together." Iguana agreed, "Well." And Leopard arranged, "For two months, you shall come and eat in my house; and then, for two months, I at your house."

And they separated, to go to their houses for sleep.

Soon the night passed, and day broke.

Leopard went to the forest and killed an Antelope (Vyâdu). He and Iguana and their families spent four days in eating it.

On another day, Leopard went to the forest and killed a Gazelle (Ihĕli). It also was finished in four days.

And again, Leopard went to the forest, and killed a Red Antelope (Ehibo). They were occupied in eating it also four days.

So, they continued all the two months. Then Leopard said, "Ngâmbi! It is your time to begin the food." Iguana replied, "I have no wild meat, only vegetables."

On the following day, Iguana got ready his food and sent word for Leopard to come to eat. He came and ate, there being on the table only vegetables and salt. Then the day darkened; and, in the evening they all came together in one place, as usual. Leopard said to Iguana, "I began my turn with meats in my house, and you ate them. I cannot eat only vegetables and salt." Iguana explained, "I do not know the arts for killing beasts." Leopard told him, "Begin now to try the art of how to catch beasts." Iguana replied, "If I begin a plan for catching Beasts, that plan will be a dreadful one." Leopard exclaimed, "Good! Begin!"

Iguana promised, "Tomorrow I will begin."

And they all went to their houses to sleep their sleep. The night passed, and day broke.

Iguana started out very early in the morning. On the way, he came to a big tree. He stood at its base, and, with a cord, he loosely tied his own hands and feet around the tree. Then he began to squeak as if in pain, "Hwa! Hwa! Hwa!" three times.

At that same time, a child of Leopard had gone wandering out into the forest. He found Iguana tied to the tree and crying. Iguana said to him, "Ah! My child! Come near me, and untie me."

The child of Leopard came near to him; and then Iguana thrust his forked tongue into the nostrils of young leopard, and pulled his brains out, so that the child died. Then Iguana untied himself, skinned the young leopard, divided it, tied the pieces in a big bundle of leaves, and took them and the skin to the village. There he gave the meat to his wife, who put it in a pot. And he went to his house, and left the skin hanging in his bedroom.

Then when the meat was cooked, he sent word for Leopard to come and eat. Leopard came and sat down at the table, and they ate. As they were eating, Leopard said, "Ah! My friend! You said you did not know how to catch beasts! What is this fine meat?"

Iguana replied, "I am unable to tell you. Just you eat it." So, they ate, and finished eating. Iguana continued that way for two weeks, killing the young leopards.

At that Leopard said to himself, "I had begotten twenty children, but now I find only ten. Where are the other ten?" He asked his children where their brothers were. They answered that they did not know, "Perhaps they were lost in the forest." The while that Iguana was killing the young leopards, he had hidden their skins all in his bedroom.

On another day, Leopard and Iguana began a journey together to a place about forty miles distant. Before he started, Iguana closed his house, and said to his children, "Njâ and I are going on a journey; while I am away, do not let anyone enter into my bedroom." And they two went together on their journey. They reached their journey's end, and were there for the duration of seven days. While they were gone, there was no one to get meat for their people, and there came on their village a great njangu (hunger for meat).

One of those days, in the village, so great was that famine that the children of Leopard were searching for rats (Betoli) for food. The rats ran away to the house of Iguana that was shut up; and the children of Leopard pursued. But the children of Iguana said to them, "Do not enter the house! Our father forbade it! Stop at the doorway!"

But the young leopards replied, "No! All the Betoli have run in there. We must follow." So, they broke down the door. There they found skins of young leopards, and they exclaimed, "So! Indeed! Ngâmbi kills our brothers!" And two days later, the two fathers came back to the village.

The young Iguanas told their father that the young leopards had broken the door, and found leopard skins hanging inside. Iguana asked them, "Really? They saw?" The young Iguanas answered, "Yes! They saw!" Then Iguana said, "Be on your guard! For Njâ will be angry with me."

Also, the young leopards said to their father, "Paia! So it is that Ngâmbi killed our brothers. We saw their skins in his bedroom." Leopard asked, "Truly?" They answered, "Yes! We saw!" He said only, "Well, let it be."

On another day, Leopard said, "This night I will go to Ngâmbi to kill him and all his children." The wife of Iguana heard this, and told him, "Tonight, Njâ will come to kill you and our children." At this, Iguana said to himself "But! We must flee, I, and my children and my wives!" So, they all went and hid in the water of a small stream.

Leopard came, in the dark of the morning, to Iguana's house, and entered it; but he saw no people, only the skins of his children. So he exclaimed, "At whatever place I shall see Ngâmbi, I will kill and eat him. We, he and I, have no more friendship!"

What Caused their Deaths?
(From the Benga people, Equatorial Guinea and Gabon)

DOG, SQUIRREL, TORTOISE and others were living in one town. They all, at that time, ate of the same kind of food. But they were at peace in that village during only two weeks. Then

Squirrel and Dog said to Tortoise, "Let us divide, and have peace each at our separate villages. You, Kudu and the others can stay at this spot if you like."

Squirrel said he would remove to a place about three miles distant north. Dog went about three miles in the opposite direction. So each had his own little hamlet.

On another day, Squirrel said to his wife, "I am going on a journey to see my friend Mbwa." He started, came to Dog's place and entered the house. Dog welcomed him, played with him and killed a fowl for their dinner. With Squirrel had come one of his wives.

While the women were cooking inside the house, Dog and Squirrel were sitting in the ikenga (reception room). They were conversing there. After a while, Dog said to Squirrel "Excuse me, I will go to see about the food." He went inside, and lay down near the fire, and Squirrel was left alone.

Dog stayed there inside the house, until the food was cooked. Then he came out to his friend, and began to set the table, while the women came in with the food, and put it on the table. Dog drew up by the table ready to eat; and Squirrel also; and Squirrel's wife, and Dog's wife also, making four at the table.

During the eating, Squirrel said to Dog, "My friend! When you left me here in the ikenga, where did you go to, the while that the women were cooking the food?" Dog answered, "Ah! My friend, you know that I like fire very much. While we were talking here, you and I, cold seized me."

Then Squirrel said, "Ah! My friend, you like fire too much; I think you will die of fire someday."

They finished the food; and after that, Squirrel prepared his return journey to his village. And he said to Dog, "My friend Mbwa, how many days before you shall come to my place?" Dog answered, "In two days, then will I come."

So, Squirrel returned to his village. His wives and children told him the daily news of what had occurred in the village while he was away. And he told them about what he had seen at Dog's. And he added, "But, there is one thing I noticed; my friend Mbwa likes fire very much."

He waited the two days; Dog came on his visit; and Squirrel killed a fowl for his guest. And he bade his woman cook the fowl. In the meanwhile, Dog and Squirrel sat in the ikenga conversing. Presently Squirrel said to Dog, "Excuse me, I am going. I will return."

Squirrel went out into his garden, and climbed up a banana stalk, and began eating the ripe fruit at the top of the bunch. After a while, he came down again. And he went into the ikenga to prepare the table for the food. When it was ready, Dog sat up at the table. With him were his wife, and Squirrel and Squirrel's wife.

Presently, Dog enquired of Squirrel, "My friend! When you left me sitting here alone, where did you go to?" Squirrel answered, "My friend! You know I like to eat bananas. So, I was up the tree," Then Dog said, "My friend! You love bananas too much; someday, you will die with them."

When they had finished their food, Dog said, "I am on my return to my village." So he returned thither. But he was arrived there only two days when he happened to fall into the fireplace. And he died in the fire. The news was carried to his friend Squirrel, "Your friend Mbwa is dead by fire." Squirrel replied, "Yes, I said so; for he loved fire too much."

On another day, in Man's town, a person went to look for food at his banana tree. And he saw that the fruit was eaten at the top, by some animal. So, that Man made a snare at the Banana tree. On the next day, Squirrel said to himself, "I'm going to eat my banana food wherever I shall find it."

He came to the town of Man, and climbed the tree. The snare caught and killed him; and he died there. The Man came and found the body of Squirrel; and he exclaimed, "Good!"

The news was carried to the village of Squirrel's children, "Your father is dead, at a banana tree."

And they said, "Yes; for our father loved bananas very much. He had said that Mbwa would die by fire because he loved fire. And himself also loved bananas."

Tortoise and the Bojabi Tree
(From the Benga people, Equatorial Guinea and Gabon)

ALL THE TRIBES of Beasts were living in one region, except one beast, which was staying in its separate place. Its name was Boa Constrictor. His place was about thirty miles away from the others.

In the region of all those Beasts, there was a very large tree. Its name was Bojabi. But none of those beasts knew that that was its name.

There fell a great famine on that Country-of-all-the-Beasts. In their search for food, they looked at that tree; and they said, "This tree has fine-looking fruit; but, we do not know its name. How then shall we know whether it is fit to be eaten?" After some discussion, they said, "We think our Father Mbâmâ will be able to know this tree's name." So they agreed, "Let us send a person to Mbâmâ to cause us to know the name of the tree." They selected Rat, and said to him, "You, Etoli, are young; go you, and enquire." They also decided that, "Whoever goes shall not go by land along the beach, but by sea." (This they said, in order to prove the messenger's strength and perseverance; whether he would dally by the way ashore, or paddle steadily by sea.) Also, they told Rat that, in going, he should take one of the fruits of the tree in his hand, so that Boa might know it. So, Rat took the Bojabi fruit, stepped into a canoe, and began to paddle. He started about sunrise in the morning. In the middle of the afternoon, he arrived at his journey's end.

He entered into the reception room of Boa's house, and found him sitting there. Boa welcomed him, and said to his wife, "Prepare food for our guest, Etoli!" And he said to Rat, "Stranger! Eat! And then you will tell me what is the message you have brought."

Rat ate and finished, and began to tell his message thus: He said, "In our country we have nothing there but hunger. But there is there a tree, and this is its fruit. Whether it is fit to be eaten or not, you will tell us." Boa replied, "That tree is Bojabi; this fruit is Njabi; and it is to be eaten."

Then the day darkened to night. And they slept their sleep.

And then the next day broke.

And Boa said to Rat, "Begin your journey, Etoli! The name of the tree is Bojabi. Do not forget it!"

Rat stepped into his canoe, and began to paddle. He reached his country late in the afternoon. He landed. And he remained a little while on the beach, dragging the canoe ashore. So occupied was he in doing this, that he forgot the tree's name. Then he went up into the town. The tribes of All-the-Beasts met him, exclaiming, "Tell us! Tell us!" Rat confessed, "I have forgotten the name just this very now." Then, in their disappointment, they all beat him.

On another day, they said to Porcupine, "Ngomba! Go you!" But they warned Rat, "If Ngomba brings the name, you, Etoli, shall not eat of the fruit."

Porcupine made his journey also by sea, and came to the town of Boa. When Porcupine had stated his errand, Boa told him, "The tree's name is Bojabi. Now, go!"

Porcupine returned by sea, and kept the name in his memory, until he was actually entering the town of his home; and, then, he suddenly forgot it. The tribes of All-the-Beasts called out to him, as they saw him coming, "Ngomba! Tell us! Tell us!" When he informed them that he had forgotten it, they beat him, as they had done to Rat.

They had also in that country, another plant which was thought not proper to be eaten. They did not know that its leaves were really good for food.

On another day, they said to Antelope, "Go you; and tell Mbâmâ, and ask him which shall we eat, this fruit or these leaves. What shall we Beasts do?"

Antelope went by sea; and came to Boa's town. And he asked Boa, "What do you here eat? Tell us." Boa replied, "I eat leaves of the plants, and I drink water; that is all I do. And the name of the tree that bears that fruit is Bojabi. You, all the Beasts, what are you to eat? I have told you."

Antelope slept there that night. And the next day, he started on his return journey. At his journey's end, as he was about to land on the beach, a wave upset the canoe, and he fell into the sea. In the excitement, he forgot the name. The anxious tribes of All-the-Beasts had come down to the beach to meet him, and were asking, "What is the name? Tell us!" He replied, "Had I not fallen into the water, I would not have forgotten the name." Then, in their anger, they beat him.

Almost all the beasts were thus tried for that journey; and they all failed in the same way, with the name forgotten, even the big beasts like Ox and Elephant. There was no one of them who had succeeded in bringing home the name.

But there was left still, one who had not been tried. That was Tortoise. So, he said, "Let me try to go." They were all vexed with him, at what they thought his audacity and presumption. They began to beat him, saying, "Even the less for us, and more so for you! You will not be able!" But Gazelle interposed, saying, "Let Kudu alone! Why do you beat him? Let him go on the errand. We all have failed; and it is well that he should fail too."

Tortoise went to his mother's hut, and said to her, "I'm going! How shall I do it?" His mother told him, "In your going on this journey, do not drink any water while at sea, only while ashore. Also, do not eat any food on the way, but only in the town. Do not perform any call of Nature at sea, only ashore. For, if you do any of these things on the way, you will be unable to return with the name. For, all those who did these things on the way, forgot the name." So Tortoise promised, "Yes, my mother, I shall not do them."

On another day, Tortoise began his journey to Boa, early. He paddled and he paddled, not stopping to eat or drink, until he had gone about two-thirds of the way. Then hunger and thirst and calls of Nature seized him. But he restrained himself, and went on paddling harder and faster. These feelings had seized him about noon; and they ceased an hour later. He continued the journey; and, before four o'clock in the afternoon, had arrived at Boa's. There Tortoise entered Boa's house, and found him sitting. Boa saluted, and said, "Legs rest; but the mouth will not. Wife! Bring food for Kudu!" The wife brought food, and Tortoise ate.

Then Boa said to Tortoise, "Tell me what the journey is about." Tortoise told him, "A great hunger is in our place. There also we have two plants; the one, this is its fruit; and this grass, the leaves. Are they eaten?" Boa replied, "The tree of this fruit, its name is Bojabi; and it is eaten. But, I, Mbâmâ, here, I eat leaves and drink water; and that is enough for me. These things are the food for All-us Beasts. We have no other food. Go and tell All-the-Beasts so." Tortoise replied, "Yes; it is well."

Then the day darkened, and they slept.

And another day came. And Tortoise began his journey of return to his home. As he went, he sang this song, to help remember the name: "Njâku! Jaka Njabi. De! De! De!" (Elephant! Eat the Bojabi fruit. Straight! Straight! Straight!) The chorus was "Bojabi", and in each repetition of the line, he changed the name of the animal, thus: "Nyati! Jaka njabi. De! De! De. Bojabi" (Ox! Eat the Bojabi fruit. Straight! Straight! Straight! Bojabi!)

He thus nerved himself to keep straight on in his journey. And, as he went, he kept repeating the chorus. "Bojabi, bojabi! Bojabi!"

He had gone about one-third of the way, when a large wave came and upset the canoe, and threw him, pwim!, into the water. He clung to the canoe, and the wave carried it and him clear ashore, he still repeating the word, "Bojabi! Bojabi!" Ashore, he began to mend the canoe; but, all the while, he continued singing, "Bojabi!" When he had repaired the canoe, he started the journey again, and went on his way, still crying out, "Bojabi"!

By that time, All-the-Beasts had gathered on the beach to wait the coming of Tortoise. He came on and on, through the surf near to the landing place of the town. As he was about to land, a great wave caught him, njim!, and the canoe. But, he still was shouting, "Bojabi!" Though All-the-Beasts heard the word, they did not know what it meant, or why Tortoise was saying it. They ran into the surf, and carried the canoe and Tortoise himself up to the top of the beach. And they, all in a hurry, begged, "Tell us!" He replied, "I will tell you only when in the town." In gladness, they carried him on their shoulders up into the town. Then he said, "Before I tell you, let me take my share of these fruits lying out there in the yard." They agreed; and he carried a large number, hundreds of them, into his house. Then he stated, "Mbâmâ said, 'Its name is Bojabi.'" And All-the-Beasts shouted in unison, "Yes! Bojabi!"

Then they all began to scramble with each other in gathering the fruit; so that Tortoise would have been unable to get any, had he not first taken his share to his mother, whose advice had brought him success.

He also reported to them, "Mbâmâ told me to tell you that himself eats leaves and grass, and drinks water and is satisfied. For that is the food of All-the-Beasts."

Had it not been for Boa, the Beasts would not have known about eating leaves. But, though that is so, the diligence and skill, in this affair, was of Tortoise.

So, All-the-Beasts agreed: "We shall have two Kings, Kudu and Mbâmâ, each at his end of the country. For the one with his wisdom told what was fit to be eaten; and the other, with his skill, brought the news."

Is the Bat a Bird or a Beast?
(From the Benga people, Equatorial Guinea and Gabon and analogous to stories from Cameroon)

BAT LIVED AT a place by itself, with only its mother. Shortly after their settling there, the mother became sick, very near to death. Bat called for Antelope, and said to him, "Make medicine for my mother." Antelope looked steadily at her to discern her disease. Then he told Bat, "There is no one who can make the medicine that will cure your mother, except Joba." Having given this information, Antelope returned to his own place.

On another day, early in the morning, Bat arose to go to call Sun. He did not start until about seven o'clock. He met Sun on the road about eleven o'clock. And he said to Sun, "My journey was on the way to see you." Sun told him, "If you have a word to say, speak!" So Bat requested, "Come! Make Medicine for my mother. She is sick." But Sun replied, "I can't go to make medicine unless you meet me in my house; not here on the road.

Go back; and come to me at my house tomorrow." So Bat went back to his town.

And the day darkened. And they all slept their sleep.

And the next day broke. At six o'clock, Bat started to go to call Sun. About nine o'clock, he met Sun on the path; and he told Sun what he was come for. But Sun said to him, "Whenever I emerge from my house, I do not go back, but I keep on to the end of my journey. Go back, for another day." Bat returned to his town.

He made other journeys in order to see Sun at his house, five successive days; and every day he was late, and met Sun already on the way of his own journey for his own business.

Finally, on the seventh day, Bat's mother died. Then Bat, in his grief, said, "It is Joba who has killed my mother! Had he made medicine for me, she would have recovered."

Very many people came together that day in a crowd, at the Kwedi (mourning) for the dead. The wailing was held from six o'clock in the morning until eleven o'clock of the next day. At that hour, Bat announced, "Let her be taken to the grave." He called other Beasts to go into the house together with him, in order to carry the corpse. They took up the body, and carried it on the way to the grave.

On their arrival at the grave, these Beasts said to Bat, "We have a rule that, before we bury a person, we must first look upon the face." (To identify it). So, they opened the coffin. When they had looked on the face, they said, "No! We can't bury this person; for, it is not our relative, it does not belong to us Beasts. This person indeed resembles us in having teeth like us. And it also has a head like us. But, that it has wings, makes it look like a bird. It is a bird. Call for the Birds! We will disperse." So, they dispersed.

Then Bat called the Birds to come. They came, big and little; Pelicans, Eagles, Herons and all the others. When they all had come together, they said to Bat, "Show us the dead body." He told them, "Here it is! Come! Look upon it!" They looked and examined carefully. Then they said, "Yes! It resembles us; for, it has wings as we. But, about the teeth, no! We birds, none of us, have any teeth. This person does not resemble us with those teeth. It does not belong to us." And all the Birds stepped aside.

During the while that the talking had been going on, Ants had come and laid hold of the body, and could not be driven away. Then one of the Birds said to Bat, "I told you, you ought not to delay the burial, for, many things might happen." The Ants had eaten the body and there was no burial. And all the birds and beasts went away.

Bat, left alone, said to himself, "All the fault of all this trouble is because of Joba. If he had made medicine, my mother would not be dead. So I, Ndemi and Joba shall not look on each other. We shall have no friendship. If he emerges, I shall hide myself. I won't meet him or look at him." And he added, "I shall mourn for my mother always. I will make no visits. I will walk about only at night, not in the daytime, lest I meet Joba or other people."

Dog, and His Human Speech
(From the Benga people, Equatorial Guinea and Gabon)

DOG AND HIS MOTHER were the only inhabitants of their hamlet. He had the power to speak both as a beast and as a human being.

One day the mother said to the son, "You are now a strong man; go, and seek a marriage. Go, and marry Eyâle, the daughter of Njambo." And he said to his mother, "I will go tomorrow."

That day darkened. And they both went to lie down in their places for sleep.

Then soon, another day began to break.

Dog said to his mother, "This is the time of my journey." It was about sunrise in the morning. And he began his journey. He went the distance of about eight miles; and arrived at the journey's end before the middle of the morning.

He entered the house of Njambo, the father of Eyâle. Njambo and his wife saluted him, "Mbolo!" and he responded, "Ai! Mbolo!" Njambo asked him, "My friend! What is the cause of your journey?" Dog, with his animal language, answered, "I have come to marry your daughter Eyâle." Njambo consented; and the mother of the girl also agreed. They called their daughter, and asked her; and she also replied, "Yes! With all my heart." This young woman was of very fine appearance in face and body. So, all the parties agreed to the marriage.

After that, about sunset in the evening, when they sat down at supper, the son-in-law, Dog, was not able to eat for some unknown reason.

That day darkened; and they went to their sleep.

And, then, the next daylight broke. But, by an hour after sunrise in the morning, Dog had not risen; he was still asleep.

The mother of the woman said to her, "Get some water ready for the washing of your husband's face, whenever he shall awake." She also said to her daughter, "I am going to go into the forest to the plantation to get food for your husband; for, since his coming, he has not eaten. Also, here is a chicken; the lads may kill and prepare it. But, you yourself must split ngândâ (gourd seeds, whose oily kernels are mashed into a pudding)." She handed Eyâle the dish of gourd seeds, and went off into the forest. Njambo also went away on an errand with his wife. The daughter took the dish of seeds, and, sitting down, began to shell them. As she shelled, she threw the kernels on the ground, but the shells she put on a plate.

Shortly after the mother had gone, Dog woke from sleep. He rose from his bed, and came out to the room where his wife was, and stood near her, watching her working at the seeds. He stood silent, looking closely, and observed that she was still throwing away the kernels, the good part, and saving the shells on the plate. He spoke to her with his human voice, "No! Woman! Not so! Do you throw the good parts, to the ground, and the worthless husks onto the plate?"

While he was thus speaking to his wife, she suddenly fell to the ground. And at once she died. He laid hold of her to lift her up. But, behold! She was a corpse.

Soon afterwards, the father and the mother came, having returned from their errands. They found their child a corpse; and they said to Dog, "Mbwa! What is this?" He, with his own language replied, "I cannot tell." But they insisted, "Tell us the reason!"

So Dog spoke with his human voice, "You, Woman, went to the forest while I was asleep. You, Man, you also went in company of your wife, while I was asleep. When I rose from sleep, I found my wife was cracking ngândâ. She was taking the good kernels to throw on the ground, and was keeping the shells for the plate. And I spoke and told her, 'The good kernels which you are throwing on the ground are to be eaten, not the husks.'"

While he was telling them this, they too, also fell to the ground, and died, apparently without cause.

When the people of the town heard about all this, they said, "This person carries an evil Medicine for killing people. Let him be seized and killed!"

So Dog fled away rapidly into the forest; and he finally reached the hamlet of his mother. His body was scratched and torn by the branches and thorns of the bushes of the forest, in his hasty flight. His mother exclaimed, "Mbwa! What's the matter? Such haste! And your body so disordered!" He replied, using their own language, "No! I won't tell you. I won't speak." But, his mother begged him, "Please! My child! Tell me!" So, finally, he spoke, using his strange voice, and said, "My mother! I tell you! Njambo and his wife liked me for the marriage; and the woman consented entirely. I was at that time asleep, when the Man and his wife went to the forest. When I rose from my sleep, I found the woman Eyâle cracking ngândâ, and throwing away the kernels and keeping the husks. And I told her, 'The good ones which you are throwing away are the ones to be eaten.' And, at once she died."

While he was speaking thus to his mother, she also fell dead on the ground. The news was carried to the town of Dog's mother's brother, and very many people came to the Mourning. His Uncle came to Dog, and said, "Mbwa! What is the reason of all this?" But Dog would not answer. He only said, "No! I won't speak." Then they all begged him, "Tell us the reason." But he replied only, "No! I won't speak."

Finally, as they urged him, he chose two of them, and said to the company, "The rest of you remain here, and watch while I go and speak to these two." Then Dog spoke to those two men with the same voice as he had to his mother. And at once they died, as she had died. Then he exclaimed, "Ah! No! If I speak so, people will come to an end!" And all the people agreed, "Yes, Mbwa! It is so. Your human speech kills us people. Don't speak any more."

And he went away to live with Mankind.

The Story of Kitinda and Her Wise Dog
(From the Congo and central Africa)

KITINDA, A WOMAN of the Basoko, near the Aruwimi river, possessed a dog who was remarkable for his intelligence. It was said that he was so clever that strangers understood his motions as well as though he talked to them; and that Kitinda, familiar with his ways and the tones of his whines, his yelps and his barks, could converse with him as easily as she could with her husband.

One market day the mistress and her dog agreed to go together, and on the road she told him all she intended to do and say in disposing of her produce in exchange for other articles which she needed in her home. Her dog listened with sympathy, and then, in his own manner, he conveyed to her how great was his attachment to her, and how there never was such a friend as he could be; and he begged her that, if at any time she was in distress, she would tell him, and that he would serve her with all his might. "Only," he said, "were it not that I am afraid of the effects of being too clever, I could have served you oftener and much more than I have done."

"What do you mean?" said Kitinda.

"Well, you know, among the Basoko, it is supposed, if one is too clever, or too lucky, or too rich, that it has come about through dealings in witchcraft, and people are burned in consequence. I do not like the idea of being burned – and therefore I have refrained often from assisting you because I feared you could not contain your surprise, and would chat about it to the villagers. Then some day, after some really remarkable act of cleverness of mine, people would say, 'Ha! This is not a dog. No dog could have done that! He must be a demon – or a witch in a dog's hide!' and of course they would take me and burn me."

"Why, how very unkind of you to think such things of me! When have I chatted about you? Indeed I have too many things to do, my housework, my planting and marketing so occupy me, that I could not find time to gossip about my dog."

"Well, it is already notorious that I am clever, and I often tremble when strangers look at and admire me for fear some muddle-headed fellow will fancy that he sees something else in me more than unusual intelligence. What would they say, however, if they really knew how very sagacious I am? The reputation that I possess has only come through your affection for me, but I assure you that I dread this excess of affection lest it should end fatally for you and for me."

"But are you so much cleverer than you have already shown yourself? If I promise that I will never speak of you to any person again, will you help me more than you have done, if I am in distress?"

"You are a woman, and you could not prevent yourself talking if you tried ever so hard."

"Now, look you here, my dog. I vow to you that no matter what you do that is strange, I wish I may die, and that the first animal I meet may kill me if I speak a word. You shall see now that Kitinda will be as good as her word."

"Very well, I will take you at your word. I am to serve you every time you need help, and if you speak of my services to a soul, you are willing to lose your life by the first animal you may meet."

Thus they made a solemn agreement as they travelled to market.

Kitinda sold her palm oil and fowls to great advantage that day, and in exchange received sleeping mats, a couple of carved stools, a bag of cassava flour, two large well-baked and polished crocks, a bunch of ripe bananas, a couple of good plantation hoes and a big strong basket.

After the marketing was over she collected her purchases together and tried to put them into the basket, but the big crocks and carved stools were a sore trouble to her. She could put the flour and hoes and the bananas on top with the mats for a cover very well, but the stools and the crocks were a great difficulty.

Her dog in the meantime had been absent, and had succeeded in killing a young antelope, and had dragged it near her. He looked around and saw that the market was over, and that the people had returned to their own homes, while his mistress had been anxiously planning how to pack her property.

He heard her complain of her folly in buying such cumbersome and weighty things, and ask herself how she was to reach home with them.

Pitying her in her trouble, the dog galloped away and found a man empty-handed, before whom he fawned and whose hands he licked, and being patted he clung to his cloth with his teeth and pulled him gently along – wagging his tail and looking very amiable. He continued to do this until the man, seeing Kitinda fretting over her difficulty, understood what was wanted, and offered to carry the stools and crocks at each end of his long staff over his shoulders for a few of the ripe bananas and a lodging. His assistance was accepted with pleasure, and Kitinda was thus enabled to reach her home, and on the way was told by the man how it was that he had happened to return to the marketplace.

Kitinda was very much tempted there and then to dilate upon her dog's well-known cleverness, but remembered in time her promise not to boast of him. When, however, she reached the village, and the housewives came out of their houses, burning to hear the news at the market, in her eagerness to tell this one and then the other all that had happened to her, and all that she had seen and heard, she forgot her vow of the morning, and forthwith commenced to relate the last wonderful trick of her dog in dragging a man back to the marketplace to help her when she thought that all her profit in trade would be lost, and when she was just about to smash her nice crocks in her rage.

The dog listened to her narrative, viewed the signs of wonder stealing over the women's faces, heard them call out to their husbands, saw the men advancing eagerly towards them, saw them all look at him narrowly, heard one man exclaim, "That cannot be a dog! It is a demon within a dog's hide. He —"

But the dog had heard enough. He turned, and ran into the woods, and was never more seen in that village.

The next market day came round, and Kitinda took some more palm oil and a few fowls, and left her home to dispose of them for some other domestic needs. When about halfway, her dog came out of the wood, and after accusing her of betraying him to her stupid countrymen, thus returning evil for good, he sprang upon her and tore her to pieces.

The Eagle Leaves the Tortoise in the Lurch
(From the Boloki people, Congo)

A LEOPARD had three young children, and she asked the Tortoise to take care of them while she was away hunting.

"Very well," said the Tortoise, "I will nurse them for you."

So the Leopard went hunting, and after a time she returned with some meat which she wished to give to her children.

"No, no, do not open the door," whispered the Tortoise, "your children are asleep. Throw the meat in at the window." The meat was passed through the window, and the Leopard went off hunting again.

While the Leopard was gone the second time, an Eagle came to the Tortoise and said: "Friend Tortoise, let us make blood-brotherhood."

The Tortoise agreed, and the friendship was properly made. After a short time the Eagle asked the Tortoise for one of the children to eat, and one was taken, and they ate it between them.

By and by the Leopard returned again from the hunt with some more meat; but the Tortoise pretended that the children were asleep; so the meat was again put through the window, and off went the Leopard to hunt in the forest.

The Eagle then came and begged for another child, and receiving it he went and ate it on a high tree.

When the Leopard returned next time, she insisted on seeing the children, but the Tortoise said: "You stop there and I will show them to you at the window."

The Tortoise then took up the only child left, and holding it at the window he said, "That is one." He put it down and held it up again, and said, "That is two." Then he showed it again at the window for the third time, and said, "That is three." The Leopard, thereupon, went away satisfied.

The Eagle came again and asked for the "other child to eat."

"What shall I do," asked the Tortoise, "when the Leopard returns and finds all her children are gone?"

"Oh, I will take care of you," said the Eagle reassuringly; "I will fly with you to a high tree." The last child was given and eaten, and then the Eagle took the Tortoise to the branch of a very high tree.

Shortly after the Eagle had carried off the Tortoise the Leopard returned, and finding all her children gone she wept very loudly for some time; then looking about her she saw the Tortoise on the top of a tree.

The Leopard gnawed at the tree, and just as it was going to fall the Tortoise called out to his friend, the Eagle, to help him. The Eagle carried him to another tree. The Leopard gnawed that one; so the Eagle removed the Tortoise to another high tree; but the Leopard gnawed that also.

The Tortoise called for his friend, the Eagle; but the Eagle replied: "I am tired of helping you, take care of yourself," and off he flew, leaving his friend in the lurch, and never returned again. The tree fell, and the Leopard killed the Tortoise. That is why the bush animals are afraid to hurt the Leopard's children.

The Kite Breaks His Promise to the Tortoise
(From the Boloki people, Congo)

WHEN THE TORTOISE and the Kite made blood-brotherhood the Kite said: "Friend Tortoise, now that we have become brothers, catch an electric fish for me."

"Friend Kite," replied the Tortoise, "when you see a skin floating on the river you will know that I have caught the fish you desire. Swoop down and take it; and, friend Kite, thou art one who lives in the air, tie up the wind and bring it to me."

By and by the Tortoise killed an electric fish (*nina*), and set it floating on the river. When the Kite saw it he said: "Ah, there is the fish my friend

Tortoise has sent me." He thereupon dropped to the river, picked up the fish, and carried it away to a high tree, where he ate it.

The Tortoise waited a long time, but the Kite never brought him the wind; so seeing the Eagle one day fishing by the river bank he said to him, "Come here, friend Eagle," and when the Eagle had alighted on a branch nearby, the Tortoise continued: "Well, my friend the Kite and I made blood-brotherhood, and he asked me to send him an electric fish, and I asked him to bring me the wind, and he agreed to this bargain. I have sent him his fish, but he has not brought me the wind. When you see the Kite remind him of his promise."

The Eagle met the Kite next day on the top of a tree and said to him: "When you make blood-brotherhood with a person you should keep your promise to him. Why don't you take the wind to the Tortoise?"

"I have not yet tied it up," said the Kite as he flew off.

The Tortoise waited, but the Kite not coming he went ashore, climbed to the roof of a house, and tied himself into a bundle like a parcel of fish.

The Kite, seeing the bundle and thinking it was some fish, swooped down on it and carried it away to a tree, and while he was undoing the bundle the Tortoise said: "Friend Kite, you have deceived me, and you have broken your promise. Where is the wind you agreed to bring to me?"

The Kite was so alarmed that he dropped the Tortoise and flew away. And because of his broken promise to his friend, he has lost the power to sail on the wind like the Eagle; but has to constantly flutter and flap his wings.

How the Squirrel Outwitted the Elephant
(From the Boloki people, Congo)

THE SQUIRREL AND THE Elephant met one day in the forest and had a big discussion about forest matters. At last the Elephant sneeringly said: "You are a Squirrel, you are only a little bit of a thing. Can you hold either my foot or my leg? No, you are too small to touch even one of my legs!"

"You may be a big thing," retorted the Squirrel, "but can you keep on eating palm nuts as long as I can?"

After much talk they decided to collect bunches of palm nuts, and when all was ready they sat down to the eating contest. Before beginning, however, the Squirrel had secreted a number of his friends in the forest near by.

The Elephant began the contest by putting a bunch of palm nuts into his mouth; but the Squirrel took the nuts one by one and ate them. And when the Squirrel was full he made some excuse and slipped away, and another squirrel took his place. In this way Squirrel after Squirrel exchanged places with each other unnoticed by the Elephant, who continued to eat all the morning, and the big pile of palm nuts grew smaller and smaller.

At last the Elephant asked: "Are you full, friend Squirrel?"

"No," answered the last Squirrel, "I feel as though I had only just begun."

"Is that so?" grunted the Elephant. "Well, you are a wonderful little thing. Why, I am getting fuller and fuller."

After that they went on eating again.

In the afternoon the Elephant asked again: "Friend Squirrel, are you full yet?"

"No," replied the last Squirrel, "I have not eaten half enough yet." And he took up some more nuts to eat.

The Elephant had not room for more than a sigh; and towards sunset he said: "I am full, and cannot eat any more palm nuts."

Thus the Elephant confessed he was beaten, and ever after that he refrained from annoying and ridiculing his friends and neighbours because they were smaller than himself.

The Spider Regrets Her Marriage
(From the Boloki people, Congo)

THERE WAS A SPIDER who lived with her parents in their town. She was unmarried, and it was very difficult to find a husband for her as she was so hard to please.

One young man asked her father for her in marriage, but he said: "You must ask her yourself." And when he said to her: "I love you. Will you be my wife?" she replied, "No," in such a way that he went back to his house very angry.

Another young man came, and she said: "I refuse all husbands, for I am going to remain as I am."

After a time another suitor came, and when the Spider declined him he said: "You refuse all offers of marriage from us; but a person will come who will not be a proper person at all, for he will have changed himself to look like a nice man. You will marry him, and you will have much trouble on going with him, for he will take you to his country, which will be far away, and you will regret that you have refused all of us."

"Be quiet!" she shouted; "you are angry because I will not marry you, and that is why you threaten me."

"Very well," said he, "you think I am telling you a lie," and away he went to his town. Now this was the Python who spoke to the girl.

The Python waited in his town for some time, and then he changed himself into another and nicer form and paid a visit to the Spider, and said to her: "Spider, I have come to marry you."

The Spider asked him: "Do you love me or not?"

He answered her: "I love you," and they were married.

After a time he said: "Spider, we must return to my town." And he deceitfully told her that he lived in a fine town, and was very rich. He also promised his father-in-law that he would return in six months – a promise he never intended to keep.

The Spider and her husband started on their journey, and went on and on and on for two months, and the wife became very tired with the long walk.

As they were nearing their town a person said to her: "The one who is travelling with you is not a real person, but a snake that has changed itself to look like a person. Do not believe in him."

They reached the husband's town, which she found was simply a tree with a large hole in it. The husband changed back to his snake form, and coiling himself up in the hole he left his wife to do the best she could outside.

The Spider was very angry, and repented having been so stupid as to refuse all the nice young men of her own town to be deceived by this snake from a distance. The poor Spider became very thin and would have died, only someone helped her back to her father.

How the Fowl Evaded His Debt
(From the Lower Congo Basin)

ONCE UPON A TIME a cock Fowl and a Leopard began a friendship, and not very long afterwards the Leopard lent some money to the Fowl. It was arranged that on a certain day the Leopard should receive the money at the Fowl's residence.

On the morning of the appointed day the Fowl ground up some red peppers, and mixed them with water so that it looked like blood, and when he heard that the Leopard was on the way to his house he went into his courtyard and said to his slaves: "When the Leopard arrives and asks for me, tell him my head has been cut off and carried to the women in the farms to be combed and cleaned." Then he hid his head under his wings and told them to pour some of the pepper water on his neck, which they did, and it fell to the ground like blood.

The Leopard arrived and asked for his friend the Fowl. The slaves repeated what they had been told, and, on the Leopard hearing it, he wished to be allowed a closer view of the marvel, and on beholding the red-pepper water dropping to the ground, he thought it was all true.

On returning later he asked the Fowl how it was done, and the Fowl replied: "When you reach your town, you cut off your head, and send it to the farm to be combed and cleaned, and there you are."

"Oh! Thank you, friend," said the Leopard, "I will astonish the natives of my town."

Away he went to his town, and told all his wives that he had been taught some wonderful magic by his friend the Fowl.

"What is it?" they asked.

"Well, my head is cut off," said the Leopard, "and then you take it to the farm to comb and clean, and then you bring it back."

"All right," they cried in chorus.

The Leopard sent messengers to all the towns in his district, inviting the folk on a certain day to come and see the wonder. On the day a great crowd of people arrived, and when all was ready the Leopard went into the centre, and his head was cut off, but his legs gave way, and he fell down.

The head was returned after being combed and cleaned, but when they put it on the neck it would not stay there. Thus died the Leopard because of his conceit in thinking he could do all that others did; and also because he did not use his common sense to perceive the foolishness of what the Fowl told him. Do not believe all you see and hear.

Why the Small-ant
Was the Winner
(From the Lower Congo Basin)

ONE DAY A FIERCE Driver-ant and a Small-ant had a long discussion as to which of them was the stronger. The Driver-ant boasted of his size, the strength of his mandibles, and the fierceness of his bite.

"Yes, all that may be true," quietly answered the Small-ant, "and yet with all your size and strong jaws you cannot do what I can do."

"What is that?" sneeringly asked the Driver-ant.

"You cannot cut a piece of skin off the back of that man's hand, and drop it down here," replied the Small-ant.

"Can't I? All of you wait and see," said the Driver-ant.

Away he climbed up the man until he reached the back of his hand. At the first bite of the strong mandibles, the man started, and, looking down at his hand, saw the Driver-ant, picked it off, and dropped it dead at his feet right among the waiting crowd of ants.

The Small-ant then climbed to the place, and gently, softly, with great patience he worked round a piece of skin until it was loose, and he was able to drop it to the ground. The waiting throng of ants proclaimed him the winner, for he had done by his gentleness and patience what the other had failed to do by his strength and fierceness.

The Gazelle Outwits the Leopard
(From the Lower Congo Basin)

ONCE UPON A TIME a Leopard and a Gazelle lived together with their wives and families in the same town. One day the Leopard said: "Friend Gazelle, let us go and buy some drums in the Zombo country." "All right," replied the Gazelle; "but where is the money?" "I have the money by me," answered the Leopard.

They started, and when they had walked a little way the Leopard growled out: "Wait here. I must return to the town, as I have forgotten something." The Leopard returned to the town and went to the Gazelle's wife and said: "My friend has sent me for his children." Mrs Gazelle gave them to him, and putting them into a bag, he returned to the place where he left the Gazelle. They started again, and when they had travelled a long distance the Leopard saw some honey in a hole in one of the trees, whereupon he said to the Gazelle: "Wait for me here while I go to eat the honey, but you must not undo the sack."

The Gazelle was left to guard the sack, which he untied, and looking in, he exclaimed: "Why, they are my children!" He put the sack on his back and hurried to the town, gave his children back to his wife, and went to the Leopard's house and said: "My friend has sent me for his children." Mrs Leopard gave them to him. He put them in the sack and returned quickly to the spot where the Leopard had left him.

After a time the Leopard arrived, licking the honey off his lips, and, picking up the bag, away they went again on their journey. By and by they reached Zombo and bought some drums, and when the Leopard paid the money for them, he whispered: "Don't undo the bag now, there are some gazelles in it."

As they were returning home they tried the drums. The Leopard beat a tune and sang: "The stupid people go on foolish journeys." For the Leopard thought the Gazelle had helped to sell his own children for drums.

The Gazelle then beat a tune and sang: "At the place where they ate honey they left their bag of wisdom." The Leopard did not know he had exchanged his own children for drums.

On their way home they played and sang in many towns, and received goats and pigs as presents for their entertainment. On reaching their town the Gazelle hurried to his house, and sent off his wife and children to hide.

The Leopard went to his house, and, looking round, he asked his wife: "Where are my children?" "Why, you sent the Gazelle for them," she replied: "and now you ask: 'Where are the children?'" The Leopard went in great rage to the Gazelle's house, but the Gazelle ran away, and as he was escaping, he cried out: "I am the wise Gazelle who has outwitted your craftiness."

How the Crow Cheated the Dove and Got into Difficulty Through It
(From the Lower Congo Basin)

ALONG TIME AGO the Crow and the Dove arranged to go hunting together. They took with them their guns, charms, dogs and chief huntsman. The dogs entered the bush and startled an animal which the Dove fired at and killed. Then up ran the Crow shouting: "It is mine, it is mine."

"No," said the Dove; "I killed it."

"It is mine," asserted the Crow, and although they tried to argue with him, he would not listen, but only shouted more loudly: "It is mine."

At last the Dove gave way, and thus it was every time they went hunting – the Crow always cheated the Dove out of his game by his loud blustering cry: "It is mine. It is mine."

One day, while hunting, the Dove accidentally shot the chief huntsman, and no sooner did the Crow hear the report of the gun than he came running and calling out: "It is mine, it is mine. I shot it," but on drawing near and seeing the body of the huntsman, he said to the Dove: "It is yours."

"No," replied the Dove; "you have said 'It is mine' every time I have killed game, and now this is yours also." They talked long and loudly about the matter, and at last they laid the case before the elders in the town.

The elders said to the Crow: "Yes, it is yours. You have claimed everything before, now take this also, and bury the body properly, and pay all the expenses of the funeral." There are many people like the Crow, who take all the credit to themselves, and leave the blame to others.

How the Civet and the Tortoise Lost Their Friendship for Each Other
(From the Lower Congo Basin)

THE TORTOISE and the Civet, although they lived in separate towns, had a great friendship for each other. Their kindness to one another was known to all the neighbours, for they never refused to help one another in sickness and trouble.

One day the Civet heard that her friend the Tortoise had given birth to a child, so at once she got ready to pay the usual visit. On arriving at the crossroad leading to her friend's town, she met a Monkey, who asked her where she was going.

The Civet said: "I am going to visit my friend the Tortoise, who has given birth to a child."

Monkey said: "Don't you go. Her child is very ill, and the 'medicine man' says that he must have the tip of your tail with which to make a charm to cure the child, and it won't be better until he has it. Of course, if you go it is your own affair."

When the Civet heard this she became very angry at the insult, and returned at once to her own house. The Tortoise was very indignant at the neglect of her friend the Civet, because from the commencement of her illness she never received a visit from her. For a very long time they never visited each other.

By and by the Tortoise heard that her friend the Civet had given birth to a child. The Tortoise said: "Although the Civet never visited me, I will not treat her in the same way, for I will go to see her."

She started on her journey, and on reaching the crossroads she met Monkey there, who asked her where she was going. On hearing she was on the way to visit the Civet, Monkey said: "You are truly very stupid. The Civet's baby is very ill, and she has sent for the 'medicine man', who says he cannot possibly cure the child unless he has the shell of the Tortoise for a charm."

On hearing this the Tortoise was dumbfounded and filled with fear, so she returned home at once.

After a very long time the Civet and the Tortoise met at the funeral festivities of a friend, and they frowned at each other and would not speak. Towards the close of the festivities, the Civet and the Tortoise told the chief and the elders all about their former love for one another, and how the friendship had been broken by each hearing what the other wanted as a charm to cure her child.

The elders restored the love they had for each other, and told the Civet and the Tortoise that in future they were not to listen to any tales, but if one did hear anything against the other she was to go and ask her friend about it, and not keep it in her heart. From that time they remained fast and true friends.

The Kingfisher Deceives the Owl
(From the Lower Congo Basin)

O NE DAY THE OWL and the Kingfisher had a long discussion as to which of them could go longest without food. The Owl proposed that they should try for ten days, and the Kingfisher agreed to it.

They tied a rope across a stream, and both birds sat on the middle of it looking down into the water. On the third day the Kingfisher began to feel hungry, and observing a fish in the water just below him, he pretended to fall, caught and gobbled the fish, but as he came up to the surface of the water he cried out: "Oh, Uncle Owl, my head turned giddy, and I fell into the stream."

The Owl replied: "Never mind, let us persevere with our contest."

But the Kingfisher continued to have these giddy fits just as fish came under the perch, and the Owl with his sleepy eyes did not notice the fish. Before many days had passed the Owl's body became thin, he lost his strength, fell into the stream and was drowned; but as for the Kingfisher he flew away, leaving his dead and cheated rival in the water.

How the Tortoise was Punished
for His Deceit
(From the Lower Congo Basin)

T HE TORTOISE set his trap, and soon afterwards caught an antelope in it, whereupon he sat down and began to cry with a loud voice. The Jackal, hearing his cries, came and asked him what was the matter, and the Tortoise said: "There is an animal killed in my trap, and I have no one to take it out."

The Jackal said: "Never mind, I'll remove it for you." So he took out the animal and set the trap again.

The Tortoise said to him: "Go and get some leaves upon which we can cut up the meat." But while the Jackal went for the leaves the Tortoise ran away with the meat to his hole in the rock.

The Jackal, on his return, called out: "Uncle Tortoise, here are the leaves;" but the Tortoise rudely cut him short by asking him: "Am I a relative on your mother's side or your father's?"

The Jackal, angry at this insult, cried out: "I will let off your trap;" and the Tortoise replied: "Touch the spring with your head, for if you put in either your arm or your leg you will die."

So the stupid Jackal put his head into the trap and was caught, and when he cried out with pain the Tortoise took his gun and shot him. In this way the Civet-cat, the Fox, the rock Rabbit and the Palm-rat were all caught and killed by the Tortoise.

One day the Gazelle heard the Tortoise crying, and went and asked him why he was crying, and the Tortoise said: "Since early morning an animal has been lying dead in my trap because I have no one to take it out for me."

"But who set your trap for you?" asked the Gazelle.

He replied: "A passerby set it for me."

"All right," kindly said the Gazelle, "I'll take it out for you;" which he did at once, and setting the trap again he dragged the animal to the Tortoise.

"Get some plantain leaves that we may divide the meat," said the Tortoise; but while he was gone the Tortoise took all the meat to his hole.

The Gazelle, on returning, called out: "Uncle Tortoise, here are the leaves," but the Tortoise laughingly asked him: "Is the Tortoise a relative on your mother's side, or your father's?"

The Gazelle was angry at this insult, and said: "I'll unset your trap."

"Very well," shouted the Tortoise, "only do it with your head, and not with your hands or your feet, or you will die."

The Gazelle, however, poked in a stick, and snap went the spring, and out loudly screamed the Gazelle, so the Tortoise thought he was caught, and came out of his hole with his gun to shoot him, but the Gazelle sprang on the Tortoise, took away his gun and killed him, and then, gathering up the meat, he went off to his own town. The Biter is eventually bit, and he who deceives others will himself be deceived.

The Leopard Pays Homage to the Goat
(From the Lower Congo Basin)

THE NATIVES SAY that there was a time when the Leopard paid homage to the Goat because of his beard and horns, but he discovered the Goat's weakness in the following manner:

One day, while the Leopard was cutting a palm tree for wine, a Billy goat arrived at the wine booth and bleated loudly: "Be—e, Leopard!"

The Leopard listened, and said, "What great chief is that calling me?"

"Be—e, Leopard," again cried the Goat.

"Yes, sir," answered the Leopard, and descending the palm tree he went softly and meekly to his wine booth and found a person there with a long beard and large horns.

"Pour me out some wine," said the Goat. This the Leopard did at once. Pouring the wine into a glass, he knelt and offered it to the Goat, who drank it off glass after glass as the Leopard crouched in a humble position before him. This happened several days running – the Goat ordering the palm wine and the Leopard offering it on his knees as to a great chief.

One day, while the Leopard was paying homage in this way to the Goat, a Gazelle arrived and stared in surprise at what he saw, and after the Goat had gone, he said to the Leopard: "Uncle Leopard, do you know who that is?"

"No," replied the Leopard; "I do not know in the least who it is, but he has a long beard and big horns."

"Oh! Oh!" laughed the Gazelle; "that is foolish. Do you not see that you are paying homage to empty size? He has no strong teeth for biting hard things and for fighting. If you do not believe me, try him tomorrow."

Next day the Goat came as usual, and demanded his palm wine. He found the Leopard and the Gazelle already there in the booth. The Gazelle took from his bag a kola nut, and, breaking it, he gave one section to the Goat, another to the Leopard, and took one himself. The Leopard crunched his section at once with his powerful teeth, and the Gazelle bit his part to pieces, but the poor Goat, having no strong teeth, turned his section of the nut over and over in his mouth, first one side and then the other.

The Gazelle made a sign with his lips to the Leopard, as much as to say: "Do you see, he has no teeth. I told you so." The Leopard thereupon jumped on the Goat and killed him without a struggle, and from that time the Leopard has never again been afraid of the Goat's long beard and big horns. A beard and horns do not make a strong animal, but a powerful mouth is necessary. Pomposity without real authority will not be respected for very long.

How the Elephant Punished the Leopard
(From the Lower Congo Basin)

THE ELEPHANT AND THE LEOPARD lived in the same town and married their wives about the same time. By and by the Leopard's wife gave birth to two children, and the Elephant's wife gave birth to one. Some time after this happened the Elephant had to go on a trading journey into a distant country, so he left his son in the care of the Leopard.

One day the Leopard, his sons, and the young Elephant all went hunting in the big bush. The Leopard showed his sons the animals' tracks, taught them where to stand and what to do; but as for the Elephant's son he took no notice of him, did not instruct him, and left him to do what he could.

In a little time an antelope started up, and the Leopard's first son fired and missed, and the second son fired and also missed. Then the antelope ran by where the young Elephant happened to be, and he shot it. Thereupon the Leopard and his sons ran up and claimed the antelope as theirs, and as the Elephant had no one to take his side he had to give way. This occurred three times, and then the young Elephant would not hunt with them anymore.

After some months the old Elephant returned from his long trading expedition, and his son told him all that had happened to him, and how he had been cheated by his guardian. When the Elephant heard it he was very angry, and said: "All right, I will punish the Leopard for defrauding you." They then dug a large hole in their house, put some twigs and branches over it, and spread a mat over the whole. Then they put the saucepans on the fire, and the Elephant bought some palm wine and asked the Leopard to come and drink with him, which invitation he at once accepted.

When the Leopard arrived they told him to sit on the mat, and as he sat down the mat gave way under him, and he fell into the deep hole underneath. The Elephant said: "I left my son with you, and instead of taking care of him you cheated him every time he went hunting with you," and he followed his words by pouring the boiling water over the Leopard. Thus died the Leopard for being false to his trust.

How the Leopard Tried to Deceive the Gazelle
(From the Lower Congo Basin)

ONCE THE LEOPARD and the Gazelle had a very bad quarrel, and ever since then the Leopard has been trying to catch and kill the Gazelle, but has failed in every attempt.

The Leopard, having tried many other ways of entrapping the Gazelle, at last pretended to be sick. He rubbed some powdered ironstone on his face and instructed his wives to send messengers for the Palm-rat, the Mongoose and all the other animals, and also for the Gazelle. When they were all gathered except the Gazelle they went in one by one to see the Leopard, and he killed them; but he thought that he had all the trouble for nothing as the Gazelle had not arrived, so he asked his wives what they were to do now to catch the Gazelle. They advised him to send for a "medicine man," and then the Gazelle would be sure to think he was really ill. While they were searching for a "medicine man" the Gazelle arrived, but he would not enter the house.

The "medicine man" arrived with his charms, and while he made "medicine" he sang:

"O Gazelle, come where the sick one is, It is your own uncle who is ill."

When the Gazelle heard this, he answered by a song:

"O uncle, come out of the house, Come out into the daylight now."

They tried by every means to persuade the Gazelle to enter the house, but he remained firm, and refused to listen to all their nice talk, and at last the Leopard, losing all patience, jumped up and rushed out of the house; but the Gazelle, noticing his anger, sprang away into the forest and escaped; but as for all the other silly ones who had been deceived by the Leopard, they were eaten by him.

The invitations and persuasions of enemies are to be received with caution.

Why the Chameleon Cut Off His Own Head
(From the Lower Congo Basin)

ONE DAY THE FROG, on going to work in her farm, left her two children in the house with plenty of food to eat. She had not been gone very long when a Chameleon arrived, and took possession of the house and the children. She dressed them with knives and bells, and made them dance. The Frog, returning from her work, found the Chameleon in her house, and when she attempted to enter, the Chameleon threatened to tread her into a pulp. **The Frog went crying to the Elephant, and he, on hearing her story, promised to get the Chameleon out of the house with his large trunk, but when he went to the door of the house, the Chameleon snarled at him, and he turned and fled.**

The Frog then went to the Leopard and told him of her trouble, and he said: "Don't worry, I will quickly have her out of the house." But no sooner did he show himself at the door than the Chameleon snarled at him, and he ran away. Thus it was with all the animals. They all boasted of what they would do, but were all afraid to do it.

As the Frog went crying she met a flock of Sparrows, and said to them: "Friend Sparrows, go and drive the Chameleon out of my house." The Sparrows went in front of the Frog's house, dried their drums at the fire, and as they began to dance they chanted a chorus: "Sparrows, when you dance, don't dance with your heads on." Some of the Sparrows then went forward, and having put their heads under their wings, they began to dance. The Chameleon, looking out of the door, saw this wonderful sight, and seeing the Sparrows dancing very nicely without any heads, she thought they had cut them off, and as she was a great dancer, and wanted to imitate the Sparrows in their marvellous dance, she cut off her own head, and fell dead. The Frog thanked the Sparrows for their help, and went into the house to nurse her children. What the big animals could not do with all their strength the Sparrows did by their cleverness.

How the Sparrow Set the Elephant and the Crocodile to Pull Against Each Other
(From the Lower Congo Basin)

WHILE THE ELEPHANT was searching for food one day he happened to pass near a sparrow's nest, and accidentally knocking against the branch, nearly threw the eggs to the ground. The sparrow thereupon said to the elephant:

"You walk very proudly, and not looking where you are going, you nearly upset my nest. If you come this way again I will tie you up."

"Truly you are a little bird," the elephant laughingly replied, "and are you able to tie up me – an elephant?" "Indeed," the sparrow answered him, "if you come this way tomorrow, I will bind you."

"All right," said the elephant, "I will now pass on, and will come back here tomorrow to look upon the strength of a sparrow." So the elephant went his way and the sparrow flew off to bathe in a neighbouring river.

On reaching the river and finding a crocodile asleep at her favourite bathing place, the sparrow said: "Wake up! This is my bathing place, and if you come here again I will tie you up."

"Can a little sparrow like you tie up a crocodile?" the crocodile asked her.

"It is true what I tell you," retorted the sparrow, "and if you return here tomorrow I will fasten you up."

"Very well," replied the crocodile, "I will come tomorrow to see what you can do." And with that the crocodile floated away, and the sparrow returned to her nest.

The next day the sparrow, seeing the elephant coming, said to him: "Yesterday I told you not to come this way again, because you endangered my nest. Now I will tie you, as I warned you."

"All right," said the elephant, "I want to see what a little thing like you can do."

The sparrow then brought a strong vine rope, put it round the neck of the elephant, and said to him: "Wait a moment while I go and have a drink of water, and then you will see how strong I am." To which the elephant replied: "Go and drink plenty of water, for today I want to see what a sparrow can do." So the sparrow went and found the crocodile basking in the sun on the river's bank.

"Oh! You are here again," she said, "I will tie you up as I warned you yesterday, because you do not listen to what you are told." "Very well," sneered the crocodile, "come and tie me up and I will see what strength you have."

The sparrow took the end of the rope and tied it round the crocodile, and said: "Wait a moment, I will go a little higher up the hill and pull." So away she flew up the hill on to a tree, and from there she called out:

"Pull elephant, pull crocodile. It is I, the sparrow." So the elephant pulled and the crocodile pulled, and each thought he was pulling against the sparrow; not knowing they were pulling against each other. All the day long they pulled, until the evening, but neither out-pulled the other. And during the whole day the sparrow was crying out: "Pull, elephant, you have the strength; pull harder, elephant." And in the same way she addressed the crocodile.

At last the crocodile said: "Friend sparrow, I cannot pull any more, come and unfasten me, and I will never come to your bathing place again." "Wait a little while," said the sparrow, "I am going up to my village." And the elephant said, as she drew near: "Now I know you are very strong. Please come and undo me, and I will never come again to shake your nest." So the sparrow loosened the elephant and then went and removed the rope from the crocodile's neck; and from that time the sparrow has never been troubled by either the elephant or the crocodile.

How the Squirrel Won a Verdict
for the Gazelle
(From the Lower Congo Basin)

WHEN THE LEOPARD and the gazelle were living in the same town each of them bought a goat – the leopard a male and the gazelle a female. One night the gazelle's goat gave birth to two kids, and the leopard, being very greedy, went and stole the two kids from the gazelle's goat and put them with his own goat.

In the morning the leopard called the gazelle and said to him: "My goat has given birth to two kids." The gazelle was very much surprised at hearing this, as male goats do not have kids, and he told the leopard so; but the leopard said: "All right, you don't believe me. We will call the judges and hear what they say." So they carried the case to the court of animals, who acted as judges, and they said: "The kids belong to the leopard's goat." For they were very much afraid of the leopard, and thought that if they gave the verdict against him he would kill them.

The gazelle went and told the squirrel all his troubles and how he was cheated out of his kids. "Tomorrow morning," said the squirrel, "put a rope across your town for me to run on." So the next morning the gazelle put a rope right by the leopard's house and courtyard, which were full of the folk who had judged the case in favour of the leopard. And by and by the squirrel came running along the rope at a great rate.

"Where are you going so quickly," asked the leopard, "that you cannot rest a little?" "I am in a hurry to fetch my mother," said the squirrel, "for my father has just given birth to twins."

"Ah! Ah!" laughed the leopard; "can a man give birth to a child?"

"Can a male goat give birth to kids?" retorted the squirrel. Whereat the leopard was so angry and felt so much ashamed of himself, that he went right away from the town and never returned, for fear of the animals laughing at him. And the gazelle carried the kids back to his own goat.

How the Fox Saved the Frog
(From the Lower Congo Basin)

A FROG, HAVING BUILT a nice town, received a visit from several well-dressed young men. The Frog welcomed them, and they very civilly answered his greetings. The Frog asked them where they were going, and they replied: "We are not going anywhere in particular; we are just walking about visiting the towns." The Frog called out his thirty wives to come and pay their respects to the visitors, and they came out of their houses and greeted the young men.

The wives asked their husband how he came to know them, and he replied: "I do not know them, but seeing them well dressed I saluted them."

"Oh! You welcomed them because they are well dressed," they retorted; "yet ever since we married you we have never received any new cloths from you."

"Never mind," he said, "I am well known as a great chief who has built a whole town and married thirty wives."

"Oh yes," they answered, "you are well known; but we work and farm, and have no cloths, only rags, hence you don't respect us like those who are well dressed." The Frog was dumb.

The Frog asked the young men where and how he could buy some cloth, and they told him that if he carried some peanuts to Mboma he could buy plenty there, and the road was not difficult to find, for if he followed the river he would reach there in a few days. The Frog was glad to hear this, and thereupon he killed six fowls and made a feast for his friends, and told each of his wives to bring him a large basket of peanuts in the morning, for he said: "Although I am a big chief of a large town I feel ashamed, because my wives have had no new cloths since I married them, and they do not dress properly."

The next morning the peanuts were brought and tied into a load, and for the journey some food was prepared, and the Frog started, telling his wives that he would be back in twenty days.

On the third day of his journey the Frog reached a large baobab tree that had fallen across the road, and while he was considering how he, a person with such short legs, could jump over it, he heard a voice say: "If you are a strong man please put down your bundle and save me, for as I was on my way to visit my wife's family this tree fell on me and has held me here for twenty months. Have pity on me and help me now from under this tree."

When the Frog heard this, he at once put down his load and went under the tree, and swelled and swelled until he lifted it and the Snake was able to crawl out; then the Frog let the tree down again, and went to pick up his load to continue his journey. The Snake, however, immediately caught him by the leg, and told him to get ready to be swallowed.

The Frog said: "What have I done that you should swallow me, for although I had a right to be paid for helping you, yet I did not ask for anything! Let me go on my way to Mboma."

While they were arguing about this an Antelope arrived, and he was asked to judge between them; but when he had heard the whole matter he was afraid to settle the affair properly, for he said to himself: "If I let the Frog go, who is right, but little, then the Snake will kill me." So the Antelope gave the verdict in favour of the Snake.

The Snake quickly said: "Do you hear that? Get ready at once and I will swallow you." But the Frog cried: "He would have given me the verdict only he is afraid of you."

While they were discussing this point a Fox arrived on the scene, and he wanted to hear all about it. When the case was laid before him, the Snake said: "Am I not in the right, for I am very hungry and want to swallow the Frog?"

But the Fox would not give the verdict until he had seen the Frog lift the tree, so he said to the Snake: "Release the Frog's leg and let him go and raise the tree," which the Frog did at once.

The Fox said: "Truly the Frog is very strong to lift so large a tree. Now, Snake, you go under it, and show us how you were lying beneath the tree." So the Snake went, thinking he would surely win the case as the judge was taking so much trouble over it, but the Snake was no sooner under the tree than the Fox called out: "Frog, let go the tree," and down it came right on the Snake, holding him so that he could not get away.

The Fox then said to the Snake: "You are entirely in the wrong, for your friend did a kindness to you in helping you in your trouble, but you want to repay him by a bad deed – you want to swallow him."

Thereupon they all went away, leaving the Snake under the tree, as no one would help him again for fear of his ingratitude.

The Frog thanked the Fox for saving him, and gave him his load of peanuts, and they became great friends.

The Antelope and the Leopard
(From the Kongo people, Congo)

THE LEOPARD ONE DAY bet his life to the antelope, that if he hid himself the antelope would never find him. "Well," said the antelope, "I accept your bet. Go and hide yourself."

And the leopard went into the woods and hid himself. Then the antelope looked for him, and after a little while found him. And the leopard was very angry with the antelope, and told him to go and hide himself, and see how easily he would find him.

The antelope agreed to this, but told the leopard that he would have his life.

After some time the leopard set out to seek the antelope. He searched the woods through and through, but could not find him. At last, thoroughly worn out, he sat down, saying: "I am too fat to walk any more; and I am also very hungry. I will pick some of these nonje nuts, and carry them to my town and eat them."

So he filled the bag he carried under his arm (called *nkutu*), and returned to his town. Once there, he determined to call his people together, and continue his search for the antelope after breakfast.

So he knocked his ngongo, and ordered all his people to assemble, from the babe that was born yesterday, to the sick men who could not walk and must be carried in a hammock. When they were all there, he ordered his slaves to crack the nonje nuts. But out of the first nut that they cracked jumped a beautiful dog.

Now, the leopard was married to four princesses. To one by common consent, to another by the rites of Boomba, to the third by the rites of Funzi, and to the fourth by those of Lembe, Each of his wives had her own cooking shed.

Now, when the little dog jumped out of the nut, it ran into the first wife's shed. She beat it, so that it ran away and entered the shed of the wife after the rites of Boomba. This wife also beat the dog, so that it took refuge with the wife after the rites of Funzi. She also beat the little dog; and thus it fled to the wife after the rites of Lembe. She killed it.

But as the dog was dying, it changed into a beautiful damsel. And when the leopard saw this beautiful maiden, he longed to marry her, and straightway asked her to be his wife.

The beautiful girl answered him and said: "First, kill those four women who killed the little dog."

The leopard immediately killed them. Then the maid said:

"How can I marry a man with such dreadful-looking nails. Please have them taken out."

The leopard was so much in love with the maiden, that he had his claws drawn.

"What fearful eyes you have got, my dear leopard! I can never live with you with those eyes always looking at me. Please take them out."

The leopard sighed, but obeyed.

"I never saw such ugly ears; why don't you have them cut?"

The leopard had them cut.

"You have certainly the clumsiest feet that have been seen in this world! Can you not have them chopped off?"

The leopard in despair had his feet taken off.

"And now my dear, dear leopard, there is but one more favour that I have to ask you. Have you not noticed how ugly your teeth are? how they disfigure you? Please have them drawn."

The leopard was now very weak, but he was so fascinated by the girl, and so hopeful now that he would obtain her by this last sacrifice, that he sent to the cooking shed for a stone and had his teeth knocked out.

The maiden then saw that the leopard was fast dying. So she turned herself into the antelope, and thus addressed him:

"My dear leopard, you thought to kill me to avoid giving your life to me, as promised, when I found you. See now how I have outdone you. I have destroyed you and your whole family." And this is why the leopard now always kills the antelope when he meets one.

How the Spider Won and Lost
Nzambi's Daughter
(From the Kongo people, Congo)

NZAMBI ON EARTH had a beautiful daughter; but she swore that no earthly being should marry her, who could not bring her the heavenly fire from Nzambi Mpungu, who dwelt in

the heavens above the blue roof. And as the daughter was very fair to look upon, the people marvelled, saying: "How shall we secure this treasure? and who on such a condition will ever marry her?"

Then the spider said: "I will, if you will help me."

And they all answered: "We will gladly help you, if you will reward us."

Then the spider reached the blue roof of heaven, and dropped down again to the earth, leaving a strong silken thread firmly hanging from the roof to the earth below. Now, he called the tortoise, the woodpecker, the rat and the sandfly, and bade them climb up the thread to the roof. And they did so. Then the woodpecker pecked a hole through the roof, and they all entered the realm of the badly dressed Nzambi Mpungu.

Nzambi Mpungu received them courteously, and asked them what they wanted up there.

And they answered him, saying: "O Nzambi Mpungu of the heavens above, great father of all the world, we have come to fetch some of your terrible fire, for Nzambi who rules upon earth."

"Wait here then," said Nzambi Mpungu, "while I go to my people and tell them of the message that you bring."

But the sandfly unseen accompanied Nzambi Mpungu and heard all that was said. And while he was gone, the others wondered if it were possible for one who went about so poorly clad to be so powerful.

Then Nzambi Mpungu returned to them, and said: "My friend, how can I know that you have really come from the ruler of the earth, and that you are not impostors?"

"Nay," they said; "put us to some test that we may prove our sincerity to you."

"I will," said Nzambi Mpungu. "Go down to this earth of yours, and bring me a bundle of bamboos, that I may make myself a shed."

And the tortoise went down, leaving the others where they were, and soon returned with the bamboos.

Then Nzambi Mpungu said to the rat: "Get thee beneath this bundle of bamboos, and I will set fire to it. Then if then escape I shall surely know that Nzambi sent you."

And the rat did as he was bidden. And Nzambi Mpurigu set fire to the bamboos, and lo!, when they were entirely consumed, the rat came from amidst the ashes unharmed.

Then he said: "You are indeed what you represent yourselves to be. I will go and consult my people again."

Then they sent the sandfly after him, bidding him to keep well out of sight, to hear all that was said, and if possible to find out where the lightning was kept. The midge returned and related all that he had heard and seen.

Then Nzambi Mpungu returned to them, and said: "Yes, I will give you the fire you ask for, if you can tell me where it is kept."

And the spider said: "Give me then, O Nzambi Mpungu, one of the five cases that you keep in the fowl house."

"Truly you have answered me correctly, O spider! Take therefore this case, and give it to your Nzambi."

And the tortoise carried it down to the earth; and the spider presented the fire from heaven to Nzambi; and Nzambi gave the spider her beautiful daughter in marriage.

But the woodpecker grumbled, and said: "Surely the woman is mine; for it was I who pecked the hole through the roof, without which the others never could have entered the kingdom of the Nzambi Mpungu above."

"Yes," said the rat, "but see how I risked my life among the burning bamboos; the girl, I think, should be mine."

"Nay, O Nzambi; the girl should certainly be mine; for without my help the others would never have found oat where the fire was kept," said the sandfly.

Then Nzambi said: "Nay, the spider undertook to bring me the fire; and he has brought it. The girl by rights is his; but as you others will make her life miserable if I allow her to live with the spider, and I cannot give her to you all, I will give her to none, but will give you each her market value."

Nzambi then paid each of them fifty longs of cloth and one case of gin; and her daughter remained a maiden and waited upon her mother for the rest of her days.

The Turtle and the Man
(From the Kongo people, Congo)

A TURTLE AND A MAN built themselves a small town, but because they had as yet planted nothing they suffered from hunger.

"Let us build a large trap," said the turtle," that we may catch an antelope." The man agreed, and they set to work and made a very large one.

"This is too large," said the turtle," let us divide it, and each have a trap of his own."

The man divided it and the turtle chose the best one. That night the man caught nothing, but a splendid antelope was found in the turtle's trap. As the turtle could not lift it, he called all the people from round about to a dance.

While they were dancing, the chimpacasi, or wild ox, came out of the wood and wanted to know what all this singing was about. And the turtle told him that he had caught an antelope, and as he could not carry it to his house, he had called in his friends. "Perhaps, good ox, you will take the antelope out of the trap for me and lift it as far as my house."

"Oh, certainly," said the ox.

"And now, please go and fetch some water."

The ox went and drew some water. They then cut up the antelope.

"Clean the plates, please," said the turtle.

And the delighted ox washed them.

"This is your share, dear ox; but you must go and got some leaves to wrap it in."

And while the ox was away in the woods, collecting leaves, the turtle lifted all the meat up and carried it into his house, which was a very strong one, and shut himself inside.

The ox returned and asked for his share, but the turtle refused to let him have it, and insulted him grossly. The ox became very angry, and told the turtle that he would destroy the trap. But the turtle had reset the trap, so that when the ox put his head in he was caught, and died after a short struggle.

"Oh, oh, Mr Ox, I told you so. You should be more careful when you are entering the turtle's trap."

He called the people again to dance and sing.

This time the leopard was attracted by the noise, and came to the turtle to find out what it was all about. And the turtle told him, and said that his hands were very sore, and that he could not carry the ox to his house; would the leopard drag him there?

Glad to oblige the turtle, the leopard at once offered his services, and in a very short time had brought the ox to the turtle's house.

"Thank you, dear leopard, will you now go to the river and fetch some water, and clean the pots?

"Certainly," said the leopard.

And when they had cooked the whole of the ox, the turtle put aside part of the meat for the leopard, and carried the rest into his shimbec.

"You would better go and fetch some leaves to wrap the meat in," said the turtle.

The leopard went. While he was away, the turtle took the meat, and shut himself within his strong house.

The leopard returned and said "Turtle, turtle, where is my meat?"

"It is here, my dear leopard."

"Then give it me."

"Nay, the ox was mine."

"Yes, but I helped you to cook it."

"Well, I shalt not give you any."

"Then I will destroy your trap."

"Take care you do not meet with the fate of the ox."

"Yes, I will take care."

And the leopard went and destroyed the trap entirely, and then, placing the rope round his neck lay down in the middle of the ruins, as if he had been entrapped.

Then the turtle went again to look at his trap and was delighted to find the leopard there.

"Ah, ah, I told you so! Why did you not take more care, my dear leopard?"

And the turtle stretched out his long neck as if to kiss the leopard. The leopard sprang upon him, and bit the turtle's head off before he had time to pull it in. He then entered his shimbec and ate up all the meat that the turtle had stored there.

Now the man wondered what the leopard was doing in the turtle's shimbec. So he went there and asked the leopard. And the leopard told him bow the turtle had tried to trick him, and how he had killed the turtle. And the man said he was quite right and might go on eating the food of the turtle.

The Rabbit and The Antelope
(From the Kongo people, Congo)

I T WAS DURING an almost rainless "hot season", when all who had no wells were beginning to feel the pangs of thirst, that the rabbit and the antelope formed a partnership to dig a deep well so that they could never be in want of water.

"Let us finish our food," said the antelope, "and be off to our work."

"Nay," said the rabbit; "had we not better keep the food for later on, when we are tired and hungry after our work?"

"Very well, hide the food, rabbit; and let us go to work, I am very thirsty."

They arrived at the place where they purposed having the well, and worked hard for a short time.

"Listen!" said the rabbit; "they are calling me to go back to town."

"Nay, I do not hear them."

"Yes, they are certainly calling me, and I must be off. My wife is about to present me with some children, and I must name them."

"Go then, dear rabbit, but come back as soon as you can."

The rabbit ran off to where he had hidden the food, and ate some of it, and then went back to his work. "Well!" said the antelope, "what have you called your little one?"

"Uncompleted one," said the rabbit.

"A strange name," said the antelope.

Then they worked for a while.

"Again they are calling me," cried the rabbit. "I must be off, so please excuse me. Cannot you hear them calling me?"

"No," said the antelope, "I hear nothing."

Away ran the rabbit, leaving the poor antelope to do all the work, while he ate some more of the food that really belonged to them both. When he had had enough, he hid the food again, and ran back to the well.

"And what have you called your last, rabbit?"

"Half-completed one."

"What a funny little fellow you are! But come, get on with the digging; see how hard I have worked."

Then they worked hard for quite a long time. "Listen, now!" said the rabbit, "surely you heard them calling me this time!"

"Say, dear rabbit, I can hear nothing; but go, and get back quickly."

Away ran the rabbit, and this time he finished the food before going back to his work.

"Well, little one, what have you called your third child?"

"Completed," answered the rabbit. Then they worked hard and as night was setting in returned to their village.

"I am terribly tired, rabbit; run and get the food, or I shall faint."

The rabbit went to look for the food, and then calling out to the antelope, told him that some horrid cat must have been there, as the food was all gone, and the pot quite clean. The antelope groaned, and went hungry to bed.

The next day the naughty little rabbit played the antelope the same trick. And the next day he again tricked the antelope. And the next, and the next, until at last the antelope accused the rabbit of stealing the food. Then the rabbit got angry and dared him to take casca (or the test bark, a purge or emetic).

"Let us both take it," said the antelope, "and let him whose tail is the first to become wet, be considered the guilty one."

So they took the casca and went to bed. And as the medicine began to take effect upon the rabbit, he cried out to the antelope:

"See, your tail is wet!"

"Nay, it is not!"

"Yes, it is!"

"No, but yours is, dear rabbit; see there!"

Then the rabbit feared greatly, and tried to run away. But the antelope said: "Fear not, rabbit; I will do you no harm. Only you must promise not to drink of the water of my well, and to leave my company forever."

Accordingly the rabbit left him and went his way.

Sometime after this, a bird told the antelope that the rabbit used to drink the water of the well every day. Then the antelope was greatly enraged, and determined to kill the rabbit. So the antelope laid a trap for the silly little rabbit. He cut a piece of wood, and shaped it into the figure of an animal about the size of the rabbit; and then he placed this figure firmly in the ground near to the well, and smeared it all over with bird lime.

The rabbit went as usual to drink the waters of the well, and was much annoyed to find an animal there, as he thought, drinking the water also.

"And what may you be doing here, sir?" said the rabbit to the figure.

The figure answered not.

Then the rabbit, thinking that it was afraid of him, went close up to it, and again asked what he was doing there.

But the figure made no answer.

"What!" said the rabbit, "do you mean to insult me? Answer me at once, or I will strike you."

The figure answered not.

Then the little rabbit lifted up his right hand, and smacked the figure in the face. His hand stuck to the figure.

"What's the matter?" said the rabbit. "Let my hand go, sir, at once, or I will hit you again."

The figure held fast to the rabbit's right hand. Then the rabbit hit the figure a swinging blow with his left. The left hand stuck to the figure also.

"What can be the matter with you, Sir? You are excessively silly. Let my bands go at once, or I will kick you."

And the rabbit kicked the figure with his right foot; but his right foot stuck there. Then he got into a great rage, and kicked the figure with his left. And his left leg stuck to the figure also. Then, overcome with rage, he bumped the figure with his head and stomach, but these parts also stuck to the figure. Then the rabbit cried with impotent rage. The antelope, just about this time, came along to drink water; and when he saw the rabbit helplessly fastened to the figure, he laughed at him, and then killed him.

The Leopard and the Crocodile
(From the Kongo people, Congo)

ONCE A MAN and his many wives lived in a certain town far away in the bush. His wives refused to work, and he was at his wit's ends to know what to do to feed them and himself.

One day a happy thought struck him, and away he went into the bush to cut palm kernels. He cut twenty bunches in all. Then he sought out the leopard, and made him his friend by presenting him with ten bunches of palm nuts. The leopard thanked him very much, and told him that if he would cut palm nuts for him, and him only, he would never more be without fresh meat to feed his wives. The man thanked the leopard, and promised to supply his wants.

Then the man went to the crocodile and presented him. with ten bunches of palm nuts. The crocodile was indeed thankful, and promised to supply the man daily with a quantity of fish, if he would only promise in his turn to cut palm nuts for him and no other.

The next day, the leopard came to the man's town and presented him with a wild pig. The crocodile came soon afterwards and brought him plenty of fish. Thus the town was full of food, and the man and his wives were never hungry.

This continued for a long time, until, in fact, the crocodile and leopard were getting tired of palm nuts, and asked the man to present them with a dog, as they had heard that dog's flesh was excellent. Hitherto neither the crocodile nor the leopard had met each other, nor had they ever seen a dog. The man did not wish to lose his dogs, so he told them that he had none. But they each day became more anxious to eat dog's flesh, and so they worried the man, until at last he promised them a dog each. But he did not mean to give them the dogs. However, they bothered and vexed him so much that they became a nuisance to him, and he determined to rid himself of them.

The next day, the leopard came and asked for a dog, which as yet he had neither seen nor tasted. The man told him that if he went to such and such a place he would there find a dog just to his taste. The leopard left him to find the dog.

The crocodile also came, bringing plenty of fish, and again asked for a dog. The man told him to go to the same place he had indicated to the leopard, and told him that he would there meet a dog that he would enjoy immensely.

The crocodile arrived at the spot first, but saw nothing that he could imagine a dog. So relying upon the word of the man he closed his eyes and basked in the hot sun. After a time the leopard came along and found the crocodile, as he thought, asleep.

"This is indeed a much larger animal than I had imagined the dog to be," he murmured.

The crocodile, aroused by the rustling noise made by the leopard as he approached, slowly opened his eyes, and thought the leopard was a very large kind of dog, if all he had heard about dogs was true. Hardly had he moved, when the leopard sprang upon him. Then there was a terrible fight, and the man called all the town to witness it. After a prolonged struggle the beasts killed each other, and the man and his people returned to town and feasted upon the food the crocodile and leopard had given him, and sang and danced until the next day.

The Bird-Messengers
(From the Kongo people, Congo)

ALL THE TOWNS in Molembo or Neotchi were suffering terribly from the awful scourge or evil wind (the disease we know by the name of smallpox). And the chief prince called the princes and people together and asked them if it were not time to ask Nzambi Mpungu why he was so cross with them? And they all agreed that it was so. But whom were they to send? They said that the Ngongongo was a wonderful bird, and could fly in a marvellous way. They sent him with a message to Nzambi Mpungu; but when he got there, and cried out, "Quang, quang, quang," it was evident that Nzambi Mpungu did not understand his tongue. So he flew back back to Neotchi and reported his failure.

Then Neotchi sent the rock pigeon (mbemba), but he could not make Nzambi Mpungu understand, and he also returned to Neotchi.

Then the prince sent the ground dove (ndumbu nkuku), and she went and sang before Nzambi Mpungu:

> *"Fuka Matenda ma fua*
> *Vanji Maloango ma fua*
> *Vanji Makongo ma fua*
> *Sukela sanga vi sia."*

> *("Mafuka Matenda is dead,*
> *Vanji Maloango is dead,*
> *Vanji Makongo is dead;*
> *This is the news that I bring.")*

And Nzambi Mpungu heard what the dove had said, but answered not.

Why The Crocodile Does Not Eat the Hen
(From the Kongo people, Congo)

THERE WAS A CERTAIN HEN; and she used to go down to the river's edge daily to pick up bits of food. One day a crocodile came near to her and threatened to eat her, and she cried: "Oh, brother, don't!"

And the crocodile was so surprised and troubled by this cry that he went away, thinking how he could be her brother. He returned again to the river another day, fully determined to make a meal of the hen.

But she again cried out: "Oh, brother, don't

"Bother the hen!" the crocodile growled, as she once more turned away. "How can I be her brother? She lives in a town on land; I live in mine in the water."

Then the crocodile determined to see Nzambi about the question, and get her to settle it; and so he went his way. He had not gone very far when he met his friend Mbambi (a very large kind of lizard). "Oh, Mbambi!" he said, "I am sorely troubled. A nice fat hen comes daily to the river to feed; and each day, as I am about to catch her, and take her to my home and feed on her, she startles me by calling me 'brother'. I can't stand it any longer; and I am now off to Nzambi, to hold a palaver about it."

"Silly idiot!" said the Mbambi, do nothing of the sort, or you will only lose the palaver and show your ignorance. Don't you know, dear crocodile, that the duck lives in the water and lays eggs? the turtle does the same; and I also lay eggs. The hen does the same; and so do you, my silly friend. Therefore we are all brothers in a sense." And for this reason the crocodile now does not eat the hen.

Weakness & Wisdom, Folly & Fancy

STORIES IN THIS section are aimed at developing in us humane and true African values. Unlike stories about 'life and death, creation and origins', which operate at high levels and usually feature mythical, metaphysical and mysterious elements, these stories are about simple matters and objects of ordinary life. They address the day-to-day sociopolitical and moral issues of our society. In other words, the stories in this category are aimed at developing in the audience the sense of communal responsibility, of society's basic philosophy of life. They also provide the audience with the knowledge and skills to solve problems of everyday life.

The stories deal with the idea that humanity's conventional understanding of foolishness and wisdom is flipped. Here the storyteller's aim is to defend the nature of weakness from those who might condemn it, suggesting that those considered to be fools and weak often act more wisely than the wise. Conversely, those considered wise often behave more foolishly than fools. Stories about stupid people may be told to get a laugh, or to warn their listeners against making similar mistakes.

In addition, the stories reflect the culture of the people in the central African sub-region, where diverse types of animals abound. As discussed earlier, the animals and birds of folktales are often accorded human attributes; it is not uncommon to find animals talking, singing or demonstrating other human characteristics, from greed and jealousy to honesty and compassion. Put differently, the animals in the tales offer examples for humans to follow or avoid. In fables that serve as standards of moral didacticism, these creatures represent various human and godly attributes. They are used to teach moral and religious lessons, or, satirically, to provide mirrors that ridicule human foibles and political corruption. Importantly for an age focused on environmental concerns, the setting in many of the stories exposes the reader to the landform and climate within the sub-region. References are often made to different seasons, such as the 'dry' or 'rainy' season, and various effects these have on the surrounding vegetation and animal life.

The Feast
(From the Cameroon, west Africa)

ONCE THERE LIVED a kind and generous chief who wished to repay his people for the long hours they had worked for him on his farm. An idea came to him that he should hold a great feast and so he sent messengers to all of the surrounding villages inviting the men, women and children to attend his home the following evening, asking only that each man bring a calabash of wine along to the celebrations.

Next day, there was great excitement among the people. They chatted noisily about the event as they worked in the fields and when they had finished their labour they returned home to bathe and dress themselves in their finest robes. By sunset, more than 100 men and their families lined the roadside. They laughed happily as they moved along, beating their drums and dancing in time to the rhythm. When they arrived at the chief's compound, the head of every household emptied his calabash into a large earthenware pot that stood in the centre of the courtyard. Soon the pot was more than half full and they all looked forward to their fair share of the refreshing liquid.

Among the chief's subjects there was a poor man who very much wanted to attend the feast, but he had no wine to take to the festivities and was too proud to appear empty-handed before his friends.

"Why don't you buy some wine from our neighbour?" his wife asked him, "he looks as though he has plenty to spare."

"But why should we spend money on a feast that is free?" the poor man answered her. "No, there must be another way."

And after he had thought about it hard for a few minutes he turned to his wife and said:

"There will be a great many people attending this feast, each of them carrying a calabash of wine. I'm sure that if I added to the pot just one calabash of water, nobody would notice the difference."

His wife was most impressed by this plan, and while her husband went and filled his calabash with water, she stepped indoors and put on her best tunic and what little jewellery she possessed, delighted at the prospect of a good meal and an evening's free entertainment.

When the couple arrived at the chief's house they saw all the other guests empty the wine they had brought into the large earthen pot. The poor man moved forward nervously and followed their example. Then he went to where the men were gathered and sat down with them to await the serving of the wine.

As soon as the chief was satisfied that all the guests had arrived, he gave the order for his servants to begin filling everyone's bowl. The vessels were filled and the men looked to their host for the signal to begin the drinking. The poor man grew impatient, for he was quite desperate to have the taste of the wine on his lips, and could scarcely remember when he had last enjoyed such a pleasant experience for free.

At length, the chief stood up and delivered a toast to his people. Then he called for his guests to raise their bowls to their lips. Each of them tasted their wine, swallowed it, and waited to feel a warm glow inside.

They swallowed some more of the wine, allowing it to trickle slowly over their tongues, and waited for the flavour to release itself. But the wine tasted as plain as any water. And now, all around the room, the guests began to shuffle their feet and cough with embarrassment.

"This is really very good wine," one of the men spoke up eventually.

"Indeed it is the best I've ever tasted," agreed another.

"Quite the finest harvest I've ever come across," added his neighbour.

But the chief of the people knew precisely what had happened, and he smiled at the comical spectacle as each man tried to hide the fact that he had filled his calabash that morning from the village spring.

The enormous earthen pot contained nothing but water, and it was water that the people were given to drink at the chief's great feast. For the chief had very wisely decided in his own mind:

"When only water is brought to the feast, water is all that should be served."

Kazaye and the Horn of Abundance
(From N'djamena, Chad, told by
Beyana Ngarbaï, storyteller)

There was once a hunter in the village of Lere, in the Mayo Kebi East area of N'djamena in Chad. He was called Kazaye. He always hunted to feed his family, and would keep fruits for them upon his return home. One fateful day during his hunting expedition, he felt itches on his body and decided to take a bath in the river. While taking his bath, he happened to touch a hard and twisted object (a horn) inside the water. He immediately took it out of the water and out of curiosity, started singing aloud to the horn asking, "What are you? Who are you?" To this question, the horn answered: "I am the giver of food". Kazaye then asked if the horn could provide him with pounded millet. As soon as Kazaye made this request, a big calabash[1] of pounded millet with meat appeared in front of him, which he ate to his satisfaction.

After this generous meal, Kazaye took the horn home, and upon arrival, called his wife, Mandjakra, and ordered her to bring a large calabash, and gather all his children in one place. When this was done, he removed the horn from his bag and repeated the questions: "What are you? Who are you?" And the horn responded again: "I am the giver of food". After this, the horn began to send out food of various types, which Kazaye and his whole family ate to their satisfaction. From here, Kazaye took the horn to the village chief, and told him to gather all the villagers, for he had something very precious for them – indeed a miracle to perform for them! The chief asked "What precious thing can you offer us, Kazaye, son of Marsuo?"[2] Kazaye answered: "Obey me and you will see." The chief insisted that Kazaye should perform the miracle first, a thing he did. He asked the magical questions to the horn: "What are you? Who are you?" And food appeared in abundance. After this the chief ordered his notables to send the message to the entire village for them to gather at the village square.

Immediately the notables beat the drum[3], the entire village gathered at the square, including animals. Kazaye stood in the middle and repeated the magical questions to the horn again: "What are you? Who are you?" The horn answered: "I am the giver of food". After this response, the horn began to produce food in very large quantities. The villagers and animals who had gathered ate to their satisfaction. At this point, the chief ordered Kazaye to stop the horn from producing food. Kazaye took his horn back home. On his way home, the horn told Kazaye that it should always be kept inside a special shelf made of bamboo[4]. Kazaye became popular in the whole village for his magical powers and was nicknamed "the satisfier of men"[5].

One day, using the magical formula, Kazaye ordered the horn to produce food, which he ate to his satisfaction as usual. Having eaten too much food, he fell asleep and forgot to put the horn on the bamboo shelf. When he woke up in the morning, he could not find the horn. Worried about the sudden disappearance of his horn, he went directly to the forest river; where he had found the horn in the first place. Luckily or unluckily for him, he found one, but it turned out not to be "the giver of food", but the "giver of lashes". When Kazaye asked the magical question to the "new" horn: "What are you? Who are you?" The "new" horn's response was, "I am the giver of lashes." Then Kazaye ordered it to demonstrate, and indeed he did by severely beating him up. When the lashes were too much to bear, Kazaye pleaded for mercy. When mercy was granted, he took the horn to the village and told the chief that he wanted to give food to the villagers again. This time around, everyone came, including disabled people who were unable to come the first time, and were transported on horseback to the village square. When all were gathered, the chief said, "Kazaye, son of Marsou, ask your horn to serve us food." Kazaye stood up and went to the middle of crowd and said the magic questions: "Wat are you? Who are you? The horn answered:" I am the giver of lashes," and lashes began to come from every direction and everybody was severely beaten, including the village chief. People tried to run in disorder, others fell trying to escape. At this point, Kazaye pleaded for mercy, and the lashing stopped. He then took the horn back to the forest. From that time, Kazaye became restless and furious against himself and was never forgiven by the villagers.

Footnotes for 'Kazaye and the Horn of Abundance'
1. In traditional communities in Africa a pumpkin is often cut and its content emptied, so that the empty shell, called a calabash, can be used as a bowl or container. In many rural places in N'djamena today, the calabash is used as a dish for food and containers to keep water.
2. Marsuo is the father of Kazaye, and in the traditional society of the Mundang people, a son is identified by his father's name.
3. The drum has long been a means of communication in traditional society in Africa. In most villages it is used to summon villagers to important social functions.
4. In traditional societies and villages in the Mundang culture, men build shelves with bamboo to store corn, beans and other foodstuffs, when they are dried. Generally, women don't have access to it. When a woman needs anything from there, she must ask the husband to get it for her.
5. The Mundang culture is highly patriarchal. And when "men" are mentioned, it implies men and women, the latter being subordinate to the former – indeed considered as property.

Why Some Bamileke Tribes Worship Skulls
(From the Bafang people, Cameroon, told by Menkwet, storyteller)

A LONG TIME AGO, there lived a troublesome young man in the Bamileke land (Bafang), who disrespected everybody including the ancestors. He was the only son of his parents and spent a great deal of his time breaking the laws of the land and being rude to people, irrespective of their origin, age or social status. He had no reverence for tradition. He did what he wanted anyhow, anywhere, any time and with anybody.

Upon observing how disappointing their lone son was, his parents started regretting having given birth to him. They did the best within their capacity to counsel him and get him on the rails to no avail, and later cursed him for such persistent ill-conduct. He cared very little about his parents' curses and continued living recklessly till they both died. It was then that he became conscious of his past life, but his parents were no more. He had no family to turn to since everybody viewed him more or less as a renegade. Life to him at this moment was a nightmare, and all his projects ended up failing. The young man started lamenting his past actions and wondering what evil would befall him as a consequence of the curses meted out on him. He wished he had apologized to his parents, but it was too late. After some years, his situation degenerated from bad to worse. There was nobody to turn to. He needed counselling but the whole village was virtually against him because of his past life. Nobody came to his assistance. As guilt was tormenting and eating him up, he became nervous and almost became insane. He kept wondering day and night, looking for an outlet to his numerous problems. He could not sleep at night. One day, after a day's hopeless venture, he went to sleep. While in his slumber, he had a dream. In the dream, a strange voice addressed him: "My son, I know you would sacrifice anything you have in order to get in touch with your parents and ask for forgiveness. You have been lamenting for a long time now. On the fifth commemoration of your late parents' death, go, dig out their skulls and prepare a worship altar for their homage. Ask them to forgive you for all your wrong deeds. Afterwards, you will treat them nicely and lovingly; from time to time, you will cater for their basic needs, that is, pour libation to them constantly, offer sacrifices to them and ensure their proper upkeep. Treat them as if they were alive, then, many doors will open to you, and you will be prosperous."

After this dream, he respected and executed all the recommendations the voice had given him. He experienced an incomparable success, prosperity and made up his mind that he would no more abandon his parents who were then represented by the skulls. After witnessing the stubborn boy's success, and what he did to attain it, the whole clan took up the practice and till date the worship of skulls is a permanent ritual among the Bamileke people of the Western region in Cameroon.

The Queen of the Pool
(From the Congo and central Africa)

IZOKA IS THE DAUGHTER of a chief of Umané whose name is Uyimba, and her mother is called Twekay. One of the young warriors called Koku lifted his eyes towards her, and as he had a house of his own which was empty, he thought Izoka ought to be the one to keep his hearth warm, and be his companion while he went fishing. The idea became fixed in his mind, and he applied to her father, and the dowry was demanded; and, though it was heavy, it was paid, to ease his longing after her.

Now, Izoka was in every way fit to be a chief's wife. She was tall, slender, comely of person; her skin was like down to the touch, her kindly eyes brimmed over with pleasantness, her teeth were like white beads, and her ready laugh was such that all who heard it compared it to the sweet sounds of a flute which the perfect player loves to make before he begins a tune, and men's moods became merry when she passed them in the village. Well, she became Koku's wife, and she left her father's house to live with her husband.

At first it seemed that they were born for one another. Though Koku was no mean fisherman, his wife excelled him in every way. Where one fish came into his net, ten entered into that of Izoka, and this great success brought him abundance. His canoe returned daily loaded with fish, and on reaching home they had as much work to clean and cure the fish as they could manage. Their daily catch would have supported quite a village of people from starving. They therefore disposed of their surplus stock by bartering it for slaves, and goats, and fowls, hoes, carved paddles and swords; and in a short time Koku became the wealthiest among the chiefs of Umané, through the good fortune that attended Izoka in whatever she did.

Most men would have considered themselves highly favoured in having such fortunate wives, but it was not so with Koku. He became a changed man. Prosperity proved his bane. He went no more with Izoka to fish; he seldom visited the market in her company, nor the fields where the slaves were at work, planting manioc, or weeding the plantain rows, or clearing the jungle, as he used to do. He was now always seen with his long pipe, and boozing with wretched idlers on the plantain wine purchased with his wife's industry; and when he came home it was to storm at his wife in such a manner that she could only bow to it in silence.

When Koku was most filled with malice, he had an irritating way of disguising his spitefulness with a wicked smile, while his tongue expressed all sorts of contrary fancies. He would take delight in saying that her smooth skin was as rough as the leaf with which we polish our spear shafts, that she was dumpy and dwarfish, that her mouth reminded him of a crocodile's, and her ears of an ape's; her legs were crooked, and her feet were like hippopotamus hooves, and she was scorned for even her nails, which were worn to the quick with household toil; and he continued in this style to vex her, until at last he became persuaded that it was she who tormented him. Then he accused her of witchcraft. He said that it was by her witch's medicines that she caught so many fish, and he knew that someday she would poison him. Now, in our country this is a very serious accusation. However, she never crossed her husband's humour, but received the bitterness with closed lips. This silent habit of hers made matters worse. For, the more patience she showed, the louder his accusations became, and the worse she appeared in his eyes. And indeed it is no wonder. If you make up your mind that you will see naught in a wife but faults, you become blind to everything else.

Her cooking also according to him was vile – there was either too much palm oil or too little in the herb-mess, there was sand in the meat of the fish, the fowls were nothing but bones, she was said to empty the chilli pot into the stew, the house was not clean, there were snakes in his bed – and so on and so on. Then she threatened, when her tough patience quite broke down, that she would tell her father if he did not desist, which so enraged him that he took a thick stick, and beat her so cruelly that she was nearly dead. This was too much to bear from one so ungrateful, and she resolved to elope into the woods, and live apart from all mankind.

She had travelled a good two days' journey when she came in sight of a lengthy and wide pool which was fed by many springs, and bordered by tall, bending reeds; and the view of this body of water, backed by deep woods all round, appeared to her so pleasing that she chose a level place near its edge for a resting place. Then she unstrapped her hamper, and sitting down turned out the things she had brought, and began to think of what could be done with them. There was a wedge-like axe which might also be used as an adze, there were two hoes, a handy Basoko billhook, a couple of small nets, a ladle, half-a-dozen small gourds full of grains, a cooking pot, some small fish knives, a bunch of tinder, a couple of fire sticks, a short stick of sugar cane, two banana bulbs, a few beads, iron bangles and tiny copper balls. As she looked over all these things, she smiled with satisfaction and thought she would manage well enough. She then went into the pool a little way and looked searchingly in for a time, and she smiled again, as if to say, "Better and better."

Now with her axe she cut a hoe handle, and in a short time it was ready for use. Going to the poolside, she commenced to make quite a large round hole. She laboured at this until the hole was as deep and wide as her own height; then she plastered the bottom evenly with the mud from the pool bank, and after that she made a great fire at the bottom of the pit, and throughout the night that followed, after a few winks of sleep, she would rise and throw on more fuel. When the next day dawned, after breaking her fast with a few grains baked in her pot, she swept out all the fire from the well, and wherever a crack appeared in the baked bottom she filled it up carefully, and she also plastered the sides all round smoothly, and again she made a great fire in the pit, and left it to burn all that day.

While the fire was baking the bottom and walls of the well, she hid her hamper among a clump of reeds, and explored her neighbourhood. During her wanderings she found a path leading northward, and she noted it. She also discovered many nuts, sweet red berries, some round, others oval and the fruit which is a delight to the elephants; and loading herself with as many of these articles as she could carry, she returned, and sat down by the mouth of the well, and refreshed herself. The last work of the day was to take out the fire, plaster up the cracks in the bottom and sides, and re-make the fire as great as ever. Her bed she made not far from it, with her axe by her side.

On the next morning she determined to follow the path she had discovered the day before, and when the sun was well-nigh at the middle of the sky, she came suddenly in view of a banana grove, whereupon she instantly retreated a little and hid herself. When darkness had well set, she rose, and penetrating the grove, cut down a large branch of bananas, with which she hurried back along the road. When she came to a stick she had laid across the path, she knew she was not far from the pool, and she remained there until it was sufficiently light to find her way to the well.

By the time she arrived at her well it was in a perfect state, the walls being as sound and well-baked as her cooking pot. After half-filling it with water, she roasted a few bananas, and made a contented meal from them. Then taking her pot she boiled some bananas, and with these she made a batter. She now emptied the pot, smeared the bottom and sides of it thickly with this sticky batter, and then tying a vine round the pot she let it down into the pond. As soon as it touched the ground, lo!, the minnows flocked greedily into the vessel to feed on the batter. And on Izoka suddenly drawing it up she brought out several score of minnows, the spawn of catfish, and some of the young of the bearded fish which grow to such an immense size in our waters. The minnows she took out and dried to serve as food, but the young of the cat and bearded fish she dropped into her well. She next dug a little ditch from the well to the pool, and after making a strong and close netting of cane splinters across the mouth of the ditch, she made another narrow ditch to let a thin rillet of spring water supply the well with fresh water.

Every day she spent a little time in building a hut, in a cosy place surrounded by bush, which had only one opening; then she would go and work a little at a garden wherein she had planted the sugar cane, which had been cut into three parts, and the two banana bulbs, and had sowed her millet, and her sesamum, and yellow corn which she had brought in the gourds, and every day she carefully fed her fish in the well. But there were three things she missed most in her loneliness, and these were the cries of an infant, the proud cluck of the hen after she lays an egg, and the bleating of a kid at her threshold. This made her think that she might replace them by something else, and she meditated long upon what it might be.

Observing that there were a number of ground squirrels about, she thought of snares to catch them. She accordingly made loops of slender but strong vines near the roots of the trees, and across their narrow tracks in the woods. And she succeeded at last in catching a pair. With other vines rubbed over with bird lime she caught some young parrots and wagtails, whose wing feathers she chopped off with her billhook. And one day, while out gathering nuts and berries for her birds, she came across a nest of the pelican, wherein were some eggs; and these she resolved to watch until they were hatched, when she would take and rear them. She had found full occupation for her mind, in making cages for her squirrels and birds, and providing them with food, and had no time at all for grief.

Izoka, however, being very partial to the fish in her well, devoted most of her leisure to feeding them, and they became so tame, and intelligent that they understood the cooing notes of a strange song which she taught them, as though they were human beings. She fed them plentifully with banana batter, so that in a few months they had grown into a goodly size. By and by, they became too large for the well, and as they were perfectly tame, she took them out, and allowed them to go at large in the pool; but punctually in the early morning, and at noon and sunset, she called them to her, and gave them their daily portion of food, for by this time she had a goodly store of bananas and grain from her plantation and garden. One of the largest fish she called Munu, and he was so intelligent and trustful in his mistress's hands that he disliked going very far from the neighbourhood; and if she laid her two hands in the water, he would rest contentedly in the hollow thus formed. She had also strung her stock of shells and beads into necklaces, and had fastened them round the tails of her favourite fish.

Her other friends grew quite as tame as the fish, for all kinds of animals learn to cast off their fears of mankind in return for true kindness, and when no disturbing shocks alarm them. And in this lonely place, so sheltered by protecting woods, where the wind had scarce power to rustle the bending reed and hanging leaves, there was no noise to inspire the most timid with fright.

If you try, you can fancy this young woman Izoka sitting on the ground by the poolside, surrounded by her friends, like a mother by her offspring. In her arms a young pelican, on one shoulder a chattering parrot, on the other a sharp-eyed squirrel, sitting on his haunches, licking his forefeet; in her lap another playing with his bushy tail, and at her feet the wagtails, wagging friskily their hind parts and kicking up little showers of dusty soil. Between her and the pool a long-legged heron, who has long ago been snared, and has submitted to his mistress's kindness, and now stands on one leg, as though he were watching for her safety. Not far behind her is her woodland home, well stored with food and comforts, which are the products of her skill and care. Swifts and sand martins are flying about, chasing one another merrily, and making the place ring with their pipings; the water of the pool lies level and unwrinkled, save in front of her, where the fish sometimes flop about, impatient for their mistress's visit.

This was how she appeared one day to the cruel eyes of Koku her husband, who had seen the smoke of her fire as he was going by the path which led to the north. Being a woodman as well as a fisher, he had the craft of such as hunt, and he stealthily approached from tree to tree until he was so near that he could see the beady eyes of the squirrel on her shoulder, who startled her by his sudden movements. It was strange how quickly the alarm was communicated from one to another. His brother squirrel peeped from one side with his tail over his back like a crest, the parrot turned one eye towards the tree behind which Koku stood, and appeared transfixed, the heron dropped his other leg to the ground, tittered his melancholy cry, *Kwa-le*, and dropped his tail as though he would surge upward. The wagtails stopped their curtseying, the pelicans turned their long bills and laid them lazily along their backs, looking fixedly at the tree; and at last Izoka, warned by all these signs of her friends, also turned her head in the same direction, but she saw no one, and as it was sunset she took her friends indoors.

Presently she came out again, and went to the poolside with fish food, and cooed softly to her friends in the water, and the fish rushed to her call, and crowded around her. After giving them their food, she addressed Munu, the largest fish, and said, "I am going out tonight to see if I cannot find a discarded cooking vessel, for mine is broken. Beware of making friends with any man or woman who cannot repeat the song I taught you," and the fish replied by sweeping his tail to right and left, according to his way.

Izoka, who now knew the woods by night as well as by day, proceeded on her journey, little suspecting that Koku had discovered her, and her manner of life and woodland secrets. He waited a little time, then crept to the poolside, and repeated the song which she had sung, and immediately there was a great rush of fish towards him, at the number and size of which he was amazed. By this he perceived what chance of booty there was here for him, and he sped away to the path to the place where he had left his men, and he cried out to them, "Come, haste with me to the woods by a great pool, where I have discovered loads of fish."

His men were only too glad to obey him, and by midnight they had all arrived at the pool. After stationing them near him in a line, with their spears poised to strike, Koku sang the song of Izoka in a soft voice, and the great and small fish leapt joyfully from the depths where they were sleeping, and they thronged towards the shore, flinging themselves over each other, and they stood for a while gazing doubtfully up at the line of men. But soon the cruel spears flew from their hands, and Munu, the pride of Izoka, was pierced by several, and was killed and dragged on land by the shafts of the weapons which had slain him. Munu was soon cut up, he and some others of his fellows, and the men, loading themselves with the meat, hastily departed.

Near morning Izoka returned to her home with a load of bananas and a cooking vessel, and after a short rest and refreshment, she fed her friends – the ground squirrels, the young pelicans, the parrots and herons, and scattered a generous supply for the wagtails, martins and swifts; then hastened with her bounties to the poolside. But, alas!, near the water's edge there was a sight which almost caused her to faint – there were tracks of many feet, bruised reeds, blood, scales and refuse of fish. She cooed softly to her friends; they heard her cry, but approached slowly and doubtingly. She called out to Munu, "Munu-nunu, oh, Munu, Munu, Munu;" but Munu came not, and the others stood well away from the shore, gazing at her reproachfully, and they would not advance any nearer. Perceiving that they distrusted her, she threw herself on the ground and wept hot tears, and wailing, "Oh! Munu, Munu, Munu, why do you doubt me?"

When Izoka's grief had somewhat subsided she followed the tracks through the woods until she came to the path, where they were much clearer, and there she discovered that those who had violated her peaceful home, had travelled towards Umané. A suspicion that her husband must have been of the number served to anger her still more, and she resolved to follow the plunderers, and endeavour to obtain justice. Swiftly she sped on the trail, and after many hours' quick travel she reached Umané after darkness had fallen. This favoured her purpose, and she was able to steal, unperceived, near to the open place in front of her husband's house, when she saw Koku and his friends feasting on fish, and heard him boast of his discovery of the fine fish in a forest pool. In her fury at his daring villainy she was nearly tempted to rush upon him and cleave his head with her billhook, but she controlled herself, and sat down to think. Then she made the resolution that she would go to her father and claim his protection – a privilege she might long ago have used had not her pride been wounded by the brutal treatment her person had received at the hands of Koku.

Her father's village was but a little distance away from Umané, and in a short time all the people in it were startled by hearing the shrill voice of one who was believed to be long ago dead, crying out in the darkness the names of Uyimba and Twekay. On hearing the names of their chief and his wife repeatedly called, the men seized their spears and sallied out, and discovered, to their astonishment, that the long-lost Izoka was amongst them once again, and that she was suffering from great and overpowering grief. They led her to her father's door, and called out to Uyimba and his wife Twekay to come out, and receive her, saying that it was a shame that the pride of Umané should be suffering like a slave in her father's own village. The old man and his wife hurried out, torches were lit, and Twekay soon received her weeping daughter in her arms.

In our country we are not very patient in presence of news, and as everybody wished to know Izoka's story, she was made to sit down on a shield, and tell all her adventures since she had eloped from Umané. The people listened in wonder to all the strange things that were told;

but when she related the cruelty of Koku, the men rose to their feet all together, and beat their shields with their spears, and demanded the punishment of Koku, and that Uyimba should lead them there and then to Umané. They accordingly proceeded in a body to the town, to Koku's house, and as he came out in answer to the call of one of them, to ascertain what the matter was, they fell upon him, and bound him hand and foot, and carrying him to their superior chief's house they put him to his trial. Many witnesses came forward to testify against his cruel treatment of Izoka, and of the robbery of the fish and of the manner of it; and the great chief placed Koku's life in the power of Uyimba, whose daughter he had wronged, who at once ordered Koku to be beheaded, and his body to be thrown into the river. The sentence was executed at the riverside without loss of time. The people of Uman and Uyimba's village then demanded that, as Izoka had shown herself so clever and good as to make birds, animals and fish obey her voice, some mark of popular favour should be given to her. Whereupon the principal chief of Umané, in the name of the tribe, ceded to her all rights to the Forest Pool, and the wood and all things in it round about as far as she could travel in half a day, and also all the property of which Koku stood possessed.

Izoka, by the favour of her tribe, thus became owner of a large district, and mistress of many slaves, flocks, goats, fowls and all manner of useful things for making a settlement by the Pool. There is now a large village there, and Izoka is well known in many lands near Umané and Basoko as the Queen of the Pool, and at last accounts was still living, prosperous and happy; but she has never been known to try marriage again.

The Story of Maranda
(From the Congo and central Africa)

MARANDA WAS A WIFE of one of the Basoko warriors, called Mafala. Maranda's father was named Sukila, and he lived in the village of Chief Busandiya. Sukila owned a fine large

canoe and many paddles, which he had carved with his own hand. He possessed also several long nets which he himself also made, besides spears, knives, a store of grass cloths and a few slaves. He was highly respected by his countrymen, and sat by the chief's side in the council place.

As Maranda grew to be fit for marriage, Mafala thought she would suit him as a wife, and went and spoke of it to Sukila, who demanded a slave girl, six long paddles ornamented with ivory caps, six goats, as many grass cloths as he had fingers and toes, a new shield, two axes and two field hoes. Mafala tried to reduce the demand, and walked backwards and forwards many times to smoke pipes with Sukila, and get him to be less exacting. But the old man knew his daughter was worth the price he had put upon her, and that if he refused Mafala, she would not remain long without a suitor. For a girl like Maranda is not often seen among the Basokos. Her limbs were round and smooth, and ended in thin, small hands and feet. The young men often spoke about Maranda's light, straight feet, and quick-lifting step. A boy's arm could easily enclose the slim waist, and the manner in which she carried her head, and the supple neck and the clear look in her eyes belonged to Maranda only.

Mafala, on the other hand, was curiously unlike her. He always seemed set on something, and the lines between the eyebrows gave him a severe face, not pleasant to see, and you always caught something in his eyes that made you think of the glitter which is in a serpent's eye.

Perhaps that was one reason why Sukila did not care to have him for his daughter's husband. At any rate, he would not abate his price one grass cloth, and at last it was paid, and Maranda passed over from her father's house into that of her husband.

Soon after, the marriage Maranda was heard to cry out, and it was whispered that she had learned much about Mafala in a few days, and that blows as from a rod had been heard. Half a moon passed away, and then all the village knew that Maranda had fled to Busandiya's house, because of her husband's ill-treatment. Now the custom in such a case is that the father keeps his daughter's dowry, and if it be true that a wife finds life with her husband too harsh to be borne, she may seek the chief's protection, and the chief may give her to another husband who will treat her properly.

But before the chief had chosen the man to whom he would give her, Mafala went to a crocodile – for it turned out that he was a Mganga, a witch-man who had dealings with reptiles on land, as well as with the monsters of the river – and he bargained with it to catch her as she came to the river to wash, and carry her up to a certain place on the river bank where there was a tall tree with a large hole in it.

The crocodile bided his chance, and one morning, when Maranda visited the water, he seized her by the hand, and swept her onto his back, and carried her to the hiding place in the hollow tree. He then left her there, and swam down opposite the village, and signalled to Mafala that he had performed his part of the bargain.

On the crocodile's departure Maranda looked about the hole, and saw that she was in a kind of pit, but a long way up the hollow narrowed like the neck of a gourd, and she could see foliage and a bit of sky. She determined to climb up, and though she scratched herself very much, she finally managed to reach the very top, and to crawl outside into the air. The tree was very large and lofty, and the branches spread out far, and they were laden with the heavy fruit of which elephants are so fond (the jackfruit). At first she thought that she could not starve because of so many of these big fruit; then, as they were large and heavy, she conceived the idea that they might be useful to defend herself, and she collected a great number of them, and laid them in a heap over some sticks she had laid across the branches.

By and by Mafala came, and discovered her high up among the foliage, and after jeering at her, began to climb the tree. But when he was only halfway up, Maranda lifted one of the ponderous fruit and flung it on his head, and he fell to the ground with his senses all in a whirl and his back greatly bruised. When he recovered he begged the crocodile to help him, and he tried to climb up, but when he had ascended but a little way, Maranda dropped one of the elephant fruit fairly on his snout, which sent him falling backwards. Mafala then begged two great serpents to ascend and bring her down, but Maranda met them with the heavy fruit one after another, and they were glad to leave her alone. Then the man departed to seek a leopard, but while he was absent Maranda, from her tree, saw a canoe on the river with two young fishermen in it, and she screamed loudly for help. The fishermen paddled close ashore and found that it was Sukila's daughter, the wife of Mafala, who was alone on a tall tree. They waited long enough to hear her story, and then returned to the village to obtain assistance.

Busandiya was much astonished to hear the fishermen's news, and forthwith sent a war canoe full of armed men, led by the father, Sukila, to rescue her. By means of rattan climbers they contrived to reach her, and to bring her down safely. While some of the war party set out to discover Mafala, the others watched for the crocodile and the two serpents. In a short time the cruel man was seen and caught, and he was brought to the riverside, bound with green withes. His legs and his arms were firmly tied together, and, after the Basoko had made Maranda repeat her story from the beginning, and Sukila had told the manner of the marriage, they searched for great stones, which they fastened to his neck; and, lifting him into the war canoe, they paddled into the middle of the stream, where they sang a death chant; after which they dropped Mafala overboard and he was never heard of more. That is all there is of the story of Maranda.

The Adventures of Saruti
(From Uganda, east Africa)

THESE ARE AMONG the things that a young Mtongolè (colonel) named Saruti related after his return from an expedition to the frontier of Unyoro, the things that he had witnessed on his journey:

Kabaka, I think my charms which my father suspended round my neck must be very powerful. I am always in luck. I hear good stones on my journey, I see strange things which no one else seems to have come across. Now on this last journey, by the time I reached Singo, I came to a little village, and as I was drinking banana wine with the chief, he told me that there were two lions near his village who had a band of hyenas to serve as soldiers under them. They used to send them out in pairs, sometimes to one district, and sometimes to another, to purvey food for them. If the peasants showed fight, they went back and reported to their masters, and the lions brought all their soldiers with them, who bothered them so that they were glad to leave a fat bullock tied to a tree as tribute. Then the lions would take the bullock and give orders that the peasant who paid his tribute should be left in peace. The chief declared this to be a fact, having had repeated proof of it.

At the next place, which is Mbagwè, the man Buvaiya, who is in charge, told me that when he went a short time before to pay his respects to the Muzimu (the oracle) of the district, he met about thirty "kokorwa" on the road, hunting close together for snakes, and that as soon as they saw him, they charged at him, and would have killed him had he not run up a tree. He tells me that though they are not much bigger than rabbits, they are very savage, and make travelling alone very dangerous. I think they must be some kind of small dogs. Perhaps the old men of the court may be better able to tell you what they are.

At the next village of Ngondo a smart boy named Rutuana was brought to me, who was said to have been lately playing with a young friend of the same age at long stick and little stick (tip-cat?). His friend hit the little stick, and sent it a great way, and Rutuana had to fetch it from the long grass. While searching for it, one of those big serpents which swallow goats and calves caught him, and coiled itself around him. Though he screamed out for help, Rutuana laid his stick across his chest, and clutching hold of each end with a hand, held fast to it until help came. His friend ran up a tree, and only helped him by screaming. As the serpent could not break the boy's hold of the stick, he was unable to crush his ribs, because his outstretched arms protected them; but when he was nearly exhausted the villagers came out with spears and shields. These fellows, however, were so stupid that they did not know how to kill the serpent until Rutuana shouted to them: "Quick! Draw your bows and shoot him through the neck." A man stepped forward then, and when close to him pierced his throat with the arrow, and as the serpent uncoiled himself to attack the men, Rutuana fell down. The serpent was soon speared, and the boy was carried home. I think that boy will become a great warrior.

At the next village the peasants were much disturbed by a multitude of snakes which had collected there for some reason. They had seen several long black snakes which had taken lodging in the anthills. These had already killed five cows, and lately had taken to attacking the travellers along the road that leads by the anthills, when an Arab, named Massoudi, hearing of their trouble, undertook to kill them. He had some slaves with him, and he clothed their legs with buffalo hide, and placed cooking pots on their heads, and told them to go among the anthills. When the snakes came out of their holes he shot them one by one. Among the reptiles he killed were three kinds of serpents which possessed horns. The peasants skinned them, and made bags of them to preserve their charms. One kind of horned snake, very thick and short, is said to lay eggs as large as those of fowls. The "mubarasassa", which is of a greyish colour, is also said to be able to kill elephants.

I then went to Kyengi, beyond Singo, and the peasants, on coming to gossip with me, rather upset me with terrible stories of the mischief done by a big black leopard. It seems that he had first killed a woman, and had carried the body into the bush; and another time had killed two men while they were setting their nets for some small ground game. Then a native hunter, under promise of reward from the chief, set out with two spears to kill him. He did not succeed, but he said that he saw a strange sight. As he was following the track of the leopard, he suddenly came to a little jungle, with an open space in the middle. A large wild sow, followed by her litter of little pigs, was rooting about, and grunting as pigs do, when he saw the monstrous black leopard crawl towards one of the pigs. Then there was a shrill squeal from a piggie, and the mother, looking up, discovered its danger, at which it furiously charged the leopard, clashing her tusks and foaming at the mouth. The leopard turned sharp round, and sprang up a tree. The sow tried to jump up after it, but being unable to reach her enemy in that way, she set about working hard at the roots. While she was busy about it the peasant ran back to obtain a net and assistants, and to get his hunting dog. When he returned, the sow was still digging away at the bottom of the tree, and had made a great hole all round it. The pigs, frightened at seeing so many men, trotted away into the bush, and the hunter and his friends prepared to catch the leopard. They pegged the net all about the tree, then let loose the dog, and urged him towards the net. As he touched the net, the hunters made a great noise, and shouted, at which the leopard bounded from the tree, and with one scratch of his paw ripped the dog open, sprang over the net, tapped one of the men on the shoulder, and was running away, when he received a wound in the shoulder, and stopped to bite the spear. The hunters continued to worry him, until at last, covered with blood, he lay down and died.

One day's journey beyond Kyengi, I came to the thorn-fenced village of some Watusi shepherds, who, it seems, had suffered much from a pair of lion cubs, which were very fierce. The headman's little boy was looking after some calves when the cubs came and quietly stalked him through the grass, and caught him. The headman took it so much to heart, that as soon as he heard the news he went straight back to his village and hanged himself to a rafter. The Watusi love their families very much, but it seems to be a custom with these herdsmen that if a man takes his own life, the body cannot be buried, and though he was a headman, they carried it to the jungle, and after leaving it for the vultures, they returned and set fire to his hut, and burnt it to the ground. When they had done that, the Watusi collected together and had a long hunt after the young lions, but as yet they have not been able to find them.

When the sun was halfway up the sky, I came from Kyengi to some peasants, who lived near a forest which is affected by the man-monkeys called nziké (gorilla?). I was told by them that the nziké know how to smoke and make fire just as we do. It is a custom among the natives, when they see smoke issuing through the trees, for them to say, "Behold, the nziké is cooking his food." I asked them if it were true that the nziké carried off women to live with them, but they all told me that it was untrue, though the old men sometimes tell such stories to frighten the women, and keep them at home out of danger. Knowing that I was on the king's business, they did not dare tell me their fables.

By asking them all sorts of questions, I was shown to a very old man with a white beard, with whom I obtained much amusement. It appears he is a great man at riddles, and he asked me a great many.

One was, "What is it that always goes straight ahead, and never looks back?"

I tried hard to answer him, but when finally he announced that it was a river, I felt very foolish.

He then asked me, "What is it that is bone outside and meat within?"

The people laughed, and mocked me. Then he said that it was an egg, which was very true.

Another question he gave me was, "What is it that looks both ways when you pass it?"

Some said one thing, and some said another, and at last he answered that it was grass.

Then he asked me, "What good thing was it which a man eats, and which he constantly fastens his eyes upon while he eats, and after eating, throws a half away?" I thought and considered, but I never knew what it was until he told me that it was a roasted ear of Indian corn.

That old man was a very wise one, and among some of his sayings was that "When people dream much, the old moon must be dying."

He also said that "When the old moon is dying, the hunter need never leave home to seek game, because it is well known that he would meet nothing."

And he further added that at that time the potter need not try to bake any pots, because the clay would be sure to be rotten.

Some other things which he said made me think a little of their meaning.

He said, "When people have provisions in their huts, they do not say, Let us go into another man's house and rob him."

He also said, "When you see a crook-back, you do not ask him to stand straight, nor an old man to join the dance, nor the man who is in pain, to laugh."

And what he said about the traveller is very true. The man who clings to his own hearth does not tickle our ears, like him who sees many lands, and hears new stories.

The next day I stopped at a village near the little lake of Kitesa's called Mtukura. The chief in charge loved talking so much, that he soon made me as well acquainted with the affairs of his family as though he courted my sister. His people are accustomed to eat frogs and rats, and from the noise in the reeds, and the rustling and squealings in the roof of the hut I slept in, I think there is little fear of famine in that village. Nor are they averse, they tell me, to iguanas and those vile feeders, the hyenas.

It is a common belief in the country that it was Naraki, a wife of Uni, a sultan of Unyoro, who made that lake. While passing through, she was very thirsty, and cried out to her Muzimu (spirit), the Muzimu which attends the kings of Unyoro, and which is most potent. And all at once there was a hissing flight of firestones (meteorites) in the air, and immediately after, there was a fall of a monstrously large one, which struck the ground close to her, and made a great hole, out of which the water spurted and continued leaping up until a lake was formed, and buried the fountain out of sight, and the rising waters formed a river, which has run north from the lake ever since into the Kafu.

Close by this lake is a dark grove, sacred to Muzingeh, the king of the birds. It is said that he has only one eye, but once a year he visits the grove, and after building his house, he commands all the birds from the Nyanzas and the groves, to come and see him and pay their homage. For half a moon the birds, great and small, may be seen following him about along the shores of the lake, like so many guards around a king; and before night they are seen returning in the same manner to the grove. The parrots' cries tell the natives when they come, and no one would care to miss the sight, and the glad excitement among the feathered tribe. But there is one bird, called the Kirurumu, that refuses to acknowledge the sovereignty of the Muzingeh. The other birds have tried often to induce him to associate with the Muzingeh; but Kirurumu always answers that a beautiful creature like himself, with gold and blue feathers, and such a pretty crest, was never meant to be seen in the company of an ugly bird that possesses only one eye.

On the other side of Lake Mtukura is a forest where Dungu, the king of the animals, lives. It is to Dungu that all the hunters pray when they set out to seek for game. He builds first a small hut, and after propitiating him with a small piece of flesh, he asks Dungu that he may be successful. Then Dungu enters into the hunter's head, if he is pleased with the offering, and the cunning of the man becomes great; his nerves stiffen, and his bowels are strengthened, and the game is secured. When Dungu wishes a man to succeed in the hunt, it is useless for the buffalo to spurn the earth and moo, or for the leopard to cover himself with sand in his rage – the spear of the hunter drinks his blood. But the hunter must not forget to pay the tribute to the deity, lest he be killed on the way home.

The friendly chief insisted that I should become his blood-fellow, and stay with him a couple of days. The witch doctor, a man of great influence in the country, was asked to unite us. He took a sharp little knife, and made a gash in the skin of my right leg, just above the knee, and did the same to the chief, and then rubbed his blood over my wound, and my blood over his, and we became brothers. Among his gifts was this beautiful shield, which I beg Mtesa, my Kabaka, to accept, because I have seen none so beautiful, and it is too good for a colonel whose only hope and wish is to serve his king.

I am glad that I rested there, because I saw a most wonderful sight towards evening. As we were seated under the bananas, we heard a big he-goat's bleat, and by the sound of it we knew that it was neither for fun nor for love. It was a tone of anger and fear. Almost at the same time, one of the boys rushed up to us, and his face had really turned grey from fear, and he cried, "There is a lion in the goat pen, and the big he-goat is fighting with him." They had forgotten to tell me about this famous goat, which was called Kasuju, after some great man who had been renowned in war, and he certainly was worth speaking about, and Kasuju was well known round about for his wonderful strength and fighting qualities. When we got near the pen with our spears and shields, the he-goat was butting the lion – who was young, for he had no mane – as he might have butted a pert young nanny goat, and baaing with as full a note as that of a buffalo calf. It appears that Kasuju saw the destroyer creeping towards one of his wives, and dashing at his flank knocked him down. As we looked on from the outside, we saw that Kasuju was holding his own very well, and we thought that we would not check the fight, but prepare ourselves to have a good cast at the lion as he attempted to leave. The lion was getting roused up, and we saw the spring he made: but Kasuju nimbly stepped aside and gave him such a stroke that it sounded like a drum. Then Kasuju trotted away in front of his trembling wives, and as the lion came up, we watched him draw his ears back as he raised himself on his hind feet like a warrior. The lion advanced to him, and he likewise rose as though he would wrestle with him, when Kasuju shot into his throat with so true and fair a stroke, that drove one of his horns deep into the throat. It was then the lion's claws began to work, and with every scratch poor Kasuju's hide was torn dreadfully, but he kept his horn in the wound, and pushed home, and made the wound large. Then the lion sprang free, and the blood spurted all over Kasuju. Blinded with his torn and hanging scalp, and weakened with his wounds, he staggered about, pounding blindly at his enemy, until the lion gave him one mighty stroke with its paw, and sent him headlong, and then seized him by the neck and shook him, and we heard the cruel crunch as the fangs met. But it was the last effort of the lion, for just as Kasuju was lifeless, the lion rolled over him, dead also. Had my friend told me this story, I should not have believed him, but as I saw it with my own eyes, I am bound to believe it. We buried Kasuju honourably in a grave, as we would bury a brave man; but the lion we skinned, and I have got his fur with the ragged hole in the throat.

The singular fight we had witnessed, furnished us all with much matter for talk about lions, and it brought into the mind of one of them a story of a crocodile and lion fight which had happened some time before in the night. Lake Mtukura swarms with crocodiles, and situated as it is in a region of game they must be fat with prey. One night a full-grown lion with a fine mane came to cool his dry throat in the lake, and was quaffing water, when he felt his nose seized by something that rose up from below.

From the traces of the struggle by the water's edge, it must have been a terrible one. The crocodile's long claws had left deep marks, showing how he must have been lifted out of the water, and flung forcibly down; but in the morning both lion and crocodile were found dead, the crocodile's throat wide open with a broad gash, but his teeth still fastened in the lion's nose.

The Search for the
Home of the Sun
(From the Songora people, central Africa)

ASTER AND FRIENDS. We have an old phrase among us which is very common. It is said that he who waits and waits for his turn, may wait too long, and lose his chance. My tongue is not nimble like some, and my words do not flow like the deep river. I am rather like the brook which is fretted by the stones in its bed, and I hope after this explanation you will not be too impatient with me.

My tale is about King Masama and his tribe, the Balira, who dwelt far in the inmost region, behind (east) us, who throng the banks of the great river. They were formerly very numerous, and many of them came to live among us, but one day King Masama and the rest of the tribe left their country and went eastward, and they have never been heard of since, but those who chose to stay with us explained their disappearance in this way.

A woman, one cold night, after making up her fire on the hearth, went to sleep. In the middle of the night the fire had spread, and spread, and began to lick up the litter on the floor, and from the litter it crept to her bed of dry banana leaves, and in a little time shot up into flames. When the woman and her husband were at last awakened by the heat, the flames had already mounted into the roof, and were burning furiously. Soon they broke through the top and leaped up into the night, and a gust of wind came and carried the long flames like a stream of fire towards the neighbouring huts, and in a short time the fire had caught hold of every house, and the village was entirely burned. It was soon known that besides burning up their houses and much property, several old people and infants had been destroyed by the fire, and the people were horror-struck and angry.

Then one voice said, "We all know in whose house the fire began, and the owner of it must make our losses good to us."

The woman's husband heard this, and was alarmed, and guiltily fled into the woods.

In the morning a council of the elders was held, and it was agreed that the man in whose house the fire commenced should be made to pay for his carelessness, and they forthwith searched for him. But when they sought for him he could not be found. Then all the young warriors who were cunning in woodcraft, girded and armed themselves, and searched for the trail, and when one of them had found it, he cried out, and the others gathered themselves about him and took it up, and when many eyes were set upon it, the trail could not be lost.

They soon came up to the man, for he was seated under a tree, bitterly weeping.

Without a word they took hold of him by the arms and bore him along with them, and brought him before the village fathers. He was not a common man by any means. He was known as one of Masama's principal men, and one whose advice had been often followed.

"Oh," said everybody, "he is a rich man, and well able to pay; yet, if he gives all he has got, it will not be equal to our loss."

The fathers talked a long time over the matter, and at last decided that to save his forfeited life he should freely turn over to them all his property. And he did so. His plantation of bananas and plantains, his plots of beans, yams, manioc, potatoes, ground nuts, his slaves, spears, shields, knives, paddles, and canoes. When he had given up all, the hearts of the people became softened towards him, and they forgave him the rest.

After the elder's property had been equally divided among the sufferers by the fire, the people gained new courage, and set about rebuilding their homes, and before long they had a new village, and they had made themselves as comfortable as ever.

Then King Masama made a law, a very severe law – to the effect that, in future, no fire should be lit in the houses during the day or night; and the people, who were now much alarmed about fire, with one heart agreed to keep the law. But it was soon felt that the cure for the evil was as cruel as the fire had been. For the houses had been thatched with green banana leaves, the timbers were green and wet with their sap, the floor was damp and cold, the air was deadly, and the people began to suffer from joint aches, and their knees were stiff, and the pains travelled from one place to another through their bodies. The village was filled with groaning.

Masama suffered more than all, for he was old. He shivered night and day, and his teeth chattered sometimes so that he could not talk, and after that his head would burn, and the hot sweat would pour from him, so that he knew no rest.

Then the king gathered his chiefs and principal men together, and said:

"Oh, my people, this is unendurable, for life is with me now but one continuous ague. Let us leave this country, for it is bewitched, and if I stay longer there will be nothing left of me. Lo, my joints are stiffened with my disease, and my muscles are withering. The only time I feel a little ease is when I lie on the hot ashes without the house, but when the rains fall I must needs withdraw indoors, and there I find no comfort, for the mould spreads everywhere. Let us hence at once to seek a warmer clime. Behold whence the sun issues daily in the morning, hot and glowing; there, where his home is, must be warmth, and we shall need no fire. What say you?"

Masama's words revived their drooping spirits. They looked towards the sun as they saw him mount the sky, and felt his cheering glow on their naked breasts and shoulders, and they cried with one accord: "Let us hence, and seek the place whence he comes."

And the people got ready and piled their belongings in the canoes, and on a certain day they left their village and ascended their broad river, the Lira. Day after day they paddled up the stream, and we heard of them from the Bafanya as they passed by their country, and the Bafanya heard of them for a long distance up – from the next tribe – the Bamoru – and the Bamoru heard about them arriving near the Mountain Land beyond.

Not until a long time afterwards did we hear what became of Masama and his people.

It was said that the Balira, when the river had become shallow and small, left their canoes and travelled by land among little hills, and after winding in and out amongst them they came to the foot of the tall mountain which stands like a grandsire amongst the smaller mountains. Up the sides of the big mountain they straggled, the stronger and more active of them ahead, and as the days passed, they saw that the world was cold and dark until the sun showed himself over the edge of the big mountain, when the day became more agreeable, for the heat pierced into their very marrows, and made their hearts rejoice. The greater the heat became, the more certain were they that they were drawing near the home of the sun. And so they pressed on and on, day after day, winding along one side of the mountain, and then turning to wind again still higher. Each day, as they advanced towards the top, the heat became greater and greater. Between them and the sun there was now not the smallest shrub or leaf, and it became so fiercely hot that finally not a drop of sweat was left in their bodies. One day, when not a cloud was in the sky, and the world was all below them – far down like a great buffalo hide – the sun came out over the rim of the mountain like a ball of fire, and the nearest of them to the top were dried like a leaf over a flame, and those who were behind were amazed at its burning force, and felt, as he sailed over their heads, that it was too late for them to escape. Their skins began to shrivel up and crackle, and fall off, and none of those who were high up on the mountain side were left alive. But a few of those who were nearest the bottom, and the forest belts, managed to take shelter, and remaining there until night, they took advantage of the darkness, when the sun sleeps, to fly from the home of the sun. Except a few poor old people and toddling children, there was none left of the once populous tribe of the Balira.

That is my story. We who live by the great river have taken the lesson, which the end of this tribe has been to us, close to our hearts, and it is this. Kings who insist that their wills should be followed, and never care to take counsel with their people, are as little to be heeded as children who babble of what they cannot know, and therefore in our villages we have many elders who take all matters from the chief and turn them over in their minds, and when they are agreed, they give the doing of them to the chief, who can act only as the elders decree.

The Adventures of Libanza; or, a Boloki Version of Jack and the Beanstalk
(From the Boloki people, Congo)

LIBANZA AND HIS SISTER, Nsongo, started on their travels in the long ago, and as they journeyed Libanza changed himself into a boy covered with yaws. A man out hunting turned aside from his party of hunters, and meeting Libanza and his sister, he exclaimed: "I have found some slaves!" He thereupon took possession of them and led them to the hunting camp.

Their new master and the other hunters were there for the purpose of snaring monkeys, and although their master caught some, yet he was not very successful. So one day Libanza said to him: "Give me the snares, and let me try to catch some monkeys."

But as he appeared to be such a poor, weak boy covered with yaws [contagious tropical disease], the master laughed at him, and twitted him with his smallness. However, on being repeatedly asked, the master gave the boy the snares, and he caught thirty monkeys in a very little time, and brought them back to the camp to be divided among the hunters.

While the hunters were busy dividing the monkeys, Libanza and his sister took some meat and ran away. After journeying for a long distance they came near to a large town, and again Libanza turned himself into a boy covered with yaws.

The people of the town were pounding sugar canes for making sugar cane wine; but a man seeing them claimed them as his slaves, and brought them and sat them on the end of the large wooden mortar in which the other men were pounding up the canes.

After a time Libanza said: "Give me a pestle, so that I may crush the canes." But the people laughed that so small a lad should make such a request.

However, after he had repeatedly asked, they gave him a pestle, and Libanza used it with such vigour that it snapped in two. They brought him two others, and taking one in each hand he pounded so strongly that they also broke; and thus he broke all they had in the town except the last one, and with that he ran away, and the people feared to follow him.

As they travelled, Nsongo caught sight of a person in the distance and wanted to marry him; but on being called the person would not come to her. So Libanza changed himself, first into a shell and then into a saucepan, and followed the man; but in these disguises Libanza was not able to catch the man for his sister because he ran away filled with fear.

Libanza then turned himself into the handle of an axe, and when the man came to pick up the handle, Libanza caught him and led him to his sister. Now this person had only one leg and simple stumps for fingers; and Nsongo, on a closer view observing these deformities, refused to have him for a husband.

Libanza and his sister, Nsongo, resumed their wanderings, and on passing a palm tree Nsongo saw a bunch of ripe palm nuts, and she implored her brother to ascend the tree and cut down the nuts. Libanza climbed the palm tree, and as he ascended it the palm tree grew higher and higher and higher, until the top was hid in the heavens, and there Libanza alighted, leaving his sister down below on the earth.

When Nsongo was left on the earth she heard a rumbling noise, which she thought was her brother, Libanza, scolding up above. She called a "wizard", and asked him how she could rejoin her brother.

The "wizard" said: "You must call a Hawk, and tell him you want to send a packet to your brother, Libanza; and then tie yourself up into a packet and put yourself on the roof of a house, and when the Hawk sees it he will say, 'That is surely the parcel I am to take,' and the Hawk will carry you up above."

Nsongo did as she was told by the "wizard," and the Hawk saw the bundle and picked it up; but twice on the way the Hawk rested and tried to open the parcel, and would have done so, but at each attempt he heard a deep sigh proceed from the interior of the bundle, and desisted.

At last the Hawk reached the place where Libanza was, and said to him, "Here is a packet which your sister has sent to you." Now when Libanza essayed to undo the parcel, out came his sister.

Libanza became a blacksmith, and there was in that country a person whose name was Ngombe, and because he swallowed people every day, he was also called Emele Ngombe (Ngombe the Swallower).

When Libanza heard about this Swallower of people, he called his bellows blower, Nkumba (Tortoise), and they heated an ingot of iron. Now as the Swallower was passing the smithy he made the sound "Kililili", and Libanza mocked him by saying, "Alalalala". Ngombe the Swallower then asked: "Who dares to ridicule me?" And again he murmured, "Kililili". And Libanza answered him by saying: "Ngalalala, I am anjaka-njaka lokwala la lotungi, Libanza, the brother of Nsongo."

The Swallower went at Libanza with his mouth wide-stretched to gulp him down, and as he went his lower jaw dragged along the ground. Libanza stirred the molten metal, the Tortoise blew the bellows, and as the Swallower rushed forward with his mouth wide open Libanza threw the liquid metal right into the gaping jaws, and the Swallower of people fell dead.

Rudeness and Its Punishment
(From the Boloki people, Congo)

THERE WAS A MAN once who built a house on an island and went fishing in its creeks and pools. He plaited a large number of fish traps, and set them in good places for catching fish.

One morning he went to look at the traps and found one full of fish, and among the fish was a Lolembe. He took them to his house, and then went to another part of the island to visit some other traps; but on his return he found some food cooked and placed in a saucepan by the fire. In his surprise he called out, "Who has cooked this food?" but there was no answer. All night he pondered this wonder in his heart, for he knew he was alone on the island.

The next morning he pretended to go to his traps, but turning back quickly he hid himself behind his house and watched through an opening in the wall. By and by he was amazed to see the Lolembe turn into a woman, who at once began to cook the food, whereupon the man showed himself to her and said: "Oh, you are the one who cooked my food yesterday!"

"Yes," she replied. They were married, and in due time the woman gave birth to two boys and a girl; and they lived with much contentment on the island.

One day the man said to one of his sons: "You come and help me with the fish traps," and away they went together to look at the various traps.

The lad was a lazy, disobedient boy who would not listen properly to what was told him, so when the father wanted to empty the water out of the canoe and told him to go to the right side, the boy went straight to the left side, because it was nearer to him than the other side. The father became very vexed, and beating him in his anger, he said: "You are too lazy and too proud to do what you are told. Do you know that your mother came out of one of these fish traps, for she was only a Lolembe?"

The boy on hearing this went crying to his mother, and told her all his father had said. The mother soothed him, but in her heart she said: "My husband jeers at me because I am only a Lolembe, yet I have been a good wife to him; perhaps some other day he will call me worse names, and when we return to the town everybody will know that I came out of one of his fish traps. I will return to my own place in the river."

She thereupon fell into the river, and changing into a Lolembe she swam away. "Therefore," says the native storyteller, "never taunt a person with being a slave."

The Water-Fairies Save a Child
(From the Lower Congo Basin)

PEDRO WAS A TRADER in birds, and travelled long distances to buy and sell them, and as he often had some left he carried them home to keep until next market day. Pedro had six

children, one of whom was a boy named Yakob, and the others were all girls. When Pedro was leaving the town one day for a trading journey to a very distant market, he said to his people: "There are some birds in that house, and if anyone lets them out and loses them I will kill him."

Soon after his father was gone Yakob thought he would like to look at the birds, so went and pushed open the door to peep in, and as he did so the birds flew out and escaped to the forest. Yakob went crying to his mother, and told her what he had done. His mother chided him for disobeying his father's orders.

By and by Pedro returned from his journey, and, going to the house where he had left his birds, he found they were gone. He was very angry, and wanted to know who had let his birds out of the house, and on being told it was Yakob, he took the boy, killed him and threw his body in the river. Some Water-fairies found the body and restored it to life, and nursed the boy, fed him and kept him with them until he grew to be a young man.

One day the Water-fairies said to him: "Yakob, you had better go for a walk and see the country." So he took his *biti* and went walking and playing his instrument. He met his sisters, and began to sing: "That which the father had cut and thought he had killed, stand out of the way, girls, and let him pass." But the sisters did not recognize him – they simply smiled at him for his song. He told them who he was, and they returned to their town and told their mother and father that they had seen and spoken with their brother, but their father said: "Oh, no, it was not your brother, it was only a passerby."

Yakob went back to his fairy mothers, and told them that he had seen his sisters, and then he gathered his things together and asked permission to return to his own people. They gave him some fine cloths to wear, and various bells, which they tied on him, so that when he walked the bells tinkled and made a pleasant sound; then they gave him a cane, and said: "When you reach the stream you hit that place and the other place." Yakob said: "I thank you with all my heart." So, bidding them goodbye, he started for his town with only three servants.

When Yakob reached the stream he did as he was told, and on beating one place, out came a band of trumpeters with ivory and brass trumpets. He hit the other place, and out came a fine hammock and carriers. He got into the hammock and sent messengers to tell the chief that he was approaching.

The chief spread his carpet and sat in his chair amid the clapping of his people, and in a short time the sound of the trumpet was heard and the carriers trotted up with Yakob's hammock, spread his carpet and arranged his chair, and then Yakob alighted from his hammock and sat down amid the shouting, drumming and clapping of the people.

On taking his seat, Yakob said: "I am your son whom you killed. What you threw away the Water-fairies picked up, and they have nursed me and kept me until this day. There is a proverb which says: 'If the Leopard gives birth to a palm rat he does not eat it.' You should have punished me for breaking your law, but you should not have killed me." The father was astonished, and went and kneeled crying before his son, and said: "My child, forgive me, for I have done wrong."

Yakob's mother was glad to see her son again; he dressed her in fine cloth, and built his own village close by his parents'.

How the Squirrel Repaid a Kindness
(From the Lower Congo Basin)

THERE WAS ONCE a man named Tunga who had a house, a wife, and a nice little baby. Tunga used to catch partridges, guinea fowls, palm rats and squirrels in his traps, and sometime he would trap three and four of these at once. One day he caught as many as fifteen partridges, and when he took them home his wife said: "We will save some of these for another day, so that our child may not be hungry should you not catch any." But Tunga said: "No, we will eat them all now, for I am sure to catch plenty of meat every day."

Some time after Tunga went to look at his traps, and found only one Squirrel in them, and this Squirrel had some bells round its neck, and just as Tunga was going to kill it, the Squirrel said: "Oh, please don't kill me, and I will help you another day."

Tunga laughed and said: "How can a little thing like you help me?"

But the Squirrel pleaded for his life and promised to help the man whenever he was in trouble, so at last Tunga let the Squirrel go. He then plucked some leaves and went home to his wife and told her what he had done. She was very angry, and quarrelled so much about there being no food for the baby to eat, that she picked up the child and went off to her own family, which lived in a distant town.

The man waited some days until he thought his wife's anger had passed away, and then he took a large calabash of palm wine and started for his wife's town. On arriving at the crossroads Tunga met an Imp that had neither arms, legs, nor body, but was all head, like a ball. The Imp said: "Let me carry your calabash for you. You are a great man and should not carry it yourself."

"How can you carry it, when you are all head and no body?" asked Tunga.

"Oh, you will see," said the Imp, as he took the calabash, balanced it on his head, and went bounding off along the road in front of Tunga.

After travelling a long way Tunga became very tired, so they sat down under a tree to rest, and while they were sitting there a Leopard came up, and noticing the palm wine, asked for a drink, and the man was too much afraid to refuse it. When Tunga was going to pour out some of the palm wine into a glass, the Leopard said: "I drink out of my own mug, not yours," and he brought out of his bag the skull of a man, and said: "Here is a mug. I have already eaten nine men and you will be the tenth."

Poor Tunga was so filled with fear that he did not know what to do; but by and by a Squirrel arrived, and after exchanging greetings he asked for some of the palm wine, and as Tunga was going to pour it out the Squirrel said: "What! Have you no respect for me? I carry my own mug," and putting his hand into his bag, he brought out the head of a Leopard, and said: "There, I have eaten nine Leopards, and this one here will be the tenth," and as he repeated the words again and again very fiercely the Leopard began to tremble, and go backwards until he was in the road, and then he turned tail and fled with the Squirrel after him.

Tunga waited, and at last he and the Imp started again on their journey. He was now glad that he had been kind to the Squirrel and had saved his life.

On reaching the town, Tunga and the Imp were welcomed by the people, a good house was given to them, and they were well feasted. After resting there some days, Tunga and his wife started on their return journey home, but before leaving the town Mrs Tunga's family gave them a goat as a parting present.

When they reached the crossroads, Tunga said to the Imp: "I will kill the goat here, and give you your half."

"All right," said the Imp; "but you must also give me half of the woman."

"No," replied Tunga; "the woman is my wife, but you shall have half the goat."

The Imp became very angry and called to his friends, and a great crowd of Imps came to fight Tunga.

While they were wrangling, the Squirrel arrived and asked what was the cause of the row. They told him, and he said: "If we divide the goat and the woman, how are you going to cook them? You have neither firewood nor water. Some of you fetch water, and others go for firewood."

He opened his box and gave to some of them a calabash in which to fetch water, but while the water was running into the calabash it sung such a magic tune that the Imps began to dance, and could not stop dancing.

Then the Squirrel opened his box again and let loose a swarm of bees that stung the other Imps so badly that they all bounded away and never returned again to trouble Tunga. Then the Squirrel said to Tunga: "You now see that if you had not been merciful to me, I should not have been able to save you from the Leopard and the Imps. Your kindness to me has saved your own life and your wife's." Tunga thanked him for his help and went his way home.

How a Child Saved His Mother's Life
(From the Lower Congo Basin)

A MAN, ONCE upon a time, cleared a large piece of bush, and then sent his wife to plant it with cassava. When the cassava was ready to pull, the bush pigs and other animals visited the farm and destroyed the roots, and it seemed as though the woman would have her trouble for nothing. The wife complained about it to her husband, and he went to dig a large pit in which to trap the wild animals that came stealing in their farm.

While the man was digging the hole an Imp came out of the forest nearby and asked him what he was doing. Upon hearing he was digging a trap for animals, the Imp said: "Let me help you." The man, fearing the Imp would kill him if he refused, accepted his offer. Thereupon the Imp said: "Let us make a bargain. All the male animals that fall into the trap are yours, but all the female ones are mine." The man agreed to this, and they then finished the hole together, after which they returned to their places.

Next morning they went to look at the hole and found one male pig in it, which the man took according to their agreement. Every morning they went and it was the same – male pigs, antelopes and buffaloes were in the trap, never any female ones, sometimes there were two males and sometimes there were five males. The man laughed, and said to the Imp: "You were foolish to make such a bargain, for did you not know that only male animals go about in search of food? You are very foolish."

The man took the animals to his town, and all the way home he was ridiculing the stupid Imp. The wife said: "Now we have plenty of meat, but no cassava bread to eat with it. Tomorrow I will go and dig up some roots in the farm with which to make some bread."

Early next morning the woman took her basket and her hoe, and went to the farm, leaving her husband at home to look after their little boy. When the woman had been gone some time the boy began to cry, so the man picked him up and followed his wife to the farm to give the child to her. As he drew near the farm he heard the Imp gleefully singing: "O my, O my, at last I have a female animal in the trap."

On reaching the trap the man asked the Imp why he was jumping, dancing and singing in that joyful fashion, and when he heard that it was because there was one female animal in the trap, the man laughed at the Imp for making so much fuss over one animal; but looking into the pit, and seeing his wife there he began to cry, and contended that the Imp was cheating him as a woman was not an animal.

They became very angry in their discussion as to whether the woman was an animal or not, that at last the boy said: "Father, you agreed to the bargain that you were to have all the male animals, and he was to have all the female ones that fell into the trap; we have had plenty of animals out of the hole, but he has not had a single one. Let him take this one."

The Imp, admiringly, said: "Is this wise judge only a boy?" and with that he jumped into the trap to get out his prize, but no sooner had he done so than the boy called out: "Look, father, there is a male animal in the trap and it is yours."

On dropping down into the trap the Imp had become, according to his own statement, an animal, and consequently belonged to the man. The Imp, to save himself, had to give up all claim to the woman, and thus the child by his smartness saved his mother's life. Never again did the man enter into an agreement until he properly understood all about the conditions.

The Story of Two Young Women
(From the Lower Congo Basin)

ONCE THERE WERE two girls whose uncle told them: "You are now old enough to marry, so you may look out for two young men." Their hearts were glad when they received this permission, and very soon they found two lovers. The elder became engaged to a poor man, and the younger to a rich one.

One day the elder girl paid a visit to her betrothed, and as he was poor he could only give her a common fish to eat and a mat to lie on for a bed; but when the younger went to see her rich lover he killed a goat for her supper, gave her a fine bed spread with blankets, and in the morning killed a pig for her breakfast; and when she was leaving to return to her home he gave her a shawl, a fine piece of blue and white cloth, a necklace of beads, and a looking glass.

The two sisters happened to meet at the crossroads, and they asked each other what presents they had received, and when the younger girl saw the poor gift received by the other, she showed her presents with much vanity, and laughed at her sister for having such a poor lover. This occurred every time they visited their young men – the younger sister laughed to scorn the poverty of the elder sister's suitor.

After due time the day of their marriage arrived, and the rich man told all his pedigree, gave a great, fat pig for the feast, and sent his bride a piece of velvet, a piece of white cloth and a piece of satin; but the poor man could only send some fowls for the feast and give his bride one piece of ordinary cloth. After the marriage festivities were over the new wives went to live in the houses of their husbands.

Before many days had passed the younger bride committed a small fault, and her husband in his anger cut off her ears. She cried out for help, but her family could not help her, as they had consented to the marriage. In a week he was angry about some other small matter, and he cut off her nose, and the next time she vexed him with some small mistake he cut off her head. Thus she did not live long to enjoy her fine things. As for the poor husband, he said to his wife: "It is not until death comes to me that we shall separate." Riches do not always bring with them happiness and contentment.

The Son Who Tried to Outwit His Father
(From the Lower Congo Basin)

A SON SAID to his father one day: "I will hide, and you will not be able to find me." The father replied: "Hide wherever you like," and then he went into his house to rest.

The son saw a three-kernel peanut, and changed himself into one of the kernels; a fowl coming along picked up the peanut and swallowed it; and a wild bush-cat caught and ate the fowl; and a dog met, chased and ate the bush-cat. After a little time the dog was swallowed by a python, that, having eaten its meal, went to the river and was snared in a fish trap.

The father searched for his son, and, not seeing him, went to look at his fish trap. On pulling it to the riverside he found a large python in it. He opened it and saw a dog inside, in which he found a bush-cat, and on opening that he discovered a fowl, from which he took the peanut, and breaking its shell he there revealed his son. The son was so dumbfounded that he never tried again to outwit his father.

The Story of the Four Fools
(From the Lower Congo Basin)

A WIZARD OUT WALKING one day met a boy crying bitterly. He asked him the reason of his tears, and the boy said: "I have lost my father's parrot, and if you can find it I will pay you well." So the wizard called a hunter, a carpenter and a thief, and told them about the loss and the reward, and they decided to search for the parrot.

"Before starting let us show our skill," said one of the four. "You, thief, go and steal an egg from that fowl without its knowledge." The thief went and stole the egg, and the fowl did not move. The hunter put up the egg as a mark, went a long distance off and proved his skill by hitting the egg. After which the carpenter showed his cleverness by putting the egg together again. Then they turned to the wizard for him to give a proof of his smartness, and after a little time he said: "The parrot has been stolen by the people in that vessel."

All four entered their glass ship and after a time caught up to the vessel. The thief went on board, and waved his charm, then he took the parrot, laid the table, and had a good feast; and when he had finished eating he picked up the parrot and returned to his glass ship.

When the people in the vessel found the parrot gone, they gave chase to the glass ship. The captain of the vessel sent down the rain and it broke the glass ship, but the carpenter mended it, and the hunter fired at the rain and killed it. The captain sent the lightning and it broke the ship, but the carpenter mended it again, and the hunter fired at the lightning and killed it. So they eventually reached the land and took the parrot to the chief's son, and said: "Here is your father's parrot."

The lad was so glad to receive it that he told them to select what they liked from his wealth, "even to the wonderful fowl which lays beads, or anything else you desire." They chose the fowl and went their way, but they had not gone very far before the wizard said: "It is my fowl, for I told you where the parrot was." The thief said: "No, it is mine, for I stole the parrot from the vessel." And the carpenter also claimed it, as he had twice mended the broken ship. Moreover, the hunter said: "Of course it is mine, for I killed the rain and the lightning." Thus they argued long and angrily, and as they could not agree, they at last did a thing that was amazingly stupid. They killed the wonderful fowl, and divided it into four pieces, each taking his share. Now who out of these four foolish ones should have had the fowl?"

Enquiry Should Come Before Anger
(From the Lower Congo Basin)

ONCE UPON A TIME a Wine-gatherer and a Fisherman became great friends; they ate together, walked and talked together, and went to work together; and when one went to collect wine from his palm trees the other would look after his fish traps in the streams and pools near to the palm trees; and after their work was finished they would meet in the booth to drink the wine and cook and eat the fish together.

One day, while thus eating and drinking, the Wine-gatherer said: "There is no one who can break the strong friendship that exists between us two," and the Fisherman assented, saying: "Why, if you had not mentioned it, I was going to remark that no one can separate us one from the other."

A frolicsome boy heard them make this covenant of friendship, and laughingly said to himself: "When they go away I will do that which will test their friendship for each other."

In a short time the two friends returned together to their town, and when they had gone the boy took the hoop and climbed up the palm trees, and removed all the small calabashes that were placed there to catch the palm wine, and then he went to the pools and streams and gathered all the fish traps, and put the calabashes in their place, and the fish traps he tied to the palm trees. Having thus changed them he returned to his town.

Next morning the Wine-gatherer and the Fisherman awoke, and calling each other they started for the valley where their work was, and there parted – one to look at his calabashes on the palm trees, and the other to visit his fish traps.

The Wine-gatherer, on arriving at the booth, took his hoop and climbed a palm tree, and there he found, not his calabash, but a fish trap; he pulled it off and threw it down in anger, and descended the palm. Thus he went from palm to palm and found nothing but fish traps, which he collected and carried to the booth, and sat down to wait for his friend, full of wrath and indignation.

While this was happening the Fisherman was going from pool to stream, finding nothing but small calabashes floating on the water where he had put fish traps the night before. In great anger he gathered them up and carried them to the booth, and there he met his friend, who said: "Those calabashes, are they not mine?"

To him the Fisherman replied: "Those fish traps, are they not mine?"

"Why did you put your useless fish traps in my palm trees?" excitedly asked the Wine-gatherer.

"Why did you put your silly calabashes in my streams and pools?" retorted the Fisherman.

And without more ado they stood up and beat each other, and cut each other, until at last they fell exhausted to the ground.

At this moment the mischievous boy arrived, and seeing their plight, said: "What! Are you not friends? Why have you been beating each other? I heard your covenant of friendship the other day, and because I wanted to try it I went and changed your things. Now you have been quarrelling with each other without talking matters over. Enquiry should come first, and anger follow after."

The Story of the Four Wonders
(From the Lower Congo Basin)

A WOMAN GAVE BIRTH to a child, who on the day it was born went by itself down to the river to bathe. While there a hunter arrived, who fired his gun.

"What are you firing at?" asked the baby. "I am shooting the mosquitoes that are eating my wife's cassava," replied the hunter.

"Whoever heard of such a thing before?" said the baby. "By shooting mosquitoes you are injuring the country."

The hunter denied this grave charge, and accused the baby of upsetting the proper order of things by bathing himself on the very day he was born.

After much discussion they submitted the case to a chief of a neighbouring town. When he had listened to their wrangling, he said: "My mouth is locked up in that room, and my wives have taken the key with them to the farms."

"Oh," they rejoined, "you, by talking when your mouth is fastened up in another room, have destroyed our country, for whoever heard of such a wonder before?"

After much debate away they went to find someone to settle the matter for them, and by and by they met a man who climbed palm trees to tap them for palm wine, and they put the case to him, each accusing the other of disarranging the proper order of earthly ways.

When they had finished the palm climber said: "I fell one day from the top of a palm tree and broke to pieces, and then I went into the town to procure men to carry all my pieces back to my house." They thereupon fell on him, accusing him of spoiling the country by his wonderful feat. They are still arguing out the matter and cannot agree as to which is worthy of the greatest blame.

The Adventures of the Twins
(From the Lower Congo Basin)

Mr Tungi built some houses and then married. When he had been married about a year he started on a journey to some distant markets to buy and trade in peanuts. He had not been gone very long when Mrs Tungi gave birth to male twins.

When the twins had grown into stout lads their mother told them that their father had gone to trade at some distant markets, but would be returning soon to his town. They at once decided to go and meet him. Their mother prepared some native bread and other food, and in a few days they set out in search of their father.

After travelling a long way they met a palm wine gatherer sitting in a palm frond drinking shelter, who welcomed them and promised to get them some fresh palm wine. He took his climbing hoop and together they went to the palm tree. Before ascending the tree the twins were astonished to see the man take out all his bones and lay them on one side, and then he climbed the tree and brought down a small calabash of palm wine for the boys, picked up his bones and put them all back again in their places. The lads asked him why he removed his bones before ascending the palm tree.

"Oh," he said, "if I were to fall I should break them, so I always leave my bones on the ground, and then, should I fall, nothing will be broken." They drank his palm wine, thanked him, and after resting a while started again on their journey.

They had not travelled very far when they met two men walking towards them whose feet were turned backwards. The twins asked them what accident had twisted their feet in that way.

They replied: "It is no accident, but we turn our feet round when travelling to keep our naked toes from knocking against the stones in the road."

The twins had hardly recovered from their surprise when they came across some men whose knees were behind, and others whose arms were at the back, and others again whose faces were at the back of their heads.

They enquired the reason for these strange things, and the first said: "We have our knees at the back of our legs so that when we fall they will not be cut by the stones."

The next replied: "We have our arms behind us so that if we fall backwards they will hold us up, and we shall not hurt ourselves."

And the last laughingly said: "Oh, we have our faces behind our heads so that the long grass by the sides of the roads will neither cut them nor get into our eyes as we push our way through it."

"Well, this is a funny country," cried the twins in amazement, "people seem to do whatever they like with their bodies."

On they went again, and during the afternoon they reached the bank of a river, where they rested under a shady tree. While sitting there they saw men and women, boys and girls coming down the hill to bathe, and they noticed that all of them took out their eyes before they entered the water and left them on the bank with their clothes. They enquired the reason for this wonderful thing, and one of the men said: "You see, we bathe here with our mothers, wives and sisters – men and women, boys and girls altogether, hence to retain our self-respect and modesty we always take out our eyes before bathing." The twins were no longer astonished at anything they saw and heard, so they silently assented to what the man told them.

They camped by the river that night, and early next morning renewed the search for their father. After three or four hours' travelling over the hills, across streams and through dense forests, they arrived at a large market, where all the people, instead of speaking, were making signs to one another as they bought and sold their goods. Upon looking at them more closely they observed that none of them had lower jaws, hence they were not able to speak. They could not enquire into this wonder, as no one was able to talk to them.

They pushed on across the market, and after walking another hour or two they reached a large river, where they saw a man, with a very heavy load, trying to cross it, and seeing he was in great difficulty they helped him over with his load, and then sat down to have a rest and chat. They told the man they were twin sons of Tungi, and were looking for their father, who left his town many years ago to trade in the distant markets.

The man said: "Why, I am Tungi, you must be my sons, and I am just returning to my town."

The sons rejoiced in this meeting with their father, and were glad they had helped him over the river, otherwise they would not have known him. They divided the load between them, and soon started for home.

As the twins walked with their father, they told him of all they had seen and heard during their journey, but they said: "In the market we passed this morning we saw people who did all their trading by signs, because they had no lower jaws. Why was that?"

Their father replied: "On the markets in this country there was so much rowing, quarrelling and fighting that they made a law that all those who went to market should leave their lower jaws at home; for if folk cannot talk they won't quarrel, and hence they will have no reason for fighting. It is talking and wrangling that lead to rows, riots and fights."

The twins and their father reached their town again safely, where they were noisily welcomed and feasted; and the twins frequently narrated the marvellous sights they had seen during their travels.

Appearances are Sometimes Deceptive
(From the Lower Congo Basin
and analogous to stories from Cameroon)

ONCE UPON A TIME a girl was betrothed by her parents to a Mr Hawk, and for a time she was satisfied with her sweetheart; but by and by she complained that his face was too black.

Her parents tried to teach her that a man was not to be accepted simply because he had a beautiful face, nor rejected for only possessing a very plain, black one; but she would not listen to them.

One day she put on her ornaments and best cloths, and went to the market, where she met a young man whose name was Oily-face, because it was polished so brightly with palm oil.

Mr Oily-face's country was a long way off, and when he left home he had a nasty body covered with pimples and scabs, and his eyes bulged out. As he passed through the towns he borrowed a face, some hair, new teeth and a nice skin; consequently when he reached the market he looked a very pleasant young man.

This Mr Oily-face saw the girl standing in the market, and said to her: "I would like to marry you." She looked at him, and seeing he had a beautiful light skin, well-plaited hair and nice white teeth, she said: "All right, come and see my parents."

When they reached her town she said to her family: "Here is a young man who wants to marry me." Oily-face looked so bashful, and showed such respect to the girl's mother, that they were all pleased with him. Very soon they were married, and shortly after started for Oily-face's country.

They had not gone very far on the road when someone called out: "Oily-face, return my hair." Another shouted: "Give me back my teeth." In another town a man requested Oily-face to return the face that he had lent him; and another said: "Give me back my stomach and take your own; it eats too much." Thus at last he was reduced to his own nasty body, pimply skin and bulging, ugly eyes.

After walking many days they reached their town, and the people came round asking Oily-face where he had procured his wife. He told them that she had come from a far country which was ten days' journey away. They welcomed her, but next morning they surrounded the house wishing to eat her.

She came outside and said: "Wait, don't eat me yet; but beat your drums and I will dance."

So she danced all day to amuse them, and sang a song about a Mr Hawk being very good, with beautiful, curving feathers; and how sorry she was for not accepting him as her husband. Every morning they wanted to kill and eat her; but she danced and sang to please them.

One day Mr Hawk passed that way, and, looking down, saw the woman, heard her song, and felt full of pity for her. He told her parents of their daughter's danger, and promised to save her. Next day, therefore, he flew off, swooped down and carried her back to her own family, who were glad to receive her amongst them again. After a time she married Mr Hawk, and never any more found fault with the colour of his face.

How the Wives Restored
Their Husband to Life
(From the Kongo people, Congo)

A CERTAIN MAN, named Nenpetro, had three wives, Ndoza'ntu (the Dreamer), Songa'nzila (the Guide), and Fulla Fulla (the Raiser of the Dead). Now Nenpetro was a great hunter; and one day he killed an antelope, and gave it to his three wives. They ate it, and after a time complained of hunger. Nenpetro went out shooting again, and killed a monkey. They ate this also, but still complained of hunger. "Oh," says Nenpetro, "nothing but an ox will satisfy you people." So off he went on the track of an ox. He followed the tracks for a long way, and at last caught sight of it as it was feeding with two or three others. He stalked it carefully, and shot it; but before he could reload, another angry ox charged him, and killed him.

Now in town they knew nothing of all this; but his wives grew very hungry, and cried for him to come back to them. Stillbe returned not. Then Ndoza'ntu dreamt that he had been killed by an ox, but that he had killed an ox before he fell.

"Come along," said Songa'nzila; "I will show you the road."

Thus they set out, and marched up hill and down dale, through woods and across rivers, until towards nightfall they came up to the place where their husband lay dead. And now Fulla Fulla went into the woods and collected herbs and plants, and set about raising him from the dead.

Then the three women began to quarrel and wonder into whose shimbec Nenpetro would first enter.

"I dreamt that he was dead," said Ndoza'ntu.

"But I showed you where he lay dead," said Songa'nzila.

"And I have brought him back to life," said Fulla Fulla, as the husband gradually gave signs of life.

"Well! Let us each cook a pot of food, and take it to him as soon as he can eat; and let him decide out of which pot he will take his first meal."

So two killed fowls, and cooked them each in her own pot, while the third cooked some pig in hers. And Nenpetro took the pot of pig that Fulla Fulla had cooked, and said: "When you dreamt that I was dead, you did not give me food, Ndoza'ntu; for I was not yet found. And when you, Songa'nzila, had shown the others the road, I was still unfit to eat; but when Fulla Fulla gave me back my life, then was I able to eat the pig she gave me. The gift therefore of Fulla Fulla is the most to be prized."

And the majority of the people said he was right in his judgment; but the women round about said he should have put the food out of the three pots into one pot, and have eaten the food thus mixed.

The Vanishing Wife
(From the Kongo people, Congo)

TWO BROTHERS LIVED in a certain town. They were called Buite and Swarmi.

Swarmi was married and had servants to wait upon him; but Buite was alone and despised. As Buite had no one to cook for him, he used to eat palm kernels, which he daily brought in from the bush.

Swarmi treated Buite very badly, never asking him to join him at his meals, or enter in any way into the festivities of his family; so that Buite determined to leave his town, and live alone far away in the bush. So one day, without saying anything, he left his brother, and walked, and walked, and walked, until at nightfall he arrived at a deep valley, fertile and thickly planted with palm trees. Far away at the bottom of this damp valley, beneath the shade of the high trees, palms and rushes, Buite built himself a little shed – a roof, supported upon sticks, about a foot in height above the ground. In this damp hovel he spread out his mat to sleep upon, and lighted his fire to cook his solitary meals.

Tired and weary of life, Buite one night fell asleep, and dreamt that a beautiful girl called him, that he rose and followed her, and that she led him through the thick jungle and woods, until they arrived at a river. Here she told him to tap on the ground three times; and to his surprise a canoe appeared. He tapped the canoe three times, and paddles made their appearance. Then she told him to go and fish, and bring her food, that she might cook it for him; but that he should cut the heads off the fish, as she could not bear to see them. And he dreamt that he did so, and returned to find the girl waiting for him to cook the fish. Then he awoke, and could sleep no longer that night.

The next morning he got up and, remembering his dream, travelled through the jungle and woods, until he came to the river he had seen in his dream. And he tapped the ground, and lo!, there appeared the canoe. He tapped the canoe, and there were the paddles. Then he went and fished, and cut the heads off the fish, and returned to his wretched hovel. But the shed had disappeared, and in its place was a large house, beautifully furnished, and all the necessary outhouses, and above everything, the beautiful girl, who came forward to meet him, just as if she had been accustomed to do so every day, and she also had nine little servants to wait upon her. And when she told him, that she had come to comfort him, he was very pleased and loved her very much.

And every day, when he went out fishing, she would send one of the little ones with him, to carry the fish. And people who passed that way were astonished at the liberal treatment bestowed upon them by Buite, and wondered where he had got his wife and riches from. His brother, Swarmi, would not believe in Buite's prosperity, and determined to visit him.

Now Buite each day went fishing, taking one of his wife's boys with him. But after a time he got tired of always cutting off the fishes' heads.

And it so happened one day that he did not cut off the heads of the fish. When the boy saw this, he cried out and protested saying that his mother did not like to see a fish's head.

But Buite asked him if it was for him, a servant, to talk in that way to his master. And the boy left for the house, carrying the fish with him. But after a time Buite ran after the boy, and caught him up just before he got home, and cut the heads of the fish off, so that his wife should not see them.

And this happened eight times with eight different servants of his wife. Each time the boy protested; each time Buite scolded him, and then, repenting, ran after the boy and cut the heads of the fish off.

The ninth time he took the youngest boy, Parrot by name, and fished, and gave the entire fish to him to carry home. And Parrot cried very much and protested, but was frightened by Buite's imperious manner, and ran away home with the fish. And Buite ran after him, and ran, and ran, and ran, but could not catch Parrot up.

And Parrot arrived, and showed the fish to the woman; and immediately the house vanished; and the outhouses, the servants, the beautiful furniture and lastly the lovely wife, all disappeared, so that when Buite arrived, all out of breath, he no longer saw his house, or wife or servants, but only his brother, Swarmi, who just then turned up to visit him.

And Buite was very sorry, and wept very much; and Swarmi more than ever despised him, and left him once more alone.

The Jealous Wife
(From the Kongo people, Congo)

TWO WIVES BUSIED themselves preparing chicoanga, or native bread, for their husband, who purposed going into the bush for six months to trade. Each of these women had a child; and

the husband, as he left them, adjured them to be very careful with the children, and see that no harm came to them. They promised faithfully to attend to his entreaty.

When it was nearly time for the husband to return, the women said: "Let us go and fish, that we may give our husband some good food when he returns."

But as they could not leave the children alone, one had to stay with them while the other fished. The elder wife went first, and stayed in the fishing ground for two or three days to smoke what she had caught. Then the younger wife left to fish, and the elder remained to take care of the children.

Now the child of the younger wife was a much brighter and more intelligent child than that of the elder; and this made the latter jealous and angry. So she determined to murder the child, and get it out of the way while its mother was fishing. She sharpened a razor until it easily cut off the hairs on her arm, and then put it away until the evening when the children should be asleep. And when it was evening and they were fast asleep, she went to the place where the child was accustomed to sleep, and killed it. The other child awoke, and in its fright ran out of the house and took refuge with a neighbour.

In the morning the elder wife went to look at her evil work, thinking to put the child away before its mother should return. But when she looked again at the child she was horror-struck to find that she had killed her own child. She wept as she picked up its little body; and wrapping it up in her cloth she ran away with it into the woods, and disappeared.

The husband returned and at once missed his elder wife. He questioned the younger one; but she could only repeat to him what her child had told her, namely, that during the night the elder wife had killed her child. The husband would not believe this story, and asked his friends, the bushmen who had come with him, to help him to search for his wife. They agreed, and scoured the woods the whole day, but without success.

The next day one of the bushmen came across a woman who was nursing something; so he hid and listened to her singing. The poor woman was forever shaking the child, saying:

"Are you always going to sleep like this? Why don't you awake? Why don't you talk? See! See! It is your mother that nurses you."

"Surely," said the bushman, "this must be my friend's wife. I will go to him and tell him that I have found her."

"Let us go," said the husband; and as they approached her they hid themselves so that she could not see them. And they found her still shaking the child and still singing the same sad song.

Then the father called in her relations, and together they went to the woods, and made her prisoner. And when they saw that the child had been really murdered, they gave casca to the woman; and it killed her. Then they burnt her body, and scattered its ashes to the wind.

Ngomba's Balloon
(From the Kongo people, Congo)

FOUR LITTLE MAIDENS one day started to go out fishing. One of them was suffering sadly from sores, which covered her from head to foot. Her name was Ngomba. The other three, after a little consultation, agreed that Ngomba should not accompany them.; and so they told her to go back.

"Nay," said Ngoniba, "I will do no such thing. I mean to catch fish for mother as well as you."

Then the three maidens beat Ngomba until she was glad to run away. But she determined to catch fish also, so she walked she hardly knew whither, until at last she came and walked, upon a large lake. Here she commenced fishing and singing:

If my mother
[She catches a fish and puts it in her basket.]
Had taken care of me,
[She catches another fish and puts it in her basket.]
I should have been with them,
[She catches another fish and puts it in her basket.]

And not here alone."
[She catches another fish and puts it in her basket.]

But a Mpunia (murderer) had been watching her for some time, and now he came up to her and accosted her:

"What are you doing here?"

"Fishing. Please, don't kill me! See! I am full of sores, but I can catch plenty of fish."

The Mpunia watched her as she fished and sang:

Oh, I shall surely die!
[She catches a fish and puts it in her basket.]
Mother, you will never see me!
[She catches another fish and puts it in her basket.]
But I don't care,
[She catches another fish and puts it in her basket.]
For no one cares for me."
[She catches another fish and puts it in her basket.]

"Come with me," said the Mpunia.

"Nay, this fish is for mother, and I must take it to her."

"If you do not come with me, I will kill you."

"Oh! Am I to die
[She catches a fish and puts it in her basket.]
On the top of my fish?
[She catches another fish and puts it in her basket.]
If mother had loved me,
[She catches another fish and puts it in her basket.]
To live I should wish.
[She catches another fish and puts it in her basket.]

"Take me and cure me, dear Mpunia, and I will serve you."

The Mpunia took her to his home in the woods, and cured her. Then he placed her in the paint house and married her.

Now the Mpunia was very fond of dancing, and Ngomba danced beautifully, so that he loved her very much, and made her mistress over all his prisoners and goods.

"When I go out for a walk," he said to her, "I will tie this string round my waist; and that you may know when I am still going away from you, or returning, the string will be stretched tight as I depart, and will bang loose as I return."

Ngomba pined for her mother, and therefore entered into a conspiracy with her people to escape. She sent them every day to cut the leaves of the mateva palm, and ordered them to put them in the sun to dry. Then she set them to work to make a huge ntenda, or basket. And when the Mpunia returned, he remarked to her that the air was heavy with the smell of mateva.

Now she had made all her people put on clean clothes, and when they knew that he was returning, she ordered them to come to him and flatter him. So now they approached him, and some called him "father" and others "uncle" – and others told him how he was a father and a mother to them. And he was very pleased, and danced with them.

The next day when he returned he said he smelt mateva.

Then Ngomba cried, and told him that he was both father and mother to her, and that if he accused her of smelling of mateva, she would kill herself.

He could not stand this sadness, so he kissed her and danced with her until all was forgotten.

The next day Ngomba determined to try her ntenda, to see if it would float in the air. Thus four women lifted it on high, and gave it a start upwards, and it floated beautifully. Now the Mpunia happened to be up a tree, and he espied this great ntenda floating in the air; and he danced and sang for joy, and wished to call Ngomba, that she might dance with him.

That night he smelt mateva again, and his suspicions were aroused; and when he thought how easily his wife might escape him, he determined to kill her. Accordingly, he gave her to drink some palm wine that he had drugged. She drank it, and slept as he put his somino (the iron that the natives make red hot, and with which they burn the hole through the stem of their pipes) into the fire. He meant to kill her by pushing this red-hot wire up her nose.

But as he was almost ready, Ngomba's little sister, who had changed herself into a cricket and hidden herself under her bed, began to sing. The Mpunia heard her and felt forced to join in and dance, and thus he forgot to kill his wife. But after a time she ceased singing, and then he began to heat the wire again. The cricket then sang again, and again he danced and danced, and in his excitement tried to wake Ngomba to dance also. But she refused to awake, telling him that the medicine he had given her made her feel sleepy. Then he went out and got some palm wine, and as he went she drowsily asked him if he had made the string fast. He called all his people, dressed himself, and made them all dance.

The cock crew.

The iron wire was still in the fire. The Mpunia made his wife get up and fetch more palm wine.

Then the cock crew again, and it was daylight.

When the Mpunia had left her for the day, Ngomba determined to escape that very day. So she called her people and made them try the ntenda again; and when she was certain that it would float, she put all her people, and all the Mpunia's ornaments, into it. Then she got in and the ntenda began to float away over the treetops in the direction of her mother's town.

When the Mpunia, who was up a tree, saw it coming towards him, he danced and sang for joy, and only wished that his wife had been there to see this huge ntenda flying through the air. It passed just over his head, and then he knew that the people in it were his. So that he ran after it in the tops of the trees, until he saw it drop in Ngomba's town. And he determined to go there also and claim his wife.

The ntenda floated round the house of Ngomba's mother, and astonished all the people there, and finally settled down in front of it. Ngomba cried to the people to come and let them out. But they were afraid and did not dare, so that she came out herself and presented herself to her mother.

Her relations at first did not recognize her; but after a little while they fell upon her and welcomed her as their long-lost Ngomba.

Then the Mpunia entered the town and claimed Ngomba as his wife.

"Yes," her relations said, "she is your wife, and you must be thanked for curing her of her sickness."

And while some of her relations were entertaining the Mpunia, others were preparing a place for him and his wife to be seated. They made a large fire, and boiled a great quantity of water, and dug a deep hole in the ground. This hole they covered over with sticks and a mat, and when all was ready they led the Mpunia and his wife to it, and requested them to be seated. Ngomba sat near her husband, who, as he sat down, fell into the hole. The relations then brought boiling water and fire, and threw it over him until he died.

The Wicked Husband
(From the Kongo people, Congo)

"CUT YOU MORE palm nuts? why, I am forever cutting palm nuts! What on earth do you do with them? I cut enough in one day to keep you for a week," said the husband to his wife.

"Nay," said the wife, "what am I to do? first, one of your relations comes to me, and asks me for a few, then another, and another, and so on, until they are all gone. Can I refuse to give them?"

"Well, as you know, it's a long way to where the palm trees grow. If you want palm nuts, you can come with me and carry them back with you."

"Nay, I cannot go so far, for I have just put the mandioca in the water."

"But you must go!"

"Nay, I will not."

"Yes, you shall!" And the husband dragged her after him.

When he got her well into the woods he placed her upon a rough table, he had constructed, and cut off her arms and legs. Then the wife wriggled her body about and sang: "Oh, if I had never married, I could never have come to this."

The husband left her, and returned to his town, telling the people that his wife had gone to visit her relations.

Now a hunter happened to hear the wife's song, and was greatly shocked to find her in such a terrible condition. He returned to town, and told his wife all about it, but cautioned her to tell no one.

Bat the prince got to hear about it, and knocked his chingongo (or bell), and thus summoned all his people together. When they were all assembled, he bade them go and fetch the wife. And they went and brought her, but she died just as she arrived in town.

Then they tied up the husband and accused him of the crime. And while they placed the wife upon a grill, to smoke and dry the body, they placed the husband beneath, in the fire, and so burnt him.

How Kengi Lost Her Child
(From the Kongo people, Congo)

NENPETRO HAD TWO WIVES, Kengi and Gunga. So he cleared a piece of ground for them, and divided it, giving each her part. And they planted maize, and beans and cassava; and soon they had plenty to eat.

One day Gunga took some beans from Kengi's plantation, and this made Kengi very cross. Gunga was sorry that she had done wrong, but pointed out that they were both married to one man, and that they ate together. After some time they came to an agreement that all that was born on the farm of the one should belong exclusively to her, and that the other should have no right to take it for her use.

Sometime after this Kengi came to Gunga's plantation, and asked her for a little tobacco, as she was in great pain and wished to smoke. Gunga told her to sit down a while, and gave her tobacco. And while Kengi was on Gunga's plantation, she bore a child. Gunga took possession of the child, and would not give it up to Kengi. Kengi wept bitterly, and sent a special ambassador to Gunga demanding her child. But Gunga refused to give the child up, and said she was ready to hold a palaver over it. Thus the two women resolved to go to the town of Manilombi and state their grievance to him.

They arrived, and Manilombi received their presents, and welcomed them. He then asked them what ailed them.

Kengi said: "I brought forth a child. Gunga has robbed me of it; let her speak."

And Gunga answered. "Nay, the child is mine; for when I took some beans from Kengi's plantation, Kengi got vexed, and made me come to an agreement with her that whatsoever was born on her plantation should belong to her, and all that was born on my plantation should belong to me, and neither of us should take anything from each other's plantation. Now, Kengi came, uncalled by me, to my plantation, and this child was born there; so that, according to our agreement, the child is mine and she cannot take it from me."

And witnesses were called, and they gave their evidence.

Then the prince and his old men went to drink water. And when they returned, Manilombi said that Gunga was acting within her right, and that therefore the child should belong to her.

The Twin Brothers
(From the Kongo people, Congo)

A CERTAIN WOMAN, after prolonged labour, gave birth to twins, both sons. And each one, as he was brought forth, came into this world with a valuable fetish, or charm. One the mother called Luemba, the other Mavungu. And they were almost full-grown at their birth, so that Mavungu, the first born, wished to start upon his travels.

Now about this time the daughter of Nzambi was ready for marriage. The tiger came and offered himself in marriage; but Nzambi told him that he must speak to her daughter himself, as she should only marry the man of her choice. Then the tiger went to the girl and asked her to marry him, but she refused him. And the gazelle, and the pig, and all created things that had breath, one after the other, asked the daughter in marriage; but she refused them all, saying that she did not love them; and they were all very sad.

Mavungu heard of this girl, and determined to marry her. And so he called upon his charm, and asked him to help him; and then he took some grass in his hands, and changed one blade of grass into a horn, another into a knife, another into a gun, and so on, until he was quite ready for the long journey.

Then he set out, and travelled and travelled, until at last hunger overcame him, when he asked his charm whether it was true that he was going to be allowed to starve. The charm hastened to place a sumptuous feast before him, and Mavuligu ate and was satisfied.

"Oh, charm!" Mavungu said, "are you going to leave these beautiful plates which I have used for the use of any commoner that may come along?" The charm immediately caused all to disappear.

Then Mavungu travelled and travelled, until at length he became very tired, and had to ask his charm to arrange a place for him where he might sleep. And the charm saw to his comfort, so that he passed a peaceful night.

And after many days' weary travelling he at length arrived at Nzambi's town. And Nzambi's daughter saw Mavungu and straightway fell in love with him, and ran to her mother and father and cried: "I have seen the man I love, and I shall die if I do not marry him."

Then Mavungu sought out Nzambi, and told her that he had come to marry her daughter.

"Go and see her first," said Nzambi,"and if she will have you, you may marry her."

And when Mavungu and the daughter of Nzambi saw each other, they ran towards each other and loved one another.

And they were led to a fine shimbec, and whilst all the people in the town danced and sang for gladness, Mavungu and the daughter of Nzambi slept there. And in the morning Mavungu noticed that the whole shimbec was crowded with mirrors, but that each mirror was covered so that the glass could not be seen. And he asked the daughter of Nzambi to uncover them, so that he might see himself in them. And she took him to one and uncovered it, and Mavungu immediately saw the perfect likeness of his native town. And she took him to another, and he there saw another town he knew; and thus she took him to all the mirrors save one, and this one she refused to let him see.

"Why will you not let me look into that mirror?" asked Mavungu.

"Because that is the picture, of the town whence no man that wanders there returns."

"Do let me see it!" urged Mavungu.

At last the daughter of Nzambi yielded, and Mavungu looked hard at the reflected image of that terrible place.

"I must go there," he said.

"Nay, you will never return. Please don't go!" pleaded the daughter of Nzambi.

"Have no fear!" answered Mavungu. "My charm will protect me."

The daughter of Nzambi cried very much, but could not move Mavungu from his purpose. Mavungu then left his newly married wife, mounted his horse and set off for the town from whence no man returns.

He travelled and travelled, until at last he came near to the town, when, meeting an old woman, he asked her for fire to light his pipe.

"Tie up your horse first, and come and fetch it."

Mavungu descended, and having tied his horse up very securely, he went to the woman for the fire; and when he had come near to her she killed him, so that he disappeared entirely.

Now Luemba wondered at the long absence of his brother Mavungu, and determined to follow him. So he took some grass, and by the aid of his fetish changed one blade into a horse, another into a knife, another into a gun, and so on, until he was fully prepared for his journey. Then he set out, and after some days' journeying arrived at Nzambi's town.

Nzambi rushed out to meet him, and, calling him Mavungu, embraced him.

"Nay," said Luemba, "my name is not Mavungu; I am his brother, Luemba."

"Nonsense!" answered Nzambi. "You are my son-in-law, Mavungu." And straightway a great feast was prepared. Nzambi's daughter danced for joy, and would not hear of his not being Mavungu. And Luemba was sorely troubled, and did not know what to do, as he was now sure that Nzambi's daughter was Mavungu's wife. And when night came, Nzambi's daughter would sleep in Luemba's shimbec; but he appealed to his charm, and it enclosed Nzambi's daughter in a room, and lifted her out of Luemba's room for the night, bringing her back in the early morning.

And Luemba's curiosity was aroused by the many closed mirrors that hung about the walls; so he asked Nzambi's daughter to let him look into them. And she showed him all excepting one; and this she told him was the one that reflected the town whence no man returns. Luemba insisted upon looking into this one; and when he had seen the terrible picture he knew that his brother was there.

Luemba determined to leave Nzambi's town for the town whence no man returns; and so after thanking them all for his kind reception, he set out. They all wept loudly, but were consoled by the fact that he had been there once already, and returned safely, so that he could of course return a second time. And Luemba travelled and travelled, until he also came to where the old woman was standing, and asked her for fire.

She told him to tie up his horse and come to her to fetch it, but. he tied his horse up only very lightly, and then fell upon the old woman and killed her.

Then he sought out his brother's bones and the bones of his horse, and put them together, and then touched them with his charm. And Mavungu and his horse came to life again. Then together they joined the bones of hundreds of people together and touched them with their charms, so that they all lived again. And then they set off with all their followers to Nzambi's town. And Luemba told Mavungu how he had been mistaken for him by his father-in-law and wife, and how by the help of his charm he had saved his wife from dishonour; and Mavungu thanked him, and said it was well.

Then a quarrel broke out between the two brothers about the followers. Mavungu said they were his, because he was the elder; but Luemba said that they belonged to him, because he had given Mavungu and them all life. Mavungu then fell upon Luemba and killed him; but his horse remained by his body. Mavungu then went on his way to Nzambi's town, and was magnificently welcomed.

Now Luemba's horse took his charm and touched Luemba's body, so that he lived again. Then Luemba mounted his horse, and sought out his brother Mavungu and killed him.

And when the town had heard the palaver, they all said that Luemba had done quite rightly.

The Chimpanzee and Gorilla
(From the Kongo people, Congo)

A NATIVE FRIEND of mine, who considers himself a great hunter and naturalist, told me that, his plantations having suffered severely from the depredations of the gorilla, he had determined to follow up his tracks, and kill him, if possible. After having journeyed a long distance, he at last came up to the gorilla's camp. The gorilla was up a tree, at the foot of which was a large heap of fruits of different kinds. He resolved upon the bold course of getting as near this fruit as he could, waiting until the gorilla should come down. Hardly had he got himself safely in his chosen position, when a chimpanzee, club in hand, came leisurely along, evidently looking about for food.

"Oh la! What fool has left his food in such a place, I wonder, right in the public footpath? I need go no further."

Thereupon the chimpanzee sat himself down, and began to enjoy a really good feed. He had not been there very long, however, before the gorilla came quietly down the tree. He quietly seated himself opposite to the chimpanzee, and commenced to eat also.

"Here, you!" said the chimpanzee, "what do you mean by eating my fruit? Can't you go and find some for yourself?"

The gorilla made no reply, but went on eating. The chimpanzee got excited, and began to abuse the gorilla. The gorilla looked at him. Then the chimpanzee struck the gorilla. The gorilla smiled, and pushed him aside. The chimpanzee took his club, and hit the gorilla with all his might. The gorilla then raised his long arm, and gave the chimpanzee one fearful blow, which stretched him dead at his feet.

"I did not wait to see any more," said my friend, "but ran away as hard as I could."

The Crafty Woman Overreaches Herself
(From the Kongo people, Congo)

I T WAS MARKET DAY, and all were intent upon going to Kitanda (the market). The first lady to arrive brought a large basket of chicoanga (native bread), placed it under the shade of the market tree, and then hid herself in the bush near at hand.

A second lady came along with a basket (or matet) of pig, and sat herself down beneath the tree.

"I wonder," said she, as she caught sight of the chicoanga, "to whom that belongs? I should very much like one piece to eat with a little of my pig. I was so busy preparing the pig for market, that I really had no time to get any chicoanga ready." She raised her voice and cried out:

"To whom does this chicoanga belong? Where is its owner?"

This she repeated many times., and then came to the conclusion that it had no owner. So she took one piece and ate it with her pig.

By and by the owner of the chicoanga came forth, and told the owner of the pig that she must pay her in pig for the chicoanga she had taken.

"No," said the owner of the pig.

And the people round about were called in; and after hearing what both had to say, they declared that the woman who owned the chicoanga was in the wrong; because she had hidden herself in the bush on purpose that her chicoanga should be taken by the owner of the pig, whom she had evidently seen coming. She had laid this trap to get some of the pig, and she deserved to lose her chicoanga.

How The Fetish Sunga Punished
My Great-Uncle's Twin Brother, Basa
(From the Kongo people, Congo)

BASA WAS my great uncle's twin brother, and a very clever fisherman. Every day he used to go out fishing in the river; and every day he caught great quantities of fish, which he used to smuggle into his house, so that none should know that he had caught any. His brother and relations used each day to ask him: "Basa, have you caught any fish?" And he would answer "No," although his house was full of fish going rotten. All this time the fetish Sunga was watching, and was grieved to hear him lie thus. So one day she sent one of her moleques, or little servants, to the place where Basa was fishing, to call him to her. It happened that upon that day Basa caught so much fish that he had to make some new matets, or baskets, to hold it all. He had already filled two, and placed them in the fork of a large tree, when he heard three distinct clappings of the hands, as if some child were saluting him, and then he heard a voice saying: "Come to my mother."

Then Basa was greatly afraid, and answered: "Which way? Please show me the way."

"Follow me," said the voice of the child, as; she led him to the river.

When they stepped into the river, the waters dried up, and all the fish disappeared, so that the bed of the river formed a perfect road for them. Even the fallen trees had been removed, that Basa might not meet the slightest difficulty in the way. When they had reached the watershed of the river, there in the great lake he saw a large and beautiful town. Here he was met by many people, and warmly welcomed. They led him to a chair, and asked him to be seated. But he was alarmed at all this ceremony, and wondered what it all meant.

Then Sunga laid a table before him, and loaded it with food and wine, and asked him to eat and drink. But he was still and told Sunga that so grand was the feast she had, afraid, placed before him that the smell alone of it had satisfied him. Then she pressed him to eat and drink, and finally he did so, drinking all the wine that there was.

Then Sunga deprived him of the power of speech, that he might lie no more, and bade him depart to his town. And so for the future he could only make his wants known by signs.

Nzambi Mpungu's Ambassador
(From the Kongo people, Congo)

NZAMBI MPUNGU heard that some one across the seas was making people who could speak. This roused his ire, so that he called the ox, the tiger, the antelope, the cock and other birds together, and after telling them the news, he appointed the cock his ambassador.

"Tell the white man that I alone am allowed to make people who can talk, and that it is wrong of them to make images of men and give them the power of speech."

And the cock left during the night, passing through a village about midnight, and only a few of the people got up to do honour to Nzambi Mpungu's ambassador, so that Nzambi Mpungu waxed wroth, and turned the inhabitants of that village into monkeys.

Nzambi's Daughter and Her Slave
(From the Kongo people, Congo)

NZAMBI HAD a most beautiful daughter, and she took the greatest care of her. As the child grew up, she was kept within the house, and never allowed to go outside, her mother alone waiting

upon her. And when she arrived at the age of puberty, her mother determined to send her to a town a long way off, that she might be undisturbed while she underwent her purification in the paint house.

She gave her child a slave; and unnoticed these two left Nzambi's town for the distant place where the paint house was situated.

"Oh, see there, slave! What is that?"

"Give me your anklets, and I will tell you," answered the slave.

The daughter of Nzambi gave the slave the anklets.

"That is a snake."

And then they walked along for some time, when suddenly the daughter of Nzambi said: "Oh, slave, what is that?"

"Give me your two new cloths, and I will tell you."

She gave the slave the two cloths.

"That is an antelope."

They had not gone far when the daughter again noticed something strange.

"Slave, tell me what that thing is? Give me your bracelets."

The girl gave the slave her bracelets.

"That thing is an eagle."

The princess thought it wonderful that the slave should know so much more than she did; and when she caught sight of a thing rising gently from the ground, she turned to her again and asked: "And what is that?"

"Give me your coral necklace."

The girl gave the slave the coral.

"That is a butterfly."

The next time she asked the slave for information, the slave made her change her clothes with her; so that while she was nearly naked, the slave was dressed most beautifully. And in this fashion they arrived at their destination, and delivered their message to the prince.

After the proper preparations they placed the slave in the paint house, with all the ceremony due to a princess; and they set the daughter of Nzambi to mind the plantations. In her innocence and ignorance the daughter of Nzambi at first thought all this was in order, and part of what she had to go through; but in a very short time she began to realize her position, and to grieve about it. She used to sing plaintive songs as she minded the corn, of how she had been mistaken for a slave, while her slave was honoured as a princess. And the people thought her mad. But one day a trade caravan passed her and she asked the trader where he was going, and he answered: "To Nzambi's town."

"Will you then take a message to Nzambi for me."

The trader gladly assented.

"Then tell her that her daughter is as a slave watching the plantations, while the slave is in the paint house."

He repeated the message; and when she had said that it was correct, he went on his way and delivered it to Nzambi.

Nzambi and her husband immediately set out in their hammock, accompanied by many followers, for the town where she had sent her daughter. And when she arrived she was greatly shocked to see her daughter in that mean position, and would have punished the prince, had she not seen that he and his people were not to blame.

They called upon the slave to come out of the paint house. But she was afraid, and would not. Then they entered, and having stripped her of all her borrowed plumes, they shut her within the house and burnt her.

The Story of a Partnership
(From the Kongo people, Congo)

THERE WERE TWO partners in trade, but they were of different tribes; one was of the tribe of Mandamba, the other of that of Nsasso. They were going to sell a goat. On their way to market the Mandamba man said to the Nsasso man: "You go on ahead, while I go into the bush; I will tie the goat up here, and catch you up shortly."

"Ah," thought the Nsasso man, "he wants to give me the slip."

So he assented and went on ahead. But when he saw that the Mandamba man had tied up the goat and gone into the bush, he came back and took the goat, and sold it quickly. Then he returned to the Mandamba man. They met, and the Nsasso man asked the Mandamba man how it was that he had been so long.

"Oh, I have lost the goat," he replied.

"Well, how stupid it was of you not to have given me charge of the goat while you went into the bush!"

"Let us go to the market," said the Mandamba, man, "we may find the goat there" (for a suspicion of what had occurred crossed his mind).

"Very well," said the Nsasso man.

On arriving at the market they saw the goat in the hands of a certain man.

"Who sold you that goat?" said the Nsasso man.

"Why, you to be sure," said the man.

"In truth then our partnership is at an end, for you have grossly deceived me," said the Mandamba man.

And they went before the king, Nteka Matunga, and the Nsasso man said he thought the Mandamba man meant to play him a trick.

"Yes," said the king, "perhaps he did intend to do so, as you are of different families, and do not trust one another; but you did play the trick, which amounts to robbery." The king condemned the Nsasso man to be burnt, but he promised to pay the price of his life to the Mandamba man, and the latter agreed to receive payment, and thus the palaver was settled.

FLAME TREE PUBLISHING